SLAY

NINA LEVINE

SLAY

Cover designed by Louisa @ LM Creations
http://lmbookcreations.wordpress.com/portfolio/

Cover Model: Scott King

Stock Image from Dollar Photo Club
www.dollarphotoclub.com

Editing by Karen Louise Rohde Faergemann at The Word Wench Editing
Services
http://wordwenchediting.wordpress.com

NINA LEVINE

**USA Today & International
Bestselling Author**

ALSO BY NINA LEVINE

STORM MC SERIES

Storm (Storm MC #1)
Fierce (Storm MC #2)
Blaze (Storm MC #2.5)
Revive (Storm MC #3)
Slay (Storm MC #4)
Illusive (Storm MC #5) – COMING 2015
Command (Storm MC #6) – COMING 2015

HAVOC SERIES

Destined Havoc (Havoc #1)
Inevitable Havoc (Havoc #2) – COMING 2015

CRAVE SERIES

All Your Reasons (Crave #1) – COMING 2015

Keep up to date with my books at my website
http://ninalevinebooks.blogspot.com.au

DEDICATION

To everyone who struggles to accept themselves

for who they truly are...

It's okay to embrace our flaws and own them,

to accept every part of ourselves,

and love ourselves,

and to let others love us, too.

"Sometimes you have to shatter to find strength.
And sometimes you have to let someone in to help
you put the pieces back together."

- Layla

A NOTE ABOUT THE STORM MC SERIES

Each book in this series continues on from the previous. While there won't be major cliffhangers in each book, there will be parts of the story that won't be resolved so please be aware of this.
It is recommended that each book be read in order.

SLAY

(Storm MC #4)

WARNING

For Mature Audience 18+
Contains Adult Sexual Situations & Language

PROLOGUE

BLADE

Twelve years old

My father was the meanest person I knew. No one even came close. I'd always thought he hated my mother and me, but the things he was saying and doing today just proved it. As I huddled in the corner of the kitchen, I chanted a prayer over and over in my mind, madly hoping God would listen.

There was a God, right?

My mother had always told me there was, but I'd never seen any proof. The only things I'd ever seen were a bare pantry, clothes that either didn't fit me anymore or had holes in them, a mother who was hardly home because she was working two jobs to keep a roof over our heads, and a mostly absent father. Further proof God probably didn't exist was when my father *did* visit, he often left us with bruises to remember him by. I wasn't sure, but I figured if there was a God, he wouldn't have let all that happen.

I didn't often call him Dad. He was Marcus to me. I knew he wasn't like a real father; he never did anything for us I saw other fathers do. And while he always had a temper, today he was really angry. Fear painted my mother's face, and dread filled my gut.

"Why the fuck is that asshole from the grocery store asking you out on a date?" he roared at my mother.

She cowered under his harsh words and furious glare. "I don't know, Marcus. I never encouraged him." Her eyes were pleading with him to believe her. I knew from experience he wouldn't.

He lashed out and slapped her face. "Don't fucking lie to me, Stella."

Her hand flew to her face. "I'm not." She tried to defend herself but he wasn't buying any of it.

The crack of his fist landing on her cheek almost made me vomit. He'd never been this violent towards her before. When he arrived at the house half an hour ago, I knew straight away he wasn't right. He was angrier than usual. And when he started going on about something he'd heard about the man at the grocery store, I knew nothing good would come of today.

He continued to rant at her and hit her. I covered my ears and started chanting prayers in my head again.

Please, God . . . if you're there, please make him leave us alone. I'll do anything, just make him stop.

I wanted to help my mother; I wanted to step up and rescue her from his violent fists. But I wasn't stupid. I was too young, too little to take my father on. Watching him now, though, watching him do the things he did to my mother, I decided there would come a day when I would challenge him. Until that day, I would be patient. I would make my plan, and I would make sure there was no way I wouldn't win when I finally gave him what he deserved for everything he'd ever done to us.

CHAPTER 1

BLADE

Eight years ago

Aged twenty-five

THE STEADY DRIP OF A LEAKING TAP SOMEWHERE IN THE warehouse was the only sound I heard as I watched the scene unfold in front of me. That and the roar of blood rushing to my head as anger took hold.

"You really wanna go there, Blade?" Leroy snarled, his lethal gaze focused solely on me.

I thought about what he'd asked even though I'd done nothing but think about that very question for the past few weeks. This was the man who'd taken me under his wing when I was a naive fifteen-year-old out dealing drugs for little more than pocket change; the man who'd taught me everything I knew today about how to survive in the dangerous underbelly we existed in. I'd lied, stolen and killed for this man. Fuck, the first time I'd taken my blade to someone had been to save Leroy's life. Ten years in his gang and I'd risen to the top, but I'd lost my humanity along the way. I didn't even question the shit I did for Leroy anymore. The darkness within had totally consumed me.

Until I met Ashley.

I took a step closer to Leroy, the adrenaline pumping through me. With a nod of my head, he'd easily be taken care of by my boys, but I wanted to be the one to do it. I needed that vengeance for what he'd tried to force upon Ashley, and for what he'd already forced upon countless other women. "Yeah, motherfucker, it seems I do."

Leroy had his loyal gang members backing him up, but I had far more of our members behind me. Once we'd discovered how Leroy was filling his brothels, we'd decided we could no longer support a filthy pig like him; a pig that refused to treat women with the respect they deserved.

His eyes were wild, his body taut; he was just as ready for this showdown as I was. "You do remember who took your sorry ass off the street and showed you what you were capable of, don't you?" He pushed his face towards mine. We were so close now that when he spat his next words out, I could smell his foul breath. "I fucking *own* you, Blade. You don't get to fucking challenge what I do."

The calmness that always took over whenever I was about to kill descended upon me. My breathing remained steady, sure. "That's where you're wrong, Leroy. You don't own me, and I sure as hell don't owe you a damn thing. Not anymore. That debt has been paid. But you and I have a huge fucking problem if you think it's okay to force women into selling their bodies so you can make money off them"

"They fucking owed me for the drugs they'd been buying off me!" he thundered, as if that made it all right. His thinking was so fucking screwed up he didn't know right from wrong anymore. Hell, in his world, there *was* no wrong. Only what he wanted, and that was always right.

"There's going to be some changes around here," I stated with the calmness I felt in my bones. This was the right thing to do.

"You're fucking dreaming if you think you can take me out and keep this organisation running, at the level of profit I've achieved, without the women."

"And you're fucking deluded if you think I'm going to let you live, so I guess I really only have one option here: kill you and find a way to make it all work, because I sure as fuck have no intention of running drugs or women anymore."

In the blink of an eye, Leroy gave his men the nod, and a second later I had five guns trained on me. In return, Leroy had twelve on him. I waited for his next play. After all, patience was my strong suit.

"If you think you can kill me with no repercussions, my boy, you might want to think again," he threatened with the confidence of a man who never made promises he couldn't keep. Leroy most certainly had shit planned for this exact outcome, but he underestimated me.

I pulled my blade out and took another step closer to him. In a low voice, I said, "It's a good thing you taught me to always keep one eye behind me, then, isn't it?"

His eyes widened slightly, and I took in the sheen of sweat on his forehead. He knew his breaths were limited. My pulse quickened as I savoured his fear and anticipated sinking my knife in his gut.

Merrick, my right-hand man, moved to speak into my ear. "Let's get this shit over with, Blade. I don't want to risk anything fucking this up, not when you've got him right where you need him."

Merrick was right, as usual, and without giving Leroy any warning, I sunk my knife into his stomach. He roared with pain and staggered back. I pulled the knife back, yanking it from his body, only to plunge it back into his stomach. My blade connected with his flesh over and over as I sought retribution for the crimes he'd committed against the women in his organisation. I heard gunshots as our boys fought it out, but all I was concentrating on was Leroy's blood. I needed more of it on my hands.

5

On my knees, surrounded by blood, my breathing ragged, Leroy lay in front of me, his body a carved canvas of death. And I was the proud and satisfied artist. No longer would he cause terror and suffering to so many.

I left him on the ground and stood. Merrick's gaze met mine, and he nodded. We were half-way to where we needed to be today.

I surveyed the casualties. There were too many; this had to be stopped before we had more. "Enough!" I bellowed. Everyone was smart enough to know that with Leroy gone, I was taking over, and they followed my command. "You all know where I stand. If that's not something you want to support, now's the time to leave."

Leroy's staunch supporter, Ricky, stepped forward. He'd taken a bullet in his arm and was beyond angry. "How the fuck do you propose to move forward, Blade? Leroy was right, there's no way to pull the kind of dollars in without the girls and the drugs. And I'm not willing to take a pay-cut."

One of the best things to ever happen, in my opinion, was for an opponent to walk straight down the path you'd already planned for them to walk down, and to do it thinking it was their own choice. Ricky Grecian was doing that right now, and all I had to do was keep leading him. "I can't promise there won't be a pay-cut, so I'd suggest you think long and hard about which way you want to go, Ricky."

He continued scowling, and I knew exactly how this was going to play out. After glaring at me for a few minutes, he announced, "I'm out. And I'll take the girls with me."

"Not fucking likely, motherfucker," I growled. "The girls stay with me."

"You said you don't want them."

"No, I said we would no longer be running them."

Merrick stepped in as planned. "You can take the drugs," he suggested. And then looking at me, he said, "That works, doesn't it, Blade? We don't want the drugs."

I took my time thinking about it; this had to appear as if we were giving up something valuable. Before I could answer, Ricky played straight into our hands. "It's either the drugs or the girls, Blade. Your fucking choice, asshole, but I'm leaving here today with one of them."

"Take the fucking drugs," I snapped. *Christ, Ricky really was a dumb fucker.*

"Right, that's settled," Ricky said. Looking around the room, he asked, "Who's with me?"

As four men left with Ricky, I turned to Merrick. "Ten years of this shit, with nothing to show for it except death and destruction," I muttered.

"Yeah, but we did a good thing here today, Blade."

Expelling a long breath, I nodded. "Things will change. I'll make fucking sure of it."

CHAPTER 2

BLADE

Present day

"BLADE!" ASHLEY SCREAMED, HER FACE CONTORTING IN pain as her attackers pressed cigarettes into her skin. Her arm reached out for me, her hand flailing around trying desperately to connect with mine. But as hard as I tried to grab hold, I couldn't do it.

I never could.

I failed.

Every fucking time.

I sat bolt upright in my bed. The bed sheet stuck to the sweat I was covered in, and I shoved it off.

I turned to the bedside clock.

Three-fifteen am.

Fuck.

Pushing myself off the bed, I stalked into the bathroom. I flicked the tap on and splashed cold water over my face. Resting my hands on the sink, I stared at my reflection in the mirror. These dreams were getting out of hand, and exhaustion ruled my life. It painted my face and clawed at my body.

The dreams had haunted me since Ashley's death, but they'd recently intensified to the point where they were hitting me hard and fast most nights. I thought they would have stopped after I'd dealt with Bullet and they *had* slowed down for a while. Fuck knew why they were back now.

I turned the tap off and scowled in the mirror. I had a lot of work to deal with today and just over two hours of sleep wasn't going to help me get through it all. However, I knew from experience sleep would prove elusive. Better just to start my day with a shower and move on from there.

When the hot water hit my shoulders a few moments later, I dropped my head and rested my chin on my chest. Closing my eyes, I savoured the heat working its way into my tired muscles. The years since Ashley's death hadn't been kind to my body. Grief, regret and a lust for revenge had taken hold of both my mind and body, inflicting weariness on me. I pushed past the exhaustion most days, but these fucking dreams were taking their toll.

Fifteen minutes later, showered and dressed, I entered the kitchen. I made coffee and logged on to my computer, checking my emails. The pain of Ashley's loss was never far away and I felt it as keenly these days as I did three years ago, but my work helped give my mind a break from it. And that was all I could ask for because I knew I'd never get over not having her in my life.

★★★

Four hours later, I parked my Jag not far from the front door of Harlow's mother's cafe, and exited it into the warm September sun. Late September in Brisbane should have been spring weather but we seemed to be moving straight into summer, just as we had last year.

The humidity in the air this morning clung to me, and I contemplated yet again moving to a cooler climate. I'd never do it, though. I was born in Brisbane and I'd die here. This city was in my blood.

"You owe me breakfast as well as coffee."

I looked up to find Madison standing on the footpath smiling at me. My sister was the happiest I'd ever seen her; marrying J had been a good decision. I cocked my head to the side. "How do you figure that, babe?"

Her smile turned into a grin that lit up her face. I liked what I saw there. Not many people meant as much to me as she did, and her happiness touched my cold heart in unexpected ways. "Well, you were supposed to have coffee with me yesterday, but you cancelled. It's only fair you buy me breakfast to say sorry."

I moved to where she was standing and draped my arm around her shoulders, pulling her closer to me. Looking down at her, I murmured, "So, just for future reference, if I cancel on you, I'm up for whatever you decide?"

She wrapped her arm around my waist, and we walked into the cafe together. "Yes! Finally, a man who gets it," she said, triumphantly.

Harlow looked up as we entered, just as Madison made her declaration. "What does he get?" she asked.

Madison let me go and moved to hug Harlow. "He gets that I call the shots if he cancels on me."

"Oh honey, I think you have your brother wrapped around your little finger. Blade might be in charge of everything else in his life, but not so much where you're concerned. He'd do anything for you."

I jerked my thumb in Harlow's direction. "She might be onto something there."

Madison hit me with a look that made most of the shit I'd been through in my life worthwhile. Having her as my sister had changed me in ways no one else had ever been able to, not even Ashley.

Madison made me want to be a better man. I was buried under a million fucking layers of darkness, and I'd embraced that for most of my life, but with her in it, I was trying hard to find a way out from under the murky depths.

She watched me watch her, and then, on a sigh, she said, "Okay, big brother, time to get your wallet out. I want pancakes and coffee today, and no skimping on the ice-cream and whipped cream."

As I pulled my wallet out, I asked, "Cream *and* ice-cream?"

"Of course." She shrugged. "Why not?"

Harlow interjected, "A girl needs a pick-me-up after her brother ditches her." She winked at me as she said this.

I shook my head and muttered, "Once. I cancelled on you once."

Madison continued to rib me. "And let the record show that you won't do it again. Right?"

This type of exchange wasn't something I was used to. Kidding around didn't come easily to me, but Madison had been teaching me how. I played along with her. "Right. Especially not if it means you'll resort to ice-cream and cream at eight o'clock in the morning."

Madison and Harlow burst out laughing as I just stood there shaking my head at their antics. I lifted my chin at Harlow. "Make it two coffees."

Harlow had worked out my moods and read me perfectly well now: I was done with the joking around. She nodded in agreement. "Done."

I moved to sit and Madison followed. As we did this, Scott entered the cafe. His focus was entirely on Harlow. He didn't see us. We both watched him, though, as he and Harlow discussed something. It looked serious, and I wondered about that, especially as they'd recently moved in together.

Turning to Madison, I asked, "All good in paradise?"

"As far as I know, yes. But that looks pretty intense, doesn't it?"

"Yeah."

"Maybe Harlow's finally worked out that Scott's not the perfect man she thought he was. Living with someone can do that."

I frowned. "Are you and J okay?" I'd never stop worrying about her, and god fucking help him if he ever screwed her over.

"Yes, but you know what it's like when you do day in, day out with someone. It's hard sometimes. There are days I could kill J, and I'm sure he feels the same way."

I thought about that, remembering back to when I lived with Ashley. She was the only woman I'd ever lived with. "Ashley used to hate the way I cooked." It was out before I had time to even filter it, and Madison was straight on it.

Her eyes widened in surprise. I never spoke about Ashley. "Why?" she asked softly.

I took a deep breath. This was the last thing I wanted to be discussing this morning. "She said I made too much of a mess, and she would have preferred I washed up as I went."

She listened but didn't say anything, and then she reminded me of one of the reasons I loved her; she let it go. Turning her attention back to Scott, she asked, "Have you spoken to him lately?"

"No."

"Will you?" Her question was short, but her eyes held all the words she hadn't spoken. She was worried about him.

I nodded slowly, hesitant to commit but wanting to put her mind at ease. "Yeah, I'll touch base with him, babe."

Her chest rose on a sigh, and some of the worry eased out of her expression. "Thank you."

"J doesn't tell me much about what's going on, and Scott's never around to talk to, so I don't really know what's happening. I hate what Griff's done to the club; to Scott and the boys. And I hate not knowing what they're going through."

I shifted forward slightly in my seat so I could bring my gaze closer to hers. "When a friend betrays you like that, it's not something you ever recover from. Not for a long time, anyway. And I know women like to talk about that shit over and fucking over, but a man doesn't want to rehash the betrayal, babe. I doubt you'll get J talking about it anytime soon, at least not with the kind of details you're looking for, so I suggest you let it go and just be there for him." I said what I had to say and then settled back in my seat, hoping she'd take it in.

"Why don't you have a woman?" she asked, throwing me with the sudden change in direction.

"I had a woman." My shoulders tensed as I answered her.

"Yeah, but why don't you date now? You give me all this advice about men and women, and you seem to know your shit, so any woman you date is going to be lucky." Her voice softened. "Ashley was awhile ago, Blade. Don't you think it's time for you to move on?"

"Are we talking dating or are we talking fucking? 'Cause I've got one of those covered, and I'm not interested in the other." My voice had hardened, and I couldn't control that as much as I may have wanted to.

"I worry about you," she said, concern clear in her tone.

"Don't worry about me. I can look out for myself; been doing it my whole fucking life."

"I know you have, but you've got me in your life now, and it's my job as your sister to worry and make sure you're okay. I think you should reconsider the dating thing."

Keeping myself under control around Madison was something I worked hard at. I didn't bother with anyone else, except my mother. However, she was pushing me today, and I feared I was about to snap. My tone was hard and firm when I said, "Madison, it's not going to happen."

She opened her mouth to say something, but I silenced her with a glare. After a moment, she said, "Okay, I'll let it be for now, but I'll revisit this at some point. Someone's gotta push you and I know you don't have anyone else who is game, so it looks like it has to be me."

At that moment, Harlow came over with our coffees and pancakes. I looked up at her. "Thank you."

She smiled. "Anytime."

I watched as she made her way back to where Scott was waiting for her. He looked our way and nodded at me before giving his attention back to Harlow.

Madison drew me back to our conversation. "Did you hear what I said?"

"Yes, and I have no doubt you'll do what you said, but babe, you need to know Ashley was everything to me, and I've never met a woman since who even came close."

"But how are you going to *know* if you're so closed off to it?"

"I'll know. Trust me, when a woman has what Ashley had, I'll fucking know."

She took that in, and finally acknowledged what I'd said. "She must have been pretty special."

Memories flooded my mind and pierced my heart. Fuck, they still managed to do that even now, and I feared they always would. "She was." I took a moment to get the words out. "She was the kindest, gentlest woman I've ever met who had a heart of gold. She accepted me and accepted what I did, but challenged me to do better. She dragged me out of that shit, and set me on a new path. If it wasn't for her, I'd still be in deep."

Madison leant across the table and reached for my hand. "I think you're amazing, Blade. You're too hard on yourself sometimes."

Fuck, if only she knew the half of it.

I pulled my hand away from hers. "I'm not, and if you knew the truth about me you wouldn't think that," I snapped.

She knew I was angry now, but she wasn't the type of woman who was easily affected by that. Having grown up surrounded by bikers would have taught her how to handle herself. She fixed a dirty glare on me and said, "Well, perhaps if you shared more about yourself with me, I would be able to show you that nothing you tell me would make me see you any differently. I love you and accept you for who you are; all of it, the good and the bad."

I was done with fucking deep and meaningful for the day. Pointing at her pancakes, I said, "Eat up, I've got shit to do today, and discussing my feelings is not on that list."

She huffed at me but did as I said.

We sat in silence until Scott joined us a few moments later. Eyeing me, he asked, "You heard from Marcus recently?"

"No," I replied, taking in the dark circles under his eyes and exhausted features.

"Me either," he murmured, deep in thought. "We should have a sit-down soon, go over where we're all at with this."

"Yeah. Work out a time with the boys and let me know."

"You free tomorrow morning? My house."

"Yeah, eight good for you?"

He nodded, then looked at Madison, and asked, "You okay?"

"Yes, apart from having brothers who don't tell me shit," she answered with a glare.

Frustration crossed Scott's face. "Right, I'm out of here. See you tomorrow."

As she watched him go, Madison blew out a long breath. They frustrated each other, and yet I could easily see the love and concern they shared. Madison's was more obvious, but Scott's was just as deep; he just showed it in his own way. Growing up, I would have done anything to have that kind of love in my life. Funny how the universe conspires endlessly against some people . . . but I'd fought back and took what I could when I had the opportunity. Having Madison's love now was something I was grateful for, and I'd always do everything necessary to keep it. Showing her my true self would almost guarantee the loss of that love, though, and I wasn't willing to take that gamble.

★★★

The rest of my day went fairly smoothly. That was, until Merrick broke news to me that pissed me off. We'd been going through my appointments for today and tomorrow when he paused for a moment before continuing in a slightly pained voice, "I've heard rumblings that Phil Deacon wants a shot at the Hurley construction job. Apparently, he'll be bidding for it, and has made threats that he'll do whatever it takes to win it over you."

Our construction company was a huge part of our organisation these days. It was one of the areas we'd branched into after we walked away from drugs and prostitution years ago. The Hurley job was massive, and I didn't intend for us to lose it.

I began pacing the room. Phil was a loose cannon; one never knew entirely what his next move would be. We'd have to tread carefully where he was concerned, because the fucker wasn't afraid of using dirty tricks or violence to get what he wanted. "Keep an eye on him. I refuse to lose the job to him so I imagine it'll get dirty for awhile."

Merrick nodded. "Yeah, I figured. I'll put Ben on him."

Ben was a good choice: brilliant at what he did and not afraid to take whatever action was needed to ensure our end goals were met. "Good."

I stopped pacing, my mood shifting as control eased back into me. "Has my mother called?"

A frown creased his forehead. "No. Doesn't she usually call your direct number?"

"Yes, but I just realised I didn't hear from her yesterday. Figured she may have called you instead."

Understanding flickered in his eyes. "I'm sure she's alright."

"I'll phone her, make sure." My mother phoned me every day, checking in and letting me know she was okay. She'd started doing it when Marcus stopped seeing her late last year. I'd been surprised as fuck when he'd made that move, and I had to admit I'd been waiting for the day he changed his mind. She'd been distraught when he'd stopped seeing her, and I knew she'd fall at his feet whenever he said the word. For her to miss a call made me consider the possibility he'd taken her back.

As he left, Merrick added, "You're a good man."

I scoffed. "Hardly." *What the fuck was up with people telling me this shit today?*

"Sure, we've been through some shit over the years, but this work we're doing now is good."

"Don't let it fool you, Merrick. The good doesn't negate the bad. And it certainly doesn't make me a good person."

He raised his eyebrows, the look on his face one of irritation. "I see things a little differently from you, Blade."

He walked out of the room, and I sat back at my desk. Surveying my office, I thought back to when we started doing this work. The day Merrick and I took matters into our own hands was burned into my memory. Ashley had been the catalyst of that, had shown me the truth of the lie I'd been living up until that point. It had been a bloody battle that day; a battle I hadn't hesitated to take charge of and do whatever was necessary to ensure victory. Justice had been served to the one who had wronged so many. The fact Ashley wasn't here to witness the results of everything we'd put in motion that day broke my fucking heart. But it just reminded me life had a way of taking the good and fucking with it when you least expected it. All you could do was savour what you had, while you had it, and hope like hell you kept it for a long time.

★★★

My childhood memories weren't happy ones. As I watched my mother lie to me the next morning, I recalled similar situations from when I was younger. I'd lost count of the number of times I begged her to stop seeing my father, and I'd lost count of the number of lies she'd told me when she agreed she would tell him to go. I knew she didn't lie to me intentionally. She lied to herself as well. There were a few times she *did* follow through and kick him out, but within a couple of months, he was always back.

Theirs was such a dysfunctional love. I could never work out why they clung to each other like they did. The moments where I glimpsed tenderness between them gave me hope, but it was always short-lived, until the day when I was a teen and I decided enough was enough. I decided there had to be more to love than false hope and bullshit promises. If the person you loved couldn't be there for you always, they weren't worthy of your time or your affection.

It had been over a year since Marcus stopped seeing my mother. She'd grieved the loss of him, and I hoped she'd grown stronger through that experience; strong enough to say no to him the day he showed up again, back at her door. He'd stayed away longer than I thought he would, but I was sure he was back now. However, mum was denying it.

"Why aren't you telling me the truth?" I demanded, a lifetime of anger flaring up.

"I *am* telling you the truth! Yes, he came around, but no, I won't take him back," she pleaded with me to believe her. She'd cried wolf one too many times, though.

"What promises did he make you this time?"

She didn't answer me. She just began folding the laundry sitting on the kitchen table in front of her. A dead fucking giveaway she was avoiding the truth.

I slammed my hand down on the table so hard it moved. She jumped, and the fear I saw in her eyes hurt like hell. I would never

18

fucking hurt her but Marcus had, over and over, to the point where any little threat scared the fuck out of her. "Fuck!" I roared, "I fucking hate what he has done to us." I rubbed the back of my neck and began pacing the small kitchen.

"Donovan, I know you think I'm weak and that I'll go back to Marcus at the drop of a hat, but this time I won't. Yes, I'm weak. I always have been." Her voice caught at that admission and my heart broke a little more for her. She turned her distraught gaze to me and bared her heart. "He promised me he would leave her; finally, after all these years. And that he would stop being so violent. I'm not taking him back, but it feels like I'm walking away from something I put my whole life into, and just when I can have what I've always wished for, I'm saying no. Do you know how hard that is?"

She was so fucking close to freedom; if he screwed with that, I would fucking move the plan up and take the bastard out myself. It was, after all, what I'd always planned to do. And to watch my father suffer at my hands would fill me with the deepest fucking satisfaction I'd ever felt.

My voice was low and controlled when I spoke. If I didn't control it, I would explode at her. "I want so much more for you, Mum. I understand that back when you had me, you had no family to support you, so you thought sticking with Marcus was the right thing, but now you have me. I can give you anything you need or want."

"You can't give me the one thing I need: the love of a man," she whispered.

The roar between my ears was deafening, and I lost my fight to control myself. "Marcus wouldn't fucking *know* love if it smacked him in the face!" I yelled, wild at him, at her, and at the fucking injustice of a world full of hateful people. "Can you not fucking see that?" I hated swearing at my mother but I couldn't help it today. I needed to get out of here before I lost my shit completely.

She began crying, and I wanted to smash my fists into the wall. All the anger and frustration inside me threatened to spill over, and I clenched and unclenched my fists over and over in an effort to stop myself.

"I know I should see that, but I can't bring myself to move past the feelings I've had for him for so long." She was sobbing now. My mother had been fucked up by her father, and those sins had set her on this fucked-up path she couldn't find a way out from.

I pulled her to me and held her. My hand smoothed her hair over and over as she clung to me. When her sobbing had subsided, I murmured, "If you need me, any time of the day, you call me. If he keeps harassing you and won't leave if you ask him to, you call me. I don't care what I'm doing; I *will* come to you if you need me. Yeah?"

The defeat I saw on her face killed me. It tore another fucking piece of my heart out. There should have been hope. After all this fucking time, she should be seeing the light and feeling real hope, but all he'd left her with was sadness and despair. "Yes," she agreed softly.

"Thank Christ," I said before hugging her again.

Relief flooded me, but the dark feelings of hatred and revenge stuck close like they always did.

Soon.

He'd be dealt with soon, and then, maybe she and I could finally find a way to move out of the darkness.

CHAPTER 3

LAYLA

I STOOD IN THE ALLEYWAY BEHIND MY BAR AND STARED UP at the inky sky. Full moon tonight. Fuck, I hoped the bar wasn't about to be invaded by the crazies. Diverting my gaze down the alleyway, I took in the two drunks passed out, completely oblivious to the thief raiding their pockets.

"Hey!" I yelled out, stalking towards him.

His head snapped up, hard eyes meeting mine. "Fuck off, cunt," he snarled, his voice full of venom.

Yeah, like fucking hell, asshole.

I ignored his directive, and when I got to where he now stood staring at me, I punched him hard in the face. The element of surprise never did me wrong. He staggered back, holding his face, surprised as fuck.

"What the fuck, bitch?"

"That was for trying to steal."

He advanced towards me, hatred blazing from his eyes. His

intent was clear, and as his arm came up to punch me, I kicked my leg out so my foot connected with his balls. At the same time, I ducked to avoid his punch and spun out to the side, away from him. The agony my kick induced, coupled with the momentum he had going with his punch, caused him to fall forward. He landed on his hands and knees, at which point I kicked him hard in the gut.

"Fuck!" He collapsed into a ball, arms around his stomach, his breathing choppy.

"*That* was for calling me a cunt."

I walked to the drunks and prodded one of them with my boot. His eye cracked open and he gave me a what-the-hell look.

"Get up," I snapped. "This asshole just tried to steal from you. It's time to go home."

Without waiting for a response, I turned back to the thief. Squatting, I said, "You think that hurt? If I see you here again, you'll know what pain is. Your balls got off lightly this time."

He grunted something unintelligible at me before attempting to stand.

I straightened and watched as he stood. My body tensed, waiting to see if he would try anything.

He glared at me. "Fucking bitch," he grumbled, still clutching his stomach.

I raised my eyebrows. "Really, dude? You want to go there with me again?"

He muttered more shit I couldn't understand before stumbling out of the alleyway. When he rounded the corner, and I could no longer see him, I allowed myself to relax.

Why did the world have to be full of scum like that?

I looked at the drunks. The one I'd woken up had passed out again. I gave him another prod. "Time to go home," I ordered. Fat lot of good it did because he didn't stir this time. Fuck it, his grave to dig, not mine to try and spare.

I headed back inside. I had better things to do than worry about people who didn't worry about themselves.

★★★

I checked the time on my watch: eleven pm. The bar was busy for a Thursday night. Thank god, because our bills were coming out of our ass at the moment. It didn't help that my business partner had disappeared two days ago. Also didn't fucking help he'd been stealing from the business for god knows how long. It had taken great strength not to do serious damage to his body when I'd discovered that shit. One almighty screaming match later, and it looked like he'd skipped town. God knew how I'd pay the bills now.

"Boss!"

I spun around to find Jess staring expectantly at me. "What?" I asked as I wiped my hands on my jeans. The wetness of the alcohol came off but the stickiness remained. Didn't bother me, though. I was used to working with sticky hands after nearly ten years of bar work.

She jerked her head in the direction of the jukebox in the corner. "Can you deal with that asshole?"

I narrowed my eyes on the guy she referred to. Seemed he had taken issue with the jukebox. When he kicked it, I turned back to Jess. "With pleasure," I replied, already heading towards him.

"Got a problem with my jukebox, buddy?" I asked as I approached him. He had that stoned look to him. Probably *was* stoned. Fucking junkies frequented the bar, but, unfortunately, it couldn't be helped: the bar was in The Valley and we bred them like mice here.

Glassy eyes focused on me. He scowled before answering. "It took my fucking money."

"No need to kick it."

23

"No need to give me shit," he spat back.

"How about you leave before this gets out of hand?" Fuck, two assholes in the space of an hour. Shit luck tonight.

He moved towards me, his bulky frame hunching up in a threatening manner. "How about you give me my fucking money back?"

I assessed the situation. He looked to have some strength on him which could be a problem with my tiny frame. There were other ways around this, though. My plan came together in my mind, however, as I went to execute it, a voice questioned from behind, "What's the problem, asshole?"

Turning my head, I found the guy I served scotch to most nights. He was one of the best-looking men I'd ever met. Also the guy I'd vote most likely to scare the fuck out of me in a dark alley. He'd been coming here for just over a year, yet we'd hardly ever spoken. He kept to himself, and it was clear to everyone he wanted to be left alone. Tonight, the scary vibes rolled off him.

"We're all good, thanks," I replied. I'd been handling my own shit for nine years now. I didn't need his help.

The thud of his heavy boot as he stepped closer to me rang out a warning. Jerking his chin to the jukebox dude, he asked, "You about to leave?"

Pretty sure it wasn't a question.

The guy squared his shoulders. I could swear, though, I saw fear flash in his eyes.

Oh dear god, he wanted to take on Scary Dude. *As if, asshole.*

A frightening energy filled the space and I knew I needed to end this before it got out of hand. As the scary dude came closer, I raised my hand to his chest to halt him. I hit rock-hard muscle. *Fuck me, built much?* My core clenched. Shit, now wasn't the time to be thinking about how much I wanted to see what his shirt hid.

He frowned at my hand on his chest. Only for a moment and then his glare returned to the asshole.

"Not till I get my money," jukebox dude answered him.

The scary dude pushed forward, easily ignoring my hand on his chest. He stepped around me, moved into the other guy's space and spoke quietly to him. I couldn't hear what he said. It must have been something significant, though, because the asshole's eyes widened, he nodded and with one last dirty look at me, he took off.

Scary Dude turned back to me. Our bodies almost touched, and the energy surrounding us turned from frightening to something else. A shiver spread down my spine and my heart rate sped up. Surely he wouldn't mind if I placed my hand on his chest again. I just needed one more touch.

"You okay?" he asked, interrupting my sexy thoughts.

I wished he would take a step away from me so I could get my brain going again. "Yeah, there's always one of them to deal with most nights."

He nodded and finally took that step back, giving me space to move and think. "I doubt he'll be back. Ever."

I didn't even want to know where his certainty came from. "Thanks."

We stood silently watching each other. His face hid his emotions well; I couldn't make out a damn thing. After a few moments in which we both sized each other up, he murmured, "Good."

Shit, a man of few words. That was too hard for me. I liked a man I could read and one I could talk to. "You want a scotch?" I asked.

He gave me a nod. "Yeah, thanks."

Well, at least he knew how to be polite even if he didn't speak much. It had become so hard to find men with manners these days.

He followed me over to the bar, and a couple of moments later, I placed a scotch in front of him. The fact he sat at the bar surprised me; he usually claimed a table in the back corner.

"That guy come in here often?" he asked after taking a swig of his drink.

"I've never seen him before."

He nodded and a thoughtful look crossed his face, but he didn't say anything.

"You know him?" I asked.

His eyes focused on mine. Guarded. I bet this dude held thousands of secrets inside. "Let's just say I know of him. He's not a man you want back in here."

He kept his eyes glued to mine while he drank some more of his scotch. His stare unnerved me. Something no one managed to do these days

Fuck, time to move away from him.

I nodded at him and said, "Well, thanks again for your help."

Without waiting for his reply, I left the bar and headed to the office out in the back. I hadn't even taken the time to make sure the staff was okay on their own. I needed a time-out so, hopefully, they'd cope without me.

★★★

Two hours later I left the office and headed back out to the front. Paperwork had consumed my last couple of hours to the point of weariness. I found the bar almost deserted. Jess and Damian were serving the last few stragglers and I began getting ready to close. It looked like we might get an early one tonight, which, in one respect, was good, because I needed sleep, but the bills wouldn't pay themselves.

As I cleaned up, I knocked a glass to the floor and it shattered everywhere.

Bloody hell, why couldn't things be easy for once?

I bent down to clean it and when I stood after getting all the glass picked up, I came face to face with a man sporting a long scar down his face. Malice clung to him and the hairs on the back of my neck raised. I feared for my safety and instinctively took a step back. When his two friends stepped forward with hostility clear on their faces, I figured we were as good as fucked.

"Dale in?" Scarface enquired.

"No."

"Where is he, sweetheart?" His voice gave me chills.

"I haven't seen him for two days so I can't help you there."

His face darkened. "Looks like we've got a problem then, you and me. He owes me a lot of money and I need that money within the next forty-eight hours."

"Fuck off. It's not my debt to clear up."

"You're Layla, right? His business partner?"

Shit, how the hell did he know that? "Even if I am, it's still got nothing to do with me."

"He used his bar as collateral so it's got everything to do with you."

"You've got to be fucking kidding me." Anger didn't begin to cover my feelings toward Dale now. I should have done some damage to him the other day.

"I don't fucking kid. When I come back in two days, I'll expect to see the twenty grand he owes me."

My head almost exploded. *Twenty fucking grand!*

"There's no way I can come up with that kind of money in two days."

"It's a pity."

"Huh?"

He dipped his head at my hands. "You'll miss those fingers, sweetheart."

"Are you fucking threatening me, asshole?" Yeah, possibly not my best move, pissing a man like him off.

Something behind Scarface caught my eye, and I diverted my

attention to see what it was. The scary dude from earlier walked towards us. I hadn't realised he was still here.

He approached Scarface, aggression written all over him. "I see you've resorted to threatening innocent women these days, Mario."

Holy god, his voice had a dangerous tone to it.

Mario glowered at him. "Fuck off, Blade. This has nothing to do with you."

Blade.

"No, but I don't like the way you're talking to her. And I'm in the mood to help a friend out."

Friend? Where the hell had that come from?

Mario quirked his brows and looked at me as he said, "You've got some friends in low places, sweetheart." I really wished he would stop calling me that.

Blade shot me a look that very clearly told me not to step into this.

"How about you leave her alone and search harder for the guy you're after," Blade suggested.

"And how about you leave me to deal with this the way I choose. Don't you have other shit to take care of?"

Blade stepped closer to Mario, his hard glare sending a very clear message. *Don't fuck with me.* "I've always got shit to take care of." He thought about something for a minute before saying, "You know, I was talking to Ice the other day, and he mentioned you owe him a bit at the moment. Asked me what I thought he should do and I told him you'd probably be good for it. I'm rethinking that advice now."

I caught the slight widening of Mario's eyes. It looked like Blade had hit gold. His face reddened with anger. "You've always fucking had it in for me. Why the fuck are you sticking your nose into this shit? You got something going on with her?"

I opened my mouth to set him straight, but Blade shook his head at me before glaring back at Mario. "None of your goddamn business, motherfucker. All you need to know is I *will* fuck with you if you fuck with her."

His last threat seemed to do the trick. Mario took a step away from the bar and motioned for his men to follow suit. He turned his gaze to me. "Looks like it's your lucky fucking day, sweetheart. But when you see Dale, you tell him I'm looking for him."

He stalked out of the bar and when I could no longer see him, I turned to Blade. "What the hell was that?"

Raising his brows, he asked, "What? No thank you?"

"I don't know who the hell you are, and what the hell you're involved in, but I figure it's not a good thing a debt collector like that asshole thinks I'm your woman."

"That's where you're wrong. Him thinking you're my woman is the best thing that happened to you tonight."

"Fuck!" I was so angry at this whole situation and the fact I had no control over any of it.

"Trust me, Layla, he won't be back to bother you."

"How the hell do you know that?"

"The guy I mentioned, Ice? He's a drug dealer and the amount of money Mario owes him is enough to get him killed if Ice feels so inclined."

Holy shit, who the fuck is this man standing in front of me to know all these shady people?

"So you'd have enough sway to convince Ice to do that?"

His stare told me everything I needed to know even if he chose not to answer me. "Let's just say you're safe and leave it at that."

My head began to pound. "Why would he be after my business partner? Like, what kind of shit does that mean Dale's gotten himself into?"

"Horses."

I placed one hand on my hip and ran the other across my forehead while I expelled a long breath. "Jesus, I knew Dale liked to gamble here and there, but I never realised he had a problem with it. I should have, though."

"Why?"

"I've worked with him for years, and then, about twelve months ago, he asked me if I wanted to buy into the bar. I knew he did that because he needed money, but I thought it was to help his ex-wife out. Then, two days ago I discovered he's been stealing from the business. Little bits here and there that I didn't miss or notice, but now there's no cash left in our bank account and it seems he's done a runner."

"He played you for a fool, huh?"

"Yeah, and I can't fucking believe I didn't see it."

Jess and Damian had stayed quiet through this whole thing but Jess interrupted us now. "You're not a fool, Layla. You trusted someone who took advantage of that trust, but it doesn't make you a fool."

"If I ever see him again, it won't be pretty," I muttered.

Jess grinned. "I can imagine." She knew me well. Knew I gave people one chance only. If they fucked with that, I didn't go back for seconds.

Blade's phone rang and he walked away to take the call. I went back to helping Jess and Damian get ready to close the bar. We were almost done and I couldn't wait to get out of here tonight. The stress of the last two days had started catching up on me, and all I wanted to do was sleep it off.

When he finished with his call, Blade came back to me. "What's your phone number?"

"Why?"

"I'm gonna check in on you, make sure Mario's not giving you grief."

"I can take care of myself, Blade," I answered, annoyed.

"Yeah, I saw that." His sarcasm was not lost on me.

"We don't need to exchange numbers."

Frustration crossed his face, but he remained patient. "Humour me, okay?"

"Oh for fuck's sake, fine," I snapped and rattled off my number to him.

He saved it on his phone and then sent me a text message. "Now you have mine, too. Use it if you need me."

I could imagine there were plenty of women who would kill to have that phone number. Blade was a good-looking man and had a mysterious sexiness about him, but there was no way in hell I would ever be using that number. However, I nodded in agreement. I figured he wouldn't leave until I agreed to that.

"Good," he murmured, and began to walk away from me.

I let my gaze drop to his ass. He had a *great* ass and the jeans he wore hugged him, accentuating it. My gaze travelled up his body. He was wearing a black t-shirt and black leather jacket. The memory of how hard his chest was came back to me, causing desire to shoot through me.

"Drinks are on the house next time you come in," I yelled out.

He turned back to me, and with a flicker of a smile, said, "Finally, she says thank you."

Fuck, he read me well. "Yeah, yeah," I said, waving a dismissive hand at him.

He gave me a chin jerk. Still no full smile, but he didn't strike me as the kind of man to give out too many of those. "Catch you later," he said, and then he was gone.

Jess yelled out from the table she was cleaning, "He's hot. You should *so* call that number."

"I second that motion," Damian chimed in.

I scowled at him. "You fucking would."

He grinned. "Can I have his number if you're not gonna use it?"

I shook my head at him. "Something tells me Blade isn't gay. I think you're shit out of luck there, dude."

"I think you might be right, boss lady. Why is it all the hot guys are straight?" he grumbled.

I snorted. "That's what she said."

He laughed and we finished closing up. As I worked, my thoughts drifted to the events of the night. I was a little concerned about Mario coming back but, at the same time, I was fairly sure Blade had sorted that out for me. Something told me he was a man you didn't mess with, even if you were a debt collector who chopped fingers off for a living. And that in itself kind of scared me, because I didn't know whether owing Blade something would come back to bite me in the ass or not.

CHAPTER 4

BLADE

I STEERED THE CAR TOWARDS SCOTT'S HOUSE. WE'D organised to meet there this morning to discuss Storm business. My mind should have been focused on that, but it wasn't. Instead, it was focused entirely on Layla. I couldn't get the dark-haired beauty out of my mind after last night. She seemed to be a strong woman, and yet I'd sensed a vulnerability to her. I was attracted to that. I didn't want to think about it, but that side of her reminded me so much of Ashley. She hid it well, though. Ashley hadn't and she'd let me in easily. I sensed Layla wouldn't be the kind of woman to do that.

Fuck, why was I even thinking about this? It wasn't like I was interested in starting something. I'd learnt women were best kept at arm's length. Since Ashley's death, I hadn't found a woman who came close to her. All I'd found were women interested in themselves, and fucked if I'd spend my life with a woman like that. I craved someone with a genuine kindness to them, someone who cared about other people as much as they cared about themself, and I'd rather end up alone than settle for less than that.

When I arrived at Scott's, he was deep in conversation with Harlow on their front lawn. Neither appeared happy, and this surprised me; from what I knew, they were tight. I watched as Scott pulled her back as she turned to leave. His grip on her wrist looked firm, and she struggled out of it but let him continue talking. Whatever was going on with them appeared to be serious.

Eventually, he finished talking and pulled her to him to lay a kiss on her forehead, and then she headed to her car in the driveway. I watched her leave as I walked to where he was standing. He'd seen me, but his gaze was fixed on Harlow, and he didn't turn to me until her car had left the street.

"Morning." He gave me a perfunctory look before turning and taking the stairs up to his house.

I followed silently. Once we were inside, he offered me coffee and as he made it, I asked cautiously, "Everything good with you and Harlow?" Being in Scott's home wasn't something I experienced often. And being alone with him even less. There was a distance between us that, as much as I'd tried to close it, had hardly changed since we'd met last year. We were both too stubborn and moody for our own good. I inwardly grimaced: a trait we shared with our father.

He glanced at me before giving his attention back to the coffee. His voice was off when he finally spoke. "No, we're going through some stuff at the moment. It's fucked." His hands stilled and his gaze hit mine. What I saw there made me suck in a breath. Whatever was going on, Scott was having a tough time at the moment because his face was a mask of torment. His eyes were hard when he added, "Everything's fucked."

I let him get it out and then let him finish making coffee. It was obvious he didn't want to talk about it so I didn't force it. A few minutes later, he placed a mug in front of me and said, "Marcus's first coke shipment hit the streets this week. Seems this has pissed some of your old friends off."

"Who?" Actually, I had a good idea who he was talking about but needed to know the name. It wasn't a name I wanted to hear, though.

"Ricky Grecian." His stare penetrated me; he knew what this name meant to me.

I acknowledged it with a quick nod. "Figured that would happen."

"What does this mean for Storm?" He asked the question but he had to know the repercussions. Everyone in Brisbane knew Ricky was a man to be avoided at all costs.

I humoured him regardless. "Let's just say Ricky will twist your balls till you wished you didn't fucking have any, because the thing about him is he likes to play with his opponents for a while. He'll eventually try to take you out but he likes to have some fun beforehand." I paused before adding, "Ricky's a sadistic fuck. Has Marcus got this covered?"

Scott raked his hand through his hair, the look on his face indicating he clearly didn't think so, but he replied, "He says he has but I have my doubts. And the division in the club at the moment won't help us."

"Where are you at with all this?" It had been a few months since Griff took over as Vice President, and I'd watched as the club had slowly begun falling apart. The support Marcus and Griff had at first was beginning to take a hit. I suspected this had to do with the direction Marcus was taking the club; he'd made a lot of promises in order to gather support, but the reality of it wasn't as rosy.

He drank some of his coffee and took his time answering me. "More of the boys have come to me with concerns about how Marcus is handling stuff. Problem is they haven't voiced that to him so he thinks they're all behind him, and still will be behind him, when shit goes down with Ricky."

"You need to deal with that, and soon."

He blew out a long breath. "Fuck, Blade, what the hell do you think I'm trying to fucking do? I've got J and Nash helping, but even between the three of us, with all the other normal club business we've got to take care of, shit's going slow."

"I'm telling you, don't fuck around with Ricky. Put your other shit to the side and take care of this first. Otherwise, you might not have a club to even worry about."

As we sat in frustrated silence, glaring at each other, a voice boomed from the front door. "Scott, why is this fuckin' cat still at your house giving me grief?"

I turned to see Nash entering the kitchen a moment later. He lifted his chin in greeting before looking at Scott with a perplexed gaze. "What's up with the cat?"

Scott shrugged. "Fucked if I know. Monty seems to like it here more than next door. Lisa's over here visiting Harlow half the fuckin' time so I guess her cat just follows. What's your problem with him?"

"He has it in for me! Tries to attack me every fuckin' time he sees me," Nash grumbled.

"Jesus Christ, Nash, he's a fuckin' cat, for god's sake. Get your shit together. We've got more important things to worry about at the moment," Scott snapped.

"Fuck you, asshole," Nash muttered.

I cut in, "I don't have time to sit around talking about a fucking cat. Nash, where are you at with that lead on Blue you mentioned to me the other day?"

He scowled before answering me. "We're thinking Blue could be an old Storm member who's now living in Western Australia. He had a heart attack years ago and moved back home. But he was tight with Marcus before they had a falling out, so, we're figuring, even if he's not Blue he might have an idea who is."

"You going to check it out?"

Nash nodded. "Yeah, heading out tomorrow."

"Good. It's way past fucking time we worked this riddle out. Whoever the hell this Blue is, he's damn good at covering his tracks. I've never had my boys come up blank when looking for someone." I drank the rest of my coffee and started heading out of the kitchen. I gave Scott one last glance. "Going back to Ricky: I've known him to kill for less than what Marcus has stirred up. Don't fuck around with this."

Scott acknowledged that with a quick nod. "I'll be in touch," he promised, and I left him and Nash to it. As I walked to my car, images of Ricky flashed through my mind. Sick, twisted images I'd done my best to forget. They'd always be there, though, because the filth of Ricky himself was stained on my soul, and as much as I'd tried to eradicate him from it, we'd seen and done too much together for me to ever be able to completely forget.

★★★

I found myself at Layla's bar again that night. I'd discovered her business a little over a year ago and came nearly every night. It was a small bar in The Valley, tucked away in a laneway and afforded me the quiet I needed after a long day. The staff left me alone as well, so that was its final selling point. Up until last night, I'd hardly spoken to any of them. As I entered, I took in how quiet it was for a Friday night. Not good for Layla if she had no cash in the bank.

She was behind the bar and gave me a nod when she saw me. As I headed towards her, she motioned for me to take a seat in my usual corner. I did as she directed, figuring she was going to make good on her offer of a free drink.

A few minutes later, she placed a scotch on the table and slid into the seat across from me. I knocked half the drink back before giving her my attention. Fuck, she really was beautiful. Long, wavy, dark hair framed her face, and curves a man could grip onto filled out her body. She wore tight jeans and a fitted t-shirt. It hugged her breasts and distracted the hell out of me.

"We had some big spenders in here today," she said, her eyes firmly on mine.

"Good to hear."

"Figured you might know something about that."

"How's that?"

"It's unusual for us to ever have that type of customer, and then, when one of them mentioned the name Blade, I figured you must have sent them. So I asked them, and fuck me if they didn't tell me they work for you."

Her irritation confused me. "I did mention your bar to some of my guys. Thought they may be interested in an out of the way place to relax after work."

"Did you also fund their little jaunt in here?"

I shrugged. "They were owed bonuses."

"Fuck," she muttered, her eyes flashing annoyance at me.

I threw back the rest of my drink. "What's the problem here, Layla? You need customers and my boys need somewhere to drink. It's a win-win for everyone," I said, still not understanding the problem.

"I don't like owing people, Blade, and now I owe you for two things."

"Consider the first debt paid."

She frowned. "How?"

I held up my empty glass. "You bought me a drink."

"Yeah, like that covers it."

"Get me another if you must, but after that we're square."

She pushed her chair back and stood. "Don't do shit for me anymore, okay? I can look after myself."

I watched her walk to the bar, that ass swaying from side to side, causing my dick to harden. Fuck, she was something else. Where did that fight in her come from? Something had to have happened to her in life for her to be that tough and independent.

When she returned with another drink, she placed it in front of me and turned to leave straight away. I reached out and grabbed her wrist, stopping her. She gave me a questioning look and I murmured, "Stay." Fuck knows why, but the urge to sit with her, talk to her, was overwhelming. I hadn't experienced this desire for a long time. Not since Ashley.

She stared at me for a few moments.

Yeah, I'd think about sitting with me too.

"Who are you?" she asked as she sat. Her eyes held a challenge in them. She had to have worked out I ran in some seedy circles if I had the ability to convince Mario to back off.

"You know my name. That's all you need to know." Fuck, even my house cleaner thought I was simply a man who owned a construction company. I didn't share my shit with anyone unless they were on a need to know basis.

"What's your real name? I doubt your mother named you Blade."

I remained silent as I filed through what I knew about her. Honesty and trustworthiness were high on her list of what she desired in a person. I figured that probably meant she possessed them.

Ah, fuck it.

"Donovan." I raised my glass to my lips and swallowed the burn of the scotch sliding down. No one got that name out of me.

"Donovan who?" Her eyes flashed more of that challenge at me. And fuck if I didn't like it.

"Brookes."

She crossed her arms in front of her and settled back into the chair. "How hard was that for you, Donovan?"

I drank the rest of my drink and slammed the empty glass on the table. She didn't even flinch, just continued to give me that hard glare of hers. I leaned forward a little and lowered my voice. "To be clear, no one gets that name. Don't go giving it out."

"Don't do me anymore favours."

"Christ, you drive a hard bargain, woman."

"Like I said, I don't like to owe anyone."

"So you're telling me, if I come in here and find you being threatened by someone, I should just let that shit happen?" It wasn't really a question, though, and she knew that.

She didn't say anything so I continued, "'Cause I'm telling you now, that's not gonna happen. Ever."

"Fine. If something like that happens, do whatever you want."

"Thank Christ we can agree on that," I muttered. Her challenging way divided me. One minute I liked it, the next it irritated the hell out of me.

"You gonna tell me who you are?"

"I already did. But you haven't told me who you are."

She pursed her lips before saying, "Layla Reed, and no, you didn't tell me what you know I'm looking for."

"You want to know how I know Mario and how I could get him to back off."

Her hands flew up in the air. "Yes!"

I shook my head. "That's not information I share with most of the people I know, let alone a woman I just met."

"So I take it that what I'm thinking you're tied up in is probably correct."

"Think what you like, Layla. Most people do."

"I don't usually spend this amount of time thinking about people, Donovan, but you've got me intrigued."

Her use of my real name jolted me back eight years. Ashley used to insist on calling me that.

I stood abruptly. "Thanks for the drinks."

She looked up at me. "Thanks for sorting Mario out for me."

"You're welcome," I murmured, giving her a long, last look.

Layla Reed could be dangerous. I savoured the deliciousness of that knowledge because danger always attracted me. I'd be back, but tonight, the ghosts of the past haunted me and I needed to be alone to deal with that.

CHAPTER 5

LAYLA

MY COUSIN, ANNIE, LIVED IN SQUALOR, AND AS MUCH AS I tried to help her, she wouldn't help herself. Ever since that fateful day nine years ago when I'd discovered her shocking secret, I'd been scrambling to help her make changes in her life. Hell, I'd fucking committed a crime for her in amongst everything else I'd done, and yet she still couldn't pull her head out of her ass.

I stood in her kitchen, assessing the mess of dirty dishes and rubbish strewn everywhere. Annie sat at the table, her head in her hands while she sobbed. The desperation of her life clung to the air around us and my skin crawled with the need to escape. But Annie needed me, so I stayed.

"Do you want some tea?" I asked. Tea always made me feel better.

Her tearstained face looked up at me and she nodded. "Yes," she choked out her answer in between sobs.

I had to wash dishes and clear space to be able to make tea. That pissed me off, and when I placed the tea in front of her, I did so with a little more force than necessary. Tea spilt over the edge of the mug, and Annie looked up at me apologetically. She knew how furious I was.

"Sorry," she mumbled, her eyes avoiding mine.

I sat at the table with her and sighed. "Annie, you know I love you. I mean, I almost fucking killed a man for you, I took you in, I paid for you to go to college...I've done every-fucking-thing I can to help you have a better life, so why the hell do you throw it in my face and continue to accept shit in your life?" My voice grew louder, more forceful. "Your boyfriend is an asshole who doesn't love you, and he treats you like you're the shit on his shoes. He does *nothing* for you and expects you to do everything for him. Fuck, look at this place. It's disgusting. You were doing better before you hooked up with him, and now you've taken so many steps backwards. I find it heartbreaking to watch."

She stared at me with wide eyes and listened to everything I had to say before starting to cry again. Her body heaved with sobs and I let her get it all out without saying a word. A very fucking hard thing to do. Eventually she said, "It's my fault. I don't want to have sex with him . . . I can't do it . . . and it upsets him . . . " Her voice trailed off as more tears fell.

My skin heated with anger and my shoulders tensed. *How fucking dare he*! "Annie, look at me," I demanded.

She didn't do what I said so I repeated myself, louder this time, "Annie, look at me!"

She jumped in her seat and quickly moved her gaze to mine. The hopelessness I saw there made me want to rip the balls off her boyfriend. I softened my voice. "You've done nothing wrong. Your father fucked you up, Annie, to the point where you have major issues with sex. That is not your fault. If you had a boyfriend who loved you and actually cared enough about you, he would help you through that.

It's not your fault he chooses, instead, to screw around on you and emotionally abuse you. Do you understand that?"

She stared at me. It was an almost vacant stare. When she slowly nodded, I knew she didn't mean it. Annie had no self-esteem.

Fuck.

I shoved my chair back and stood. Looking down at her, I said, "We're leaving."

Her eyes turned frantic and she madly shook her head. "No . . . I can't leave . . . where will I go?" Tears began falling again, and I moved to her so I could place my hand on her shoulder.

I squatted so I was at her eye level. "Annie," I said in a gentle tone, "you can stay with me. I will look after you and help you get back on your feet." I should have made her come live with me years ago, but I was always focused on helping her gain independence. What I should have focused on was getting her mind to a good place before sending her out into the world on her own. I'd do that this time. She needed to see a psychologist to begin working through the shit weighing her down.

She didn't seem convinced, but nevertheless, she stood and nodded. "Okay."

I quickly packed some clothes in a bag for her. I didn't want to risk her changing her mind, so I worked fast to get her out of there. For a twenty-five year old woman, she owned very little so it didn't take me long. Fifteen minutes later, I bundled her into my car and made the half-hour drive home. Annie sat next to me staring out the window, not saying a word. I prayed like hell she would run with this plan and not slink back to her boyfriend.

★★★

I lived above the bar. It had been my home for six months. The decision to move here had been made in desperation when the house

I rented was sold and I had nowhere to go. My intention had never been for it to become a permanent home, it had just worked out that way over time. I liked it, though, and couldn't see myself moving out anytime soon.

It was three o'clock when Annie and I arrived back there. Jess was working and she gave me a sad smile when she saw me follow behind Annie. She knew Annie's story, and also knew I'd spent years trying to help her to no avail. "Hi Annie," she greeted her with kindness in her voice.

"Hi Jess," Annie replied, so softly I doubted Jess would have heard it.

"I'll meet you upstairs soon, hon," I said to Annie. "You unpack your stuff and get settled, and I'll see you in a couple of minutes."

"Okay," she murmured before giving me a small smile and heading upstairs.

With a heavy heart, I walked over to where Jess was at the bar.

"She moving in?" Jess inquired.

"Yeah. Her boyfriend is a dick and has been cheating on her and treating her like shit. I need to find her a psychologist and get her head sorted."

"You take too much on, Layla. She's a grown woman. Maybe it's time she started looking out for herself rather than relying on you to always swoop in and fix her problems."

I perched on a stool and rested my elbows on the bar. Blowing out a long breath, I said, "I know what you're saying, but I feel like I've never given her the tools to do that. And god fucking knows her parents didn't either, so she's almost like a child just floating aimlessly through life with no idea how to be an adult. I think if we can work with a professional, Annie might finally be able to gain the belief in herself and the skills she needs to move forward, you know?"

Jess considered what I'd said. "Maybe. Promise me, though, if you do this and put the time into it, and it doesn't work, you need to stop putting yourself through that. Annie's not only hurting herself here."

I knew she was coming from a good place, but she didn't have anyone in her life that needed her like Annie needed me, so she couldn't understand why I would never give up on my cousin. "I can't promise that, Jess."

We were both quiet for a few moments. Then she said, "I'm here if you need anything, okay?"

I smiled. Jess had worked here for a couple of years and we'd become good friends. We were the same age, twenty-seven, but where I had no family around me, except for Annie, she was surrounded by loving parents and five siblings. She'd taken me under her wing and introduced me to her family when she discovered I had no one. They'd welcomed me and made me an honorary member of their family. She always came through for me, even if she didn't agree with the choices I made. "Thank you," I said.

"Always."

I jumped off the stool. "I'm gonna head up and make sure she's okay. Just call if you need me."

She nodded. "Will do. What time is Damian coming in?"

"Seven, so I'll make sure I'm back down by five unless you call."

"Okay, boss," she said, waving her hands to indicate I should leave her to it.

I climbed the stairs slowly. Dealing with Annie was weary work, and while I never resented it, I didn't necessarily look forward to it. I found her in my spare bedroom, curled up on the bed, asleep, so I left her and headed back down to the bar.

Jess frowned as she caught sight of me. "Why aren't you upstairs?"

"She's asleep so I thought I would help you get the bar ready for tonight."

"Thanks."

I began helping her stock the bar and she asked, "Have you heard from Dale at all?"

"No." Anger swirled in my stomach just at the thought of him. *I'd hate to see my reaction if he walked back in here.*

"Do you think he's gone for good?"

I put the bottle that was in my hand down and contemplated her question. "I wouldn't be surprised. That's a lot of cash he owes and I can't think of anyone he knows who could lend it to him. If I were him, I wouldn't come back."

"Yes, you would," she stated, matter-of-factly. "You're too good of a person to do what he's done to you."

"Yeah, but if a bookie had me in his sights for that much, I think I'd run."

"Layla, you wouldn't. You're the kind of woman who gets shit done and finds a way when the rest of us think we've run out of options. But this conversation is a waste of time anyway, because you wouldn't get yourself in that kind of shit to begin with. And you certainly wouldn't steal from your friend."

"Well, there is that. You're damn right I wouldn't steal from a friend."

Her eyes lit up as if she just remembered something. "Have you heard from that guy? You know, the one who helped you the other night. The arm porn dude."

"The what?" *Arm porn?* Jess really did come out with some weird shit sometimes.

She grinned. "Did you get a look at his fucking arms? They're like looking at porn, babe. Guaranteed to get you off on sight."

I had to laugh. "I guess that's one way to think about it. And yeah, I did get a look at them."

"And?" She had that excited energy about her which usually meant she was formulating plans in her head.

I put my hand on my hip and gave her a stern look. "And what?"

"Oh god, Layla! Do you even notice when men are interested in you?" she asked me, looking exasperated.

"He's not interested in me," I muttered, trying to ignore the flutter in my belly. I may have been attracted to him, but to get involved with him could only be a bad idea. The shit he seemed to be involved in wasn't anything I wanted to be near.

Jess pulled a face. "He is. You'll see."

Yeah, we'd see, but I had no interest in pursuing anything.

Well, maybe sex. That couldn't hurt, could it?

★★★

He stepped through the front door of the bar at near midnight that night, and my tummy fluttered again. Just at the sight of him.

Dear lord.

I stood at the bar and watched as he strode toward me. He was wearing his standard outfit – jeans and black t-shirt teamed with his heavy boots. Tattoos peaked out from under his sleeves, and they only served to accentuate his muscles.

And turn me on.

"You okay?" he asked when he met me at the bar. Concern creased his face, and I wondered if I should be worried.

"Yeah, why?"

"Just checking. You haven't seen or heard from Mario?"

"No," I answered him, and then added, "Should I have?"

He raked his hand through his hair. Not that he had a lot of hair; it was cut quite close to his head. I had a thing for bald men, so I loved that. Pushing out a breath, he said, "Sorry, didn't mean to worry you. Been a long day with a lot of shit going down, so I just wanted to make sure Mario was keeping his end of the bargain."

I relaxed and pulled out the scotch to pour him a drink. It seemed he needed one. "You looking for a reason to get those fists out?"

His brows rose. "Am I that easy to read?"

I slid his scotch across the bar, our eyes fixed on each other. "Just a little."

He picked up his drink and held it for a moment while maintaining eye contact with me. I couldn't shift my gaze even if I'd wanted to. And it seemed he couldn't, either. He finally drank some of the scotch, his eyes still on mine. Placing the glass on the bar, he murmured, "Knew you were dangerous."

What he said didn't make any sense, but before I could ask him what he meant, he said, "I'm gonna take a seat. Can you keep the drinks coming?"

"Sure."

I watched as he walked away.

What the hell did he mean by that statement?

I didn't have time to contemplate it because Annie came down to the bar and distracted me. She'd been crying again, and my gut seized with apprehension.

Had that asshole been in contact with her?

I placed my hand gently on her arm. "What's wrong?"

"He rang me and told me not to bother coming home." She spoke through sniffles.

I checked my frustration and controlled my voice to keep the annoyance out of it. "Annie, you don't *want* to go back. Remember?"

She nodded. "Yes, but it's hard. We were together for ages, and, besides you, he's all I had."

I put my hand out. "Give me your phone."

"What?"

"Give me your phone so he can't ring you and fuck with your head again."

She stared at me with indecision. The thing with Annie was I could totally control her if I tried, and while I hated what I was doing, it would be for the best when all was said and done.

I clicked my fingers and snapped, "Now."

She quickly reached into her back jean pocket, pulled her phone out and gave it to me. It was better I controlled her for a while than some asshole only looking out for his own needs.

"Good," I said, placing her phone in my pocket. "Now, I want you to go up to bed because tomorrow you start work."

She stiffened. "Work?"

"Yes, you can work here while you stay with me."

"I don't know anything about working in a bar." Panicked features stared back at me.

I ignored her worry. "It'll be fine. I'll show you everything you need to know. Promise."

She relaxed a little. Whenever I promised something, I always came through, and she knew that. "Okay, Layla."

I waited until she'd gone upstairs before shaking my head and expelling a frustrated breath.

Lord help us.

"Layla."

I turned to see Jess watching me. "She okay? We can cope down here without you if you want to go up and sit with her."

I shook my head. "Thanks, but I think she'll be alright by herself."

Jess's attention shifted to something behind me, and I looked around to find her looking at Donovan. *Blade.* I liked his given name better.

His gaze pierced me, stirring my lust. "Oh, shit," I muttered as the lust unfurled through me.

"What?" Jess asked.

"I was supposed to keep his drinks coming."

She grinned. "Well, you better get onto that then."

I groaned at her subtlety. "I should send you over."

"Nope, can't do it. I've already got too much to do. You'll have to take care of Mr Arm Porn." She kept grinning as she brushed past me to get back to work.

"I'll remember this," I muttered as I poured his scotch.

When I placed it in front of him a couple of moments later, he asked, "Who's the redhead?"

Momentarily confused, I frowned. "Who?"

He jerked his chin toward the bar. "The little redhead you were just talking to."

Annie.

"She's my cousin." I narrowed my eyes at him. "Why?"

He shrugged. "I like to know who all the players are."

"Who all the players are? What the fuck?"

"Layla, you're in some serious shit here. I'm keeping an eye on everyone involved, so when I see a new face, I like to know who we're dealing with."

Seriously?

I pulled the spare seat back and sat down, glaring at him. "I'll tell you who the fuck we're dealing with, Donovan. Her name's Annie and she's my cousin. I've just moved her in with me to get her away from her deadbeat asshole of a boyfriend. Annie is the sweetest girl, but she struggles in life due to the shit her father dealt her growing up. She has absolutely nothing to do with Mario so you can stop wondering about her. Annie wouldn't hurt a fly." My pulse sped up, racing through my body while my heart pounded in my chest. I wouldn't have Annie involved in this shit.

He shifted forward in his seat and dipped his head a little to bring his gaze closer to mine. "I didn't think she would. I'm more concerned about Mario sniffing her out if he comes back here. That he'd use her against you. Anyone can see the girl is vulnerable."

Shit.

I slumped in the chair, my body returning to its normal state. *Some days it just felt like all the shit was piling up and I had no way out from under it.* "Does life ever get to you?" I asked. He seemed so in control all the time.

He stared at me. I couldn't read him, though. Couldn't figure out what thoughts were running through his mind. Finally, he admitted, "Some days, yes." And down came his guard a little. The hard lines of his face softened, and as he scrubbed a hand over his face, I noticed his exhaustion.

"Only some days?"

His lips curved into a small smile. "Perhaps more often than that."

"I don't know, Donovan...It just seems like every time I think life is going well, shit happens and screws it up. The two steps forward turn into three steps back some days."

"Diamonds are made under pressure," he murmured, eyes glued to mine, and I held my breath for a moment as I processed what he'd said. No one had ever given me a compliment like that, and I didn't know what to make of it.

As I scrambled for what to say, he continued, "No one calls me Donovan anymore. I like it on your lips." He drank some more of his scotch, eyes still on me.

God, he was something else. I'd never met a man like him. One who had the ability to make me want him even when I wanted nothing to do with him at the same time. One who threatened to set my panties on fire with words alone.

"I prefer it to Blade. How'd you get that name?" I asked.

He finished his drink, and carefully placed the glass back on the table before looking at me. "Probably best if I don't share that story with you." The intense way he looked at me sent shivers through my body.

I really wanted to know that story.

"Try me," I challenged.

His eyes searched mine, looking for what, I wasn't sure.

"Not much surprises me anymore, Donovan," I added.

"Yeah? You'd be surprised at what surprises me."

"Like what?"

"Like discovering I've been drinking at a bar for a year or so now, and never knew that the woman serving me drinks would turn out to be the most fascinating woman I've met in eight years."

I couldn't see them, but I was sure my eyes must have bulged out of my head. I didn't say a word. Mostly because my mouth felt glued shut, but also because I had no idea what to say to that.

His lips twitched, not quite forming into a full smile, but it gave me a glimpse of what he'd look like if he actually did smile. I had no doubt that when Donovan Brookes smiled, it would open his face up into the most beautiful face I'd ever seen on a man.

"Surprised?" he asked, and he surprised me again with the playfulness I heard in his tone. Only slight, but I caught it.

"Twice. Don't do it again or I might fall off my chair," I joked. It'd be interesting to see if he played along. I wasn't sure he had it in him.

His small smile spread across his face, and I was right. Donovan *was* the most beautiful man I'd ever met. My core agreed and desire shot through me.

Oh god, where was this leading?

"Duly noted," he murmured.

I returned his smile. "Good." I pushed my chair back and stood. "I should get back to work," I said, even though it was the last thing I wanted to do.

He grabbed my wrist to stop me. His firm grasp sent more shivers through me as I imagined his hands on me, holding me. "You want me to have a word with Annie's boyfriend? Sort him out so he doesn't give her anymore grief?"

I knew what he was asking, and while I kind of liked the idea of that asshole getting *sorted out* by Donovan, I wanted to be there, too,

53

because I had some words to say to him first. "As long as I can tag along."

He was silent for a moment, and I could just imagine all the thinking going on in his head. I doubted his thoughts ever gave him a moment's peace. "Okay, but you do what I say if shit goes south."

He had a lot to get to know about me.

I ignored that and asked, "When?"

"Tomorrow. I'll drop by about three and pick you up if that works for you?"

"Sure."

Bring it on. I wasn't sure if my excitement stemmed more from telling Annie's boyfriend off or spending time with Donovan.

CHAPTER 6

BLADE

I GRIPPED THE BATHROOM VANITY AND STARED IN THE mirror. Fucking three am, and I was awake again because of another fucking dream. And, once again, sweat covered me.

Fuck.

I turned the shower on and stepped in. If only I could cleanse the bad memories from my mind as easily as the sweat from my body. *Why the hell didn't killing Bullet give me fucking peace?* 'Cause it sure as fuck hadn't.

The night gave way to day as I dealt with my emails, phone calls, and meetings with Merrick and my boys. There was nothing out of the ordinary today. Three o'clock rolled around, and exhaustion called my name. But as I stepped through the front door of Layla's bar, I felt pumped. The dual thoughts of seeing her and kicking someone's ass if they needed it fuelled my newfound energy.

Thursday afternoon seemed to be a quiet time. There were only ten customers by my count. I slowed my approach as I made my way to where Layla stood at the bar. Her ass was on full display while she bent over picking something up from the floor. *Fuck, her curves were sexy.* My gaze stayed glued to them until she retrieved whatever she was after and straightened. She spun around on the spot and caught me staring at her.

"Fuck, do you always creep up on people like that?" she asked, her hand going to her chest and her eyes wide.

"Sorry, didn't mean to frighten you," I apologised.

She calmed herself down and waved my apology away. "No, it's all good, I was in my own little world and then heard you. You didn't frighten me, just made me jump a little."

I followed her to the end of the bar where she had her bag. "You ready?" I watched her rummage through it like a madwoman. What the hell women kept in their bags was beyond me.

"Yeah, just gotta tell the girls I'm going out. I'll be right back." She slung her bag over her shoulder and ducked out of sight through a doorway.

Within a couple of minutes she was back, and I followed her outside. She came to a stop and I realised she needed to know which car belonged to me.

"The black Jag," I said, pointing towards it.

She dropped her head slightly and raised her brows at me. "I probably could have worked out which car it was without the colour."

I scanned the street. She had a point; there were no other Jags to be seen. I ignored her statement, though, and opened the door for her. This earned me another eyebrow raise. "What?" I asked.

She slid into the seat before looking up at me. "It's not often a man opens the door for a woman anymore."

"There should be more of it," I said.

"I agree."

Once she had her seatbelt on, I closed her door and walked around to my side. I had no idea where we were going today, but I hoped it wasn't close by. The more time alone with her, the better, as far as I was concerned.

A couple of minutes later, I pulled away from the kerb, and we were silent until she said, "I always wondered why people would spend so much on a car. Still don't really get it, but this is pretty damn comfortable."

I found her honesty refreshing. Glancing at her, I asked, "Did you grow up with money?"

"Yes."

"But they didn't spend it on cars?"

"They did. They had so much money and bought anything and everything they wanted or thought I wanted." She paused before adding softly, "We were the most miserable people you could ever meet. Money did that to us."

"And that's why you wonder why people spend so much on cars."

"Bingo. If my parents had spent their time like they spent their money, happy would have been my middle name." She shifted in her seat, and I glanced across to see her looking at me. "How about you, Donovan? Did you have money growing up?"

"No. My mother worked her ass off just to give me the basics, let alone anything else."

"So, it was just you and your mother?"

"Yeah."

"And your Dad? Where was he?"

Usually, I hated being pushed to talk about Marcus, so it stunned the hell out of me when I found myself answering her question. "Marcus was married to another woman and had another family. He visited us when it suited him and hardly gave my mother any money."

She sat silently next to me. When she still hadn't said anything a couple of moments later, I turned to look at her. She was staring at me with a look I couldn't place. I frowned. "What?"

"No offence to you, because you strike me as one of the good guys, but fuck, men can be assholes sometimes."

I nodded and murmured, "Yeah."

If only she knew the half of it.

We retreated from each other, lost in our own minds for the remainder of the trip. It was an easy silence. Hell, although Layla could be stubborn and argumentative, being with her *was* easy. The half-hour drive passed quickly, and when she directed me to the rundown house in a shitty suburb I knew well, I cursed under my breath.

The past always came back to bite you in the ass.

I cut the engine and looked at Layla. "Why don't you wait here while I go in and deal with this?"

"Like hell. I told you I wanted to be here for this. I've got shit I want to say to him, too."

I squeezed my fingers around the steering wheel. Why did she have to choose now to dig her heels in? "Layla, I told you, if shit went south you had to do as I said."

"Shit hasn't gone south yet."

"Yeah, well, it's about to."

She narrowed her eyes on me. "Why? What are you about to do?"

I shook my head. "It's not what I'm about to do. It's what Gary's about to do." Gary was a loose cannon. Fuck knew how he'd handle me showing up here.

I watched as she processed my words and saw the moment she realised exactly what I was saying in not so many words. "Shit! You know Gary."

"Yeah."

"Well, so do I, and he's a fucking asshole I need to have words with, so until shit *really* goes south, I'm coming in," she declared and exited the car.

Fuck.

I got out as well and hurried to catch up to her. She was nearly at the front door and I had to stop her before she barged in and caused no end of fucking problems. I caught her by the wrist and pulled her back. "Layla," I hissed, "I'm not kidding when I say you need to let me handle this."

She scowled at me and yanked her wrist out of my grip. "And I'm not kidding when I say I have something to tell him."

We stood glaring at each other, neither backing down. And then Gary ripped the door open and stepped outside.

"Blade? What the fuck?" Confusion plastered his face as he looked between Layla and me. To her, he said, "I'm done with you and that bitch cousin of yours so you can fuck off."

That did it for Layla. She shoved past me and got in his face. "Don't come anywhere near Annie ever again. You've spent the last year shredding what little self-esteem she had to pieces. You're a fucking asshole, and I hope the next woman you fuck with squeezes the shit out of your balls and screws you over."

I thought she was done, but she wasn't. Once she'd said her piece, she caught him off guard with a knee to the balls. As he doubled over in pain, she placed her hands on his shoulders and pushed him so hard he fell on his back. Hell, this was a woman on a mission, and I stood back and enjoyed the show. She wasn't quite finished yet and took a determined step forward so she could press her boot to his dick. Bending down slightly, she threatened, "You come near Annie again, and I'll find ways to make you hurt worse than this."

Goddamn, I was growing hard watching her.

She pressed harder on his dick, and he screamed in pain. "Tell me you understand, motherfucker," she demanded, and he nodded his head furiously. Oh yeah, he understood. She removed her foot and said, "Good."

When she turned to look at me, I raised my brows. "You finished?"

Her chest heaved and she blew out a breath. "Yes."

I jerked my head towards the car. "Wait for me in the car."

I waited for her to protest, but she didn't. For once, she did what she was told and left us alone. I waited until she was settled in the car before reaching down to pull Gary up by his shirt. "You sorry sack of shit. Never did know how to treat a woman right, did you?" Memories of his past behaviour flooded my mind, and I had to restrain myself from doing some serious damage.

The pain Layla had inflicted was stamped on his face but he put on a show of being unaffected. He spat on the ground at my feet and sneered, "Ricky always did say you were a fucking pussy where women were concerned. Seems he was right."

Ricky Grecian.

Will I ever fucking escape him?

"There's such a thing as treating a woman right, asshole. Sadly, men like you and Ricky haven't got a fucking clue how to do it. If you come near Annie again, I will personally make sure you never have the ability to fuck with anyone again."

He stared at me. Probably weighing which step to take now. "I'm not fucking interested in her anyway. Fucking cunt wouldn't open her legs for me."

Blood roared in my head, and it threatened to explode with anger. My muscles tensed, ready to knock him the fuck out. I wanted his blood, fucking craved it for what he'd said and the way he'd treated Annie and the women before her. I dug my fingers into his shirt and gripped it hard. Pulling him to me, I roared, "Women weren't put on this earth for your fucking pleasure, motherfucker. If I so much as hear a whisper that you're up to your old tricks, so help you god." I maintained my hard grip on him for a few more moments before shoving him away from me.

He stumbled backwards but when he got his bearings, he stalked back towards me and got in my face. "You should watch your fucking back, Blade. Ricky's got plans to take you out, asshole, and I can't fucking wait to see that day. He should have done it years ago after you kicked him out."

The crunch of bone I heard when my fist connected with his face was the most satisfying sound I'd heard all day. I backed it up with a couple more punches until Gary was sprawled on the grass, his face a bloody mess. Standing over him, I growled, "Ricky can plan shit all he likes, but he doesn't have the backing he'd need to take me out. And you're wrong about one other thing: *I* shouldn't have let *him* walk away all those years ago."

I stalked to the car before I allowed my inner demons out to finish him off. He had no idea how close he'd come to death today. Possibly the only thing holding me back was Layla. Judging by her reaction to my blood-covered shirt when I slid into the seat next to her a moment later, she may not have cared.

Her gaze focused on my shirt. "I see you sorted him out."

I waited for her to shift her eyes to mine before answering. "Yeah, I sorted him out."

"Good," she said, and reached for her belt, clipping it in. "Now take me the hell home. I don't want to spend another fucking minute in this dump."

I couldn't agree with her more.

★★★

After I dropped Layla off back at her bar, I turned the car towards my mother's house. I wanted to check in on her, make sure she hadn't caved and let Marcus back in. On the drive there, I called Merrick.

"I want everything you can find about Layla Reed," I said when he answered.

"I'm one step ahead of you."

"You've got it already?" I asked, surprised he'd beaten me to it.

"Still gathering it, but yeah, almost done."

"Anything interesting so far?"

"Her family is Reed's Mining."

"Fuck." She wasn't kidding when she said she came from money. Her family was at the top of the social ladder. Everyone in Australia knew Reed's Mining.

"She dropped out of the public eye when she was eighteen, though. Cut all ties to her family and no one knows why. It was all very hush-hush at the time, but what seems odd is that her cousin, Annie, also dropped out at the same time."

"Where does Annie fit into all this?"

"Their fathers are brothers. They inherited the company together from their father."

"Something happened that concerned both of them, yeah?"

"That's my guess. It must have been bad, because Layla walked away from it all, both the family and the money. You ever hear of someone walking away from that kind of money?"

No one walked away from millions unless they had a damn good reason.

"Never."

"I'll keep digging, see what we can come up with," he promised.

"How the hell did you know I'd want this information?"

"Blade, you've been frequenting her bar for over a year, and now you've involved yourself with her problems, putting yourself out for her. You need me to go on?"

Fucker knew me better than I knew myself sometimes.

"No," I snapped.

"Where are you going now?"

"I'm gonna check in with my mother and then head over to see

Madison. Call me if you need me or have anything else to report about Layla."

"Will do," he said, and we ended the call.

The more I learnt about Layla, the more I wanted to get to know her and spend time with her. At the same time, it confused the fuck out of me. Ashley still haunted me, and I knew in my gut I hadn't dealt with that fully yet. To even consider opening up to someone new was madness.

CHAPTER 7

LAYLA

MIDNIGHT.

Friday night.

I stood at the bar and surveyed the room.

Where the fuck was all our customers?

"You want a drink, boss?"

I turned to Jess. She held vodka in her hand: my usual drink. Not tonight, I decided. Tonight was a tequila night. I shook my head and pointed at the tequila. "Pour me a shot of that. And you're having one with me. Damian can run the bar by himself with the amount of fucking people in here tonight."

She grinned. "Hell, yeah." She swapped the vodka for tequila and poured two shots.

After she passed me one, she raised her shot. "To good friends and good men."

I raised my shot as well, and we drank them down together. When I was done, I lined my shot glass up for another and asked,

"What's with that toast? Good men?"

She poured more drinks and explained, "You need to get laid, and it's been over a week since your man has been in here. Now, I'm not sure what happened there, so I'm toasting to good men in the hopes that either he comes back or someone else walks in."

I didn't wait for her this time; I threw the shot back, placed the glass on the bar and slid it her way for more. Eyeing her, I said, "Nothing happened with him, that's the weird thing. He was all about helping me, and then he just disappeared."

She shrugged and poured more drinks. "So odd. I would have bet money he was gonna make a move on you."

Damian finished with his customer and joined us. "You ladies getting trashed tonight?"

Jess grinned at him, held her shot up and drank it. "Sure are. Boss lady is in the mood. I can't say no to that."

He rolled his eyes. "Jess, when have you ever said no to alcohol? Seriously, some days I worry you're working in the wrong place. I often wonder how long until we'll have to check you into rehab."

She poked her tongue at him. "Very funny."

I drank my shot and slammed the empty glass down. "He's got a point, Jess."

"Oh my god! I hate it when you two gang up on me."

I clicked my fingers to indicate I needed more tequila. "Quick, get some more alcohol in you. It makes it all better."

Damian muttered something under his breath and left us to take care of the customer now waiting at the other end of the bar.

Jess poured another shot. As she handed it to me, she asked, "Is Annie okay?"

"As far as I know. Why?"

"She just seemed a little quiet today."

"It's been a big week for her. She hasn't had a job for so long now and I think she's struggled a bit this week with learning it all."

"She's doing really well, though," Jess said, and that meant something. Jess didn't blow wind up anyone's skirt.

"Yeah, I think so, too. Glad you can see it as well. My goal is to give her as much confidence as possible, and if she can master some new skills, that will help."

"Are you going to call that psychologist you got the name for the other day?"

I drank the shot. "I called her today, and Annie has her first appointment early next week."

She smiled at me. "You're a good woman, Layla. She's lucky to have you."

I thought about growing up with Annie. She'd been my constant companion when our parents dumped us with babysitters so they could go out to parties. We'd been like sisters back then, sharing everything from clothes, to makeup, and secrets. Annie had been there for me every time I needed her. Looking at Jess, I said, "I can't abandon her. She's the only family I have, and we always look out for each other."

"Yeah, but you seem to do all the giving in that relationship. Annie would be lost without you."

"I don't keep score, Jess. You can't live your life like that. I'm here for Annie for whatever she needs for as long as she needs it. Who's to say in five years it won't be the other way around?"

"True." She held up the tequila. "You want another one?"

"One more, and I think that will be enough." The effect of the alcohol was slowly making its way through my body, and I was feeling much more relaxed.

Thank fuck.

I drank the shot she passed me a moment later, and as I downed it, my core clenched at the sight I glimpsed.

Donovan.

His eyes found mine, and he headed my way, not letting my gaze go.

"Evening," he murmured when he was standing in front of me.

My tummy fluttered as his voice slid through me. Commanding would be how I'd describe it best. It affected me so much I almost lost my balance. Never in my life had I come across a man who could do that from the sound of his voice alone.

Jess cut into my thoughts. "I'll leave you to it." She took the tequila and headed over to where Damian was. I didn't take much notice, though, because my attention was completely on Donovan.

"It's been a week since I've seen you," I stated.

And I've missed you.

"I've been busy."

"Bullshit." Fuck, the tequila was doing all the talking now.

Surprise touched his face, and he remained silent for a couple of moments. Finally he agreed, "Yeah, bullshit." He scrubbed a hand over his face, and I didn't pursue it. His honesty was all I needed.

"You want a drink?"

He gave a quick nod. "Thanks."

I jerked my chin at his table in the corner. "I'll bring the bottle over."

I watched his sexy ass as he left me. God, I wanted to hold that ass in my hands. I moved my gaze up his body. His shirt was fitted against his hard muscles. I wanted to take that shirt off and run my hands over those muscles.

Shit.

Put your tongue back in your mouth, woman.

I grabbed a glass and the bottle of scotch and joined him a moment later. Sitting across from him, I passed him both. "You can pour your own tonight."

He raised his brows. "This how you treat all your customers?"

"No, only the ones I want to fuck."

He didn't even blink. Instead, he picked up the bottle, poured himself a drink and knocked it back before asking, "Are there many on that list?"

I leaned across the table and whispered, "It's a new thing I've started and there's only one on it so far."

His stare was intense as he said, "Keep it that way."

A shiver ran down my spine at his words and I squeezed my legs together.

He spoke again before I could think of what to say to that. "Why'd you walk away from your family?"

Totally wasn't expecting that.

"How'd you know that?"

He poured another drink and took a sip, drinking this one much slower than the last. "Layla, I'm sure you've worked out by now I get to know everything I can about the people in my life."

"I figured as much, but I'm not really in your life."

He stared at me with a hint of frustration. "What would you call it, then?"

"I don't know. You visit my bar and help me out when I need it."

"And is that not what you'd call a friendship?"

"Okay, so we're friends. Do you really investigate all your friends?"

"I do. So tell me, what happened with your family?"

Unease stirred in my gut. I hated talking about this stuff, because it meant I actually had to dredge the shitty memories up. And usually I had to censor the story, but something told me I could share the full truth with Donovan if I really wanted.

Did I want to?

He waited silently for me to talk. I took a deep breath and began. "Annie and I grew up almost as sisters. Our parents hardly spent any time with us, always leaving us with babysitters so they could attend social functions or go on holidays. So we had that strong bond, you know?" He nodded his understanding, and I continued. "When I was eighteen and Annie was sixteen, I discovered her father had been molesting her for years. She was fucked-up, and I finally dragged the truth out of her." I took another breath and looked at him. He was watching me intently, waiting patiently for me to get it out. I still hadn't decided how much to share with him. "I . . . " my voice drifted off as I struggled with what to tell him.

"What did you do?" He tried to coax it out of me, and as I looked at him, I knew he could handle the truth and not judge me for it.

"I tried to kill her father. I walked in on them and couldn't stop myself. They were in their kitchen and I grabbed a knife... I stabbed him a couple of times and slashed his face but the bastard didn't die. Annie tried to stop me. She didn't want me to go to jail, but I didn't care about that. I just wanted her safe from him forever. In the end, his wife came home and saved him. I'll never understand a mother who puts a husband like that above their *child*." Memories assaulted my mind and I thought I might vomit. To this day, it still made me sick to think about what Annie endured throughout her childhood.

"Did her mother know it was going on all that time?" Donovan seemed as sickened by it as I was.

"No, but I screamed it at her while she tried to stop me from killing him. She wouldn't listen."

"So he didn't die?"

"Not from what I did to him, but he killed himself a week later."

"Why did you two walk away from your family if he was dead?"

I took another deep breath. "In the week between my attack and his suicide, our families covered it all up. I tried to go to the police to have him charged for what he did to Annie but my parents wouldn't let me and her mother made her stay silent too. They were more concerned with their social standing and good reputation in business than with looking after Annie. After he killed himself, the reporters came sniffing around, wanting to know why. I'll never forget the day my father threatened to disown me and cut me out of his will if I breathed a word of it." My chest ached with hurt and sadness, and I looked up into Donovan's eyes to find softness there. I'd never seen it in him before, not like that.

He understands.

"You cut yourself out of it anyway," he murmured.

"Yes, and I took Annie with me. She was so broken and fucked-up, and her mother was useless. The worst mother I've ever met. She grieved a husband who didn't deserve any grief and ignored a child who needed her unconditional love." I blinked back the tears that threatened to fall every time I thought about how they'd screwed Annie up. Staring at him, I asked, "Who the fuck does that?"

He poured the rest of his scotch down his throat and then surprised me by sharing something personal. "My father beat my mother and ignored me for most of my life. Some people should not have the privilege of being parents." His voice was tight and controlled, but there was a vulnerability to it that I caught. He still battled with this.

I moved my hand across the table and clasped his. Instinctively, I knew the physical contact would be soothing, and I was right. Donovan's touch calmed me. When he intertwined our fingers a moment later, I knew he felt it, too.

"Do you have anything to do with your father these days?" I asked.

His face hardened and his shoulders tensed. I waited for him to pull his hand away from mine, but he didn't. "He's in my life but not by my choice. My mother is weak where he's concerned. He stopped seeing her about a year ago but he's back, sniffing around at the moment." He tried to hide his brokenness with his tough exterior, but the survivor in me knew that, on the inside, he fought his demons. By the exhaustion on his face, I figured it was a fight he wasn't currently winning.

"I'm guessing you're close to your mother." I loosened my grip on his hand and let my finger trace lazy patterns over his.

His gaze dropped to our hands and he stared at them for a few moments. He seemed unsure, almost like he wanted to push me away, but he didn't. Looking back up at me, he answered, gruffly, "Yeah."

"Any brothers or sisters?"

"Half brother and half sister. I knew about them while growing up but we never had any contact. They didn't know about my mother and me. It all came out a little over a year ago and I've since grown close to my sister, Madison."

I watched as lightness crossed his face while he talked about Madison. It looked good on him. "And your brother?"

He sighed. "That's a hard relationship. We're not close, but we are in contact."

I stopped tracing patterns on his hand and squeezed it instead. "Madison sounds wonderful," I said softly.

He allowed himself a smile. "She's the kind of woman who loves to drive you crazy with her demands, but I wouldn't have her any other way."

I returned his smile. "You deserve that."

He stilled at my words and I wasn't sure what I'd said wrong. Letting go of my hand, he stood. He grabbed the bottle of scotch and his glass from the table and stalked to the bar with them. After he gave them to Jess, he stalked back to me. The feral look in his eyes shot straight to my core. *God, I want him.*

I stood and waited for him. When he moved into my space, he slid a hand around my waist and pulled me to him. His hand snaked all the way around to my ass and he dipped it to curve around one of my cheeks. His other hand landed on my stomach and slowly made its way up to cup my breast, a finger pulling the top of my t-shirt down so he could run his finger along my skin.

My body burned with desire, and when he moved his hand to

slide it up under my tee to cup my breast, I wondered if I might explode from the desire. His strong fingers kneaded me and I imagined how good they would feel all over my body.

"I want you," he growled. Then his hand glided down my body to my pussy where it stilled. "Now," he commanded in that voice of his that said he'd take what he wanted and to hell with what anyone said.

Oh, fuck me.

I closed my eyes and swayed a little while his hand remained firm on my pussy. The thought briefly crossed my mind that we were in public, but I couldn't bring myself to worry about people watching; his hand felt too damn good on me. He rubbed it up and down me until I couldn't take it any longer, and I reached down, stopping him. I opened my eyes and found him staring into my face with a look of pure need. "Upstairs," I breathed out, and his nostrils flared.

He let me go, and I led him up to my bedroom. As he followed me into my room, he kicked the door shut and reached his hand around my waist. Next minute, my back was against his front and his lips were on the back of my neck.

"Fuck," he muttered as he trailed kisses up my neck. His spare hand came up to cup my face and turn it to the side so he could press a kiss to my lips.

He tasted like scotch and home. I hardly knew this man, and yet, I knew him like the back of my hand. He kissed me slowly at first, letting our lips and tongues explore each other. Slowly, he deepened the kiss until I was begging him with my mouth to take me harder, at which point he growled into my mouth and turned me in his arms so our fronts were pressed hard against each other. He pulled his lips from mine for a moment and stared at me. "How hard do you want this?"

I grasped his head with both hands, ground myself against him and pulled his face back to mine. "As hard as you wanna give it."

He hissed; his desire for that was clear in his eyes. Strong hands moved down to cup my ass, his grip hard, and he rasped, "You sure you know what you're asking for, baby?"

Baby.

That word from his mouth was like a match to my flame.

I wanted this man more than I'd wanted any man.

I wanted to sink into him, to take everything from him, to let him take everything from me.

Oh god, where was this going to end up?

He was danger in all its glory, and yet he was safety and shelter at the same time. I knew that in my bones. And I knew I wanted it all.

"Yes," I finally said.

Determination flared in his eyes, and a growl came from his chest. He kissed me again, his lips insistent against mine. I opened my mouth to his and he devoured me with a force that threatened to steal my breath away.

When he broke the kiss, he let me go and took a step away from me. Hungry eyes feasted on me and I enjoyed the thrill, knowing this powerful man wanted me. *Me.*

He pulled his t-shirt off and I sucked in a breath when his rock hard muscles were revealed to me. I let my gaze roam over them as I committed his body to memory. Ink covered one side of his chest in a tribal tattoo of some sort. It extended down his arm as well.

Arm Porn.

Jess was right when she compared Donovan's arms to porn. I could barely tear my gaze away from them. They mesmerised me and held my attention until his voice broke the spell.

"Take your top off," he commanded in a rough voice.

I did as he said and let my top fall to the floor.

"Bra."

His eyes were fixed on mine, and I wondered how long until they would drop to my chest.

I want your eyes on my body.

Reaching behind me, I unsnapped my bra and let it fall away to reveal my breasts to him.

His eyes didn't move, but he did. He came to me and crushed a kiss to my lips. Then, after one final glance at my face, he dropped his gaze to my chest. His sharp intake of breath uncurled more desire in me. I thought I might shatter a moment later when he sucked one of my nipples into his mouth and teased it with his tongue.

I moaned his name and he sucked me harder. My hands threaded through his hair and I pulled his head towards me. He gently bit my nipple as one of his hands reached down to my jeans and rubbed my pussy through them.

"Fuck," I moaned. *Feels so damn good.* I moved my hand to undo my jeans and he helped me by pulling the zip down.

Our movements grew frantic as we rushed to rid ourselves of all clothes. When we stood naked in front of each other a moment later, I couldn't hold myself back. The need to touch him overwhelmed me. I took his cock in my hand and stroked it, firm but slow. His breathing grew ragged while I worked my strokes into a faster pace.

As his body jerked with the pleasure, I moved to bend so I could take him in my mouth, but he stopped me. A firm hand came around me neck and he gripped me there, hard. His intense stare while he remained silent caused a new round of sensations to fire through me. My body sizzled with the need to have him, but he seemed intent on slowing me down.

He began walking us backwards until my back hit the wall. His hand still circled my neck in a strong hold. Not tight enough to choke me, but tight enough to restrict my breathing a little.

Tight enough to excite my dark fantasies.

I watched as he bent his mouth to my neck to suck and bite me. His bite was hard enough to mark me. Hard enough to make me shiver with anticipation of what he would do next. I wanted that mouth all over me, biting and marking me everywhere.

"Donovan . . . " I murmured, and waited for his reply.

He kept sucking and biting as he said, "Mmm?"

I ran my hand down his spine as far as I could and said, "I want your teeth everywhere."

He lifted his head and took my mouth in another hard kiss, biting my lips as he went. "Yeah, baby, that's what I want, too."

Baby.

There it was again.

I could get used to that.

He relaxed his hold on my neck and then moved his hands to cup both my breasts. "Here?" he asked, his eyes firmly on mine. "You want my teeth on your breasts?"

Oh good god, I want that.

"Yes." I bit my lip in hope.

He didn't waste any time and moved his mouth to my breasts, kissing, sucking and biting me into a crazed state of need. My arms went around him and I dragged my fingernails down his back, hard enough to draw blood. He hissed and snapped his head up to look at me.

"Fuck," he muttered, but I knew it wasn't in anger. He liked that, and the proof was when he slid his hands down to take hold of my ass and roughly lift me up against the wall.

I wrapped my legs around him and dug my nails in his back again as I held on tight.

"Bite me," he ordered.

Yes.

My teeth connected with the flesh of his neck a second later and I sucked and bit him while he groaned in my ear, his body grinding against mine. My pussy was so wet and ready for him, and I was growing frantic in my need for his cock.

I pulled away from his neck and begged him. "I need you in me, now."

His eyes flashed his own need, but I could tell from the way he restrained himself, he had more planned for me before he would give me what I wanted. Without a word, he moved us away from the wall. He held me tight in his strong arms as he walked us to the bed.

"I'm gonna place you on the bed, and then I'm going to fuck you, but not with my cock. You get to choose, my tongue or my fingers."

Oh fuck. What to choose?

My arms were around him, my face close to his, and I couldn't think straight. "Your fingers." I'd choose his tongue next time.

He gave me a quick nod before placing me gently on the bed. I loved how he mixed his soft in with his rough. "Move up the bed," he said and watched as I did.

Once I was settled with my head on the pillow, he knelt on the bed and placed his hands on my legs, spreading them. I watched his eyes take in my pussy and caught his intake of breath at the sight. He trailed a finger along the inside of my leg, all the way from my knee to my pussy, and then he trailed it lightly over me there. Slowly, he worked me into such a state with his feather-light touch all over my sex until I was writhing on the bed in front of him.

Almost about to beg him to stop teasing me, I jolted with pleasure when he finally pushed his finger inside. My back arched up off the bed and I moaned out his name. He added another finger and rubbed my clit with his thumb. My eyes shut as I let the bliss from his touch take over my body.

When Donovan shifted on the bed, I lazily opened my eyes to find him positioning himself so he could take me with his tongue. He obviously wanted that as much as I did, and I was ecstatic he'd chosen to give me both his fingers and his tongue. His hands slid under my ass and he gripped me hard while he pulled my pussy to his mouth. A second later, his tongue traced my entrance before pushing inside.

Oh god.

This must be what heaven is like.

He ate me until I could hardly stand it any longer. The pleasure had taken over, sending sensations I'd never felt before all through me. Every inch of my body was alight with need.

A need for Donovan.

A need unlike any other I'd ever experienced.

I scrunched my fingers in his hair and pulled hard. His head shot up and he glared at me. A hungry glare that challenged me to stop him from what he wanted to do.

"I need you to fuck me now," I demanded.

He continued to glare at me, his mouth wet from my pussy, and then he moved. Like a wild animal stalking its prey, he moved over me. I throbbed with excitement.

Yes.

When he'd moved half-way over me, he grasped my neck and yanked me to a sitting position. My heart beat faster at the raw desire I saw on his face. "We need to get one thing straight," he growled, tightening his hold on my neck. "When I'm in the middle of fucking you with my mouth, you don't interrupt. You can have my cock, but it'll be when I decide it's time. Do you understand?"

I'd never had a man speak to me this way during sex.

I needed more.

"And what happens if I do interrupt?" I challenged him, wanting to know how far he would take this. Needing him to take it much, much further.

His brows rose, and the vein in his neck pulsed. "You really want to push this? I'm not sure you'll like where it goes."

I struggled to breathe as he squeezed his fingers a little harder around my neck.

Yes.

My pussy danced with delight. Staring hard into his eyes, I nodded. "Yes, show me who you are, Donovan."

77

He uttered a string of words I couldn't make out and raked his free hand through his hair. It seemed like he was weighing something in his mind, and then, suddenly, he let me go and moved off the bed. He strode to where his jeans were on the floor, scooped them up and grabbed a condom out of his wallet.

I held my breath.

Waiting.

Watching.

Coming back to me, he stood at the end of the bed and watched me while he ripped the foil packet and put the condom on. He climbed onto the bed and moved to where I was. A moment later, he'd flipped me onto my stomach, his hand had gone around my waist and he'd pulled my ass up into the air while I rested on my hands and knees. He knelt behind me and ran his hands over my ass, gently to begin with and then more roughly. I pushed myself back against him, desperate to have his cock, but he had other ideas. He kept one hand on my ass while the other one grabbed my hair into a ponytail and yanked my head back.

His mouth came to my ear. "You might regret knowing who I am." His words and his warm breath on my skin made me shiver.

"Never," I breathed out, welcoming the pain his grip caused.

He growled and bit down on my shoulder.

Hard.

I screamed.

He bit harder.

Fuck. Yes.

When his mouth moved from my shoulder, I wanted to demand he bring it back. However, he kept giving me what I craved when he thrust hard inside me.

No warning.

No more foreplay.

One hand pulling my hair back, one hand clawing at my ass, and his cock ramming into me over and over.

This man was made for my pleasure.

He moved me closer to my release with his rough fucking, and just as I felt myself tipping over the edge, he pulled out, let go of me, and flipped me onto my back. His movements were fluid and fast; for a man of his size he had a surprising agility.

I stared disbelievingly up into his eyes as he straddled me.

I was so close.

He shook his head and silenced my words with his finger over my lips. "*This* is what you get when you drag me away from your pussy."

Oh.

His eyes moved to my breasts and he bent his face to my chest so he could suck and bite my nipples while he massaged my breasts. His hands slid down to my hips, and he shifted so he could kiss and bite his way down my body, ending at my inner thighs.

His punishment was both maddening and exquisite.

I wanted him to stop.

I *needed* him to keep going.

He spread my legs once again, looked up at me, and asked, "Will we have a problem if I finish what I started?" His voice had that growly quality to it that was like a shot of pure ecstasy in my veins.

I shook my head, and he grunted his approval before burying his face back in my pussy and setting me on fire with his tongue. I lay back and didn't dare complain. Not because I didn't like his form of punishment, but rather I didn't want to delay having his cock in me any longer, and I knew I wouldn't get it until he'd gotten what he wanted. And it seemed what Donovan wanted was to get his fill of my pussy first.

It didn't take long for him to bring me to orgasm, and I squeezed my eyes shut and gripped his head as it hit. He didn't waste time once I'd come; he prowled back up my body until our faces were centimetres apart. I'd barely had time to open my eyes, and I blinked to focus. The untamed look in his eyes spoke straight to my core.

It was time.

Finally.

I expected him to thrust straight in, but his unpredictability was fast becoming his signature move. He moved fast again, pulled me up, and flipped me around so I was on my knees facing the headboard of the bed. His hands grasped mine and he positioned them so they were gripping onto the top of the headboard. A moment later, his front pressed against my back, and he murmured against my ear, "Your cunt is so fucking tight this might not last long."

My pussy clenched.

His words had the power to bring me to my knees.

I was sure of it.

A strong arm came around my waist and moved me so my ass tilted back. His cock rubbed against my entrance only for a moment, before he thrust in, hard, fast and to the hilt. He grunted, and the sound caused another ripple of pleasure to course through me. There seemed to be no end to it, and as he thrust in and out, balls slapping against me, I began to think I might never recover from tonight.

He's going to kill me with bliss.

Donovan had been wrong when he said he might not last long. His dick had stamina. The longer he lasted, the rougher his thrusts became. His fingers dug into my skin, and his teeth sunk into my flesh as he chased his release. When he finally came, he roared it for the world to hear. The sound he made was the best thing I'd heard for a long time.

Passion and rage all rolled into one.

My kindred spirit.

CHAPTER 8

BLADE

I WATCHED LAYLA SLEEP AS I PULLED ON MY CLOTHES. She had the ability to look as sexy asleep as she did awake. Her long, dark hair fanned out over her bare back and the bed. My gaze travelled down her body, and my dick threatened to harden again at the sight of her waist, ass and legs. Everything about her was spectacular. But her physical beauty paled in comparison to her inner beauty.

Kind, nurturing and resilient; I was drawn to her.

We shared a connection I struggled to understand.

But I *felt* it.

I sat on her bed to put my boots on, and the shifting of the bed woke her. She rolled to her side, propped herself on her elbow and watched me silently.

We don't need words.

I gave her my eyes for a couple of moments before focusing back on my boots. When I stood, she murmured, "Thank you."

I turned. "For the sex?"

"No, for not judging me."

Fuck.

I'd never judge her.

I nodded. "I'll check in with you tomorrow, make sure you're okay."

"Okay," she said softly. Sleepily.

"Do you have to close up?"

"No, Jess and Damian can do it."

"Good. Get some sleep," I said. With one last look at her, I turned and headed downstairs.

The bar was nearly empty. Over the last few months, I'd noticed a steady decline in business, and wondered how Layla kept it running.

"Blade!"

I turned and found Jess staring at me. "Yeah," I said, walking towards her.

"Is Layla coming down?"

"No. Said you guys would close up."

She grinned. "You knocked her flat, huh?"

I ignored that. "I'll see you later," I said and started heading towards the door.

"Don't fuck her around," she yelled at me.

I stopped. Turning, I said, "That's not my M.O."

She nodded. "Good."

Once we had that settled, I left. As I stepped outside, I scanned the street. It looked clear tonight. I hadn't mentioned anything to Layla, but I had concerns Mario would be back. Tomorrow, I'd put some eyes on her in case he did. That motherfucker wouldn't fucking want to, though.

★★★

"Blade!"

I turned to the familiar voice screaming my name.

Ashley.

I smiled at her and began jogging to her. She kept moving, though. I thought she was so close, but the more I ran, the further away she seemed. The smile on her face turned into a frown the longer I took.

"Ashley!" I yelled, extending my arm for her to grab hold of.

She reached her hand to try and grab onto it, but the harder we both tried, the further away our hands seemed.

"Blade, where did you go?" Her eyes grew sad, and when I saw the first tear fall, my heart constricted.

"Nowhere, baby. I'm right here," I promised, wanting to take all her tears away.

Why does she think I went somewhere?

"No, you're not. You went away. You left me," she accused.

My foot hit something while I was running, and I fell.

The last thing I saw was her tears.

I was falling.

Falling into the darkness.

I sat bolt upright, my heart almost beating out of my chest.

Fuck.

The sheet stuck to my sweat.

Again.

I turned to the bedside clock.

Four fifteen am.

I scrubbed my hand over my face as I recalled the dream. I had no idea what it meant, and no desire to figure it out. Pushing the sheet off, I left the bed to take a shower.

Maybe it's time for sleeping pills.

A couple of hours of sleep wouldn't cut it today.

★★★

Three hours later, I pulled my car out of my driveway and drove to Harlow's café for breakfast with Madison. When I arrived, she was standing on the footpath waiting for me.

I stepped out of the car, locked it and walked to her. "Morning." I smiled at her.

She returned my smile. "Hey, big brother." Her arms came up around my neck as she kissed me on the cheek.

I fought the instinct to pull away from her embrace.

"You're getting better at this," she said with a wink after she let me go.

"You've no idea," I muttered, and began walking to the café.

She grabbed my arm and stopped me. "Wait! What does that mean?"

Expectation covered her face while she waited for my reply. Not ready to share my thoughts, I said, "Nothing."

"That was *not* nothing," she insisted, and I mentally berated myself for my words.

"Leave it, Madison," I cautioned.

Her eyes widened. "Oh my god! You're seeing someone, aren't you?" Her excitement levels shot through the roof, and I almost expected her to start jumping up and down on the spot.

"Leave it," I growled and stalked into the café without waiting for her.

Harlow looked up as I entered and smiled at me. I jerked my chin at her, and began walking to where she was at the counter.

"Good morning," she greeted me. Harlow always had a smile on her face. I wondered if she had many bad days, because it seemed like she didn't. Except for lately when I'd seen her and Scott arguing.

I scowled at her. "Morning."

"Having a bad morning?" she asked softly.

"Sorry," I apologised, not wanting to take it out on her.

"He's shitty with me for asking him about who he's dating."

I turned to Madison who had come up behind me. If I didn't give her what she wanted, she'd keep pushing until she got an answer. "*Yes*, I've met someone, but I don't know what it is yet, so can we just leave it for now?"

She stared at me, stunned. And then a huge smile spread across her face. "Yes! Of course we can. I'm just so happy for you."

Thank Christ.

Harlow stepped in and led Madison away from that conversation. "Are we still on for shopping tomorrow? I really need a new swimsuit."

I tuned out their shopping conversation and let my mind wander to my day ahead. Merrick wanted to discuss the new construction job we were bidding for, and Ben, my head of security, wanted to discuss a new lead on Blue he had.

"Blade!"

I focused back on the conversation to find Madison staring at me, waiting for me to say something. "Sorry. What?"

"Do you want anything to eat or just coffee?"

She'd give me grief if I didn't order food. "Eggs on toast and coffee, please," I said to Harlow.

"I'll bring it over soon," she promised, and we made our way to a table.

I waited for Madison to interrogate me further, but she surprised me by leaning in close and asking me, "Do you know if everything is okay between Scott and Harlow?"

"I'm not sure." I wasn't one to break a confidence so I didn't divulge the tiny piece of information he'd shared with me recently.

"I think there's something going on with them. Harlow hasn't been her usual self lately."

"I guess, whatever it is, it's between them. She'll share with you when and if she's ready."

"I don't want them to be having problems." She sighed. "She's so good for him. He better not fuck this up."

"How's J?" I asked, wanting to change the subject.

She grinned. "He's an ass, but I love him."

I snorted. "You two really *were* made for each other, weren't you?"

"Yep."

"You guys talking babies yet?"

"Oh god, he keeps bringing it up, but I'm in no hurry." She grew serious. "I just want to enjoy him all to myself for a while longer, you know what I mean? We spent so many years stuffing around with what we had . . . I need more time with him before we add kids to the mix."

"Smart move, babe."

Harlow brought our breakfast over, and Madison spent the next half an hour while we ate filling me in on what she'd been up to. I listened to everything she said, but my mind kept shifting to Layla, wondering how she was this morning. Wondering whether I was ingrained on her soul as much as she was on mine.

One night, and she can do that to me.

Fuck.

"Blade!"

I blinked.

"What?"

She shook her head at me. "You're so far away today, but you're not gonna tell me where you are, are you?"

If I didn't give her something, she'd never leave me alone. "No, babe, it's for me at the moment. If it goes anywhere, I promise you'll be the first to know."

She slowly nodded. "Okay."

We finished eating and headed out to our cars after saying

goodbye to Harlow. Madison hugged me and made me promise to have breakfast again in a couple of days.

My phone rang, distracting me from watching her leave. "Hello," I answered it, not recognising the number on the screen.

"Blade."

The voice on the other end was one I hadn't heard in years. One I'd never wanted to hear again. "Ricky."

"Your father's playing with fire. You might want to tell him to back the fuck off," he threatened.

"I don't have anything to do with my father so I suggest you tell him yourself." Even after all these years he still managed to piss me off.

"This was just a friendly suggestion between old friends. I don't intend to waste my time talking to Marcus."

"You and I were never friends, Ricky."

"It pains me you feel that way, Blade. Way I remember it, we were. We've certainly got a shitload of shared memories. You know, like that time I lied for you to that Judge."

His meaning wasn't lost on me. It was a clear threat.

Fuck.

"What do you want, motherfucker?" I snapped.

"I don't want to share my territory. Talk to Storm," he ordered, and he hung up on me.

I held my phone away from my ear and just stared at it.

Like fuck I'd roll over and give in to his threats.

CHAPTER 9

LAYLA

JESS TOOK ONE LOOK AT ME AND RAISED HER BROWS. "I take it he marked your neck."

My hand went to the scarf around my neck. He'd marked me in more than one place. No way was I going out in public today without the scarf. I scowled at her but didn't say anything.

She'd just arrived at work and went to put her bag out in the back. Damian had called in sick today so Jess had agreed to come in to help Annie and me. Annie stood at the other end of the bar, stacking glasses. I watched her for a moment. She was doing well, even seemed to be okay with the fact Gary hadn't come after her. I'd given her phone back to her, and she hadn't called him. I checked up on that every day just to be sure.

She looked up at me and smiled. "Who is he?" she asked.

It was the first time she'd asked anything about me since she'd moved in. Up until this point, she'd been completely engrossed in herself and her problems to have it in her to think of anyone else. I took it as a good sign. "His name's Donovan, and he's a customer who's been coming here for about a year."

Jess came back out to the front of the bar and started helping us get ready to open.

Annie kept the conversation going. "What's he like?" She had that dreamy look in her eyes. Annie was a born romantic. Probably the reason she flitted from guy to guy with hardly a break in-between. She craved love and didn't do well on her own. She was so different from me.

"He's complex. Unlike any man I've ever met." I paused to think about him. "I don't know him that well yet, but I think he's like those sour lollies you like: sour at first, but sweet when you get to the centre."

"I can't wait to meet him, Layla. You deserve someone good."

I smiled at her. "Yeah, I do."

Jess joined the conversation. "When are you seeing him again?"

"I don't know. He said he'd call today. We'll see."

"He will," Jess said, adamantly, like she knew something I didn't.

"Do you have a crystal ball?"

She winked. "No, but I told him not to fuck you around last night, and he assured me he wouldn't."

"It's so unlike you to trust anything a guy says," I mused.

"I know," she said, quietly. "But there's something about him that makes me totally believe everything he says."

Me, too.

We finished getting the bar ready and opened about fifteen minutes later. A couple of customers wandered straight in, and I sent a prayer to the universe that we'd be busy today. My bank balance needed it.

The three of us worked well together and had some fun. I loved watching Annie loosen up, and I especially loved seeing the smile on her face. It'd been too long.

A couple of hours after opening, the day went to shit.

Mario and his goons came in, and I sucked in a breath. The look of malice on his face scared the shit out of me.

My hand went to my phone in my pocket.

I need Donovan.

Mario's face curved into a sneer as he said, "Seems we meet again."

"What do you want?"

He slammed his hand on the counter, making me jump. "I want my fucking money!"

My heart fell into my stomach. "I told you, I don't have your money, and I haven't heard from Dale."

My words seemed to really piss him off. "You're a smart bitch, aren't you? Fucking feeding me lies about having no money."

What's he talking about?

"I'm not feeding you any lies. Look around my bar. Does it look like I have enough customers to make me rich?"

He leant across the bar at me, his foul breath polluting the air between us. "I know who your family is," he spat out.

Fuck.

My stomach rolled.

He expected me to go to my family for the money.

He gave me a smug look as he stepped away from the bar. "Two days, bitch, and then I'm coming for you."

I watched him leave, my legs almost buckling from the dread surging through my body. I staggered back against the wall behind me and clutched my stomach as it threatened to expel its contents.

"Shit." Jess gave me a worried look. "You need to call Blade."

I pulled my phone out and dialed him. "Layla," he answered, his voice tight as if he was distracted.

"Mario came back."

I was met with silence and then, "Fuck."

I waited.

"You okay?" he asked, the concern clear in his voice.

I blew out the breath I'd been holding in.

Donovan will fix this.

"Yeah," I said.

"I'm gonna send someone over to stay with you until I can get there, okay?"

"Okay."

Silence.

And then, "Call me if you need me. I don't care what the fuck it is, you ring me. Yeah?"

I nodded even though he couldn't see me. "Yes."

"I'll be there as soon as I can."

"Thank you."

He ended the call, and I placed my phone down on the bar. I looked up at the girls who were staring at me expectantly. "He's taking care of it."

"Thank fuck," Jess muttered.

Annie's eyes were wide with fear and I went to her. I put my arms around her and pulled her close. Smoothing my hand over her hair, I murmured, "It's going to be okay, honey. Donovan will help us. We don't have to do this on our own."

Her body was tense. I knew her reaction must be from remembering the shit we'd been through together. We'd come a long way since then and I'd learnt how to defend myself. How to defend us.

I won't let you down again.

She pulled away from me. "Okay," she whispered, but I could tell from her hesitation I hadn't convinced her.

I placed my hands on her shoulders and stared into her eyes. "I promise."

She answered me with a small smile and nod.

It was the best I'd get out of her.

Turning to Jess, I said, "I'm gonna lock the front door until Donovan's guy gets here. If any customers want to leave, we'll let them out, but no one else gets in, okay?"

She nodded. "Good idea."

I locked the door and we waited.

How the fuck do I get myself into these situations?

★★★

Banging on the front door twenty minutes later startled all of us. The bar was empty now after the last customer left five minutes ago.

"Might be Blade's guy," Jess suggested.

"Let's hope so," I said, and went to check it out.

Thank god for the glass panel in the door.

Two bikers stood on the other side, staring at me.

Shit.

I hesitated, not sure whether they'd been sent by Mario or Donovan.

One of them spoke. "Blade sent us, babe. Open up."

I eyed him. Ink pretty much covered every inch of his skin, and although I didn't usually go for that look, I had to admit he was gorgeous. I shifted my gaze to the other guy. He was more my type, with less ink, and had the looks sure to melt any woman's panties. But they both oozed a don't-fuck-with-me attitude.

That's what I need.

I unlocked the door and let them in before locking it again after them.

The heavily-inked one looked at me. "You can leave it open, babe. We'll stay till Blade comes."

Gratitude overwhelmed me. "Thank you." It came out almost as a whisper.

His grin lit his face and that was when I appreciated fully what he

92

had going on. He was breathtaking with that grin. "You're welcome." He pointed to himself, "I'm Nash, and this dickhead is J." He pointed at J as he introduced him.

J jerked his chin at me. "You ladies okay? I haven't heard from Mario again since you spoke to Blade?"

They followed me to the bar where Jess and Annie were waiting. "No, he hasn't been back," I answered.

"Good to hear," J said as he settled on a bar stool.

"You guys want a drink?" Jess asked, her eyes roaming all over Nash. She had a weakness for bad boys, and I figured he was hitting all her buttons.

They both declined.

Nash pulled up a stool as well and scanned the room before giving his attention to me. "You had the bar long?"

"I've been part-owner for about a year now. Before that I worked here for years."

"You do well?"

"We used to but the last few months have been slow."

He turned his gaze back to the far corner and then looked at me. "Ever thought about putting a stage over there and bringing live music in? I've always thought this place would do well with that."

"You've been here before?" I'd never seen him here.

J snorted. "Highly doubt that, babe. You don't have any skin on show in here, hardly Nash's preference."

Nash ignored him. "I've been here a few times over the years, but I keep up with all the bars in the area. We've got a strip club not far from here so it pays to know what's happening out and about. Not much live music around, so you could do well."

It paid to never judge a book by its cover. My parents never taught me that, but once I was on my own in the world, I'd quickly discovered it. I loved meeting people who proved it. Smiling at Nash, I said, "Thank you, I'll put some thought into it."

He grinned at me again. "Anytime. Gotta look after Blade's woman."

Blade's woman.

I was far from his woman, and yet Nash's words shot delicious warmth through me. I had no idea where last night would lead, or what it meant to Donovan, but I wanted more.

I needed more like I needed air.

★★★

When Donovan strode into the bar a little over an hour later, his face said it all.

Anger and concern all rolled into one.

He came straight to me. His hand cupped my chin, and his eyes bored into mine. "You okay?"

I am now.

"Yes."

His chest heaved. "Thank fuck."

Letting go of me, he turned to Nash and J. "Thanks for coming."

"Anytime, man. You want us to tag along when you go see Mario?" Nash asked. From the gleam in his eye, I was betting he hoped Donovan said yes.

"Heading over there now. You got time?" Donovan asked. Turned out I was right because Nash jumped at the opportunity. I didn't even feel sorry for Mario. As far as I was concerned, he deserved whatever they did to him.

J interrupted, "You got eyes on this place now?"

Donovan nodded. "Yeah, two of my guys are sitting outside."

"Thank you," I murmured.

He turned to me, and his gaze softened. "I'm gonna give you their numbers. You ring them first if you need them, but you *always* ring me after. Yeah?"

It stunned me how much I loved his protective streak. After years of looking out for myself, I hated relying on anyone or needing anyone. Donovan was different. I looked deep into his eyes. "Yeah."

He keyed their numbers into my phone, inspected the place to make sure we were secure, and then the three of them left.

To take care of Mario.

Deep down, I knew what that meant.

And I had zero problems with it.

CHAPTER 10

BLADE

I PULLED UP OUTSIDE MARIO'S PLACE. THE MOTHER-fucker lived in a dive. Paint peeled from the house, overgrown grass hid the ground, and rubbish littered the footpath. He'd fallen a long way from the place he used to live.

That's what drugs do to you, asshole.

Slamming the door of the Jag as I exited it, I surveyed the street.

Quiet.

No one around.

Fucking perfect.

"What's the plan, boss?"

I turned to Ben. I'd brought him and two of my other guys with me. Nash and J, too. "You three take the back. I'll keep Nash and J with me at the front."

He nodded his agreement.

"I get to finish the asshole, Ben," I added.

"I figured," he said, his face a mask of intent.

I watched the three of them head around the back and then motioned for J and Nash to follow me. A moment later, I banged on the front door.

We stood back and waited.

When Mario opened the door, he looked at J and Nash before smirking at me. "Brought your back-up, I see. Won't make a difference, though, asshole. Your bitch owes me money, and I fucking want it."

My fist collided with his cheek so hard he staggered backwards. I stepped inside his house and punched him again. Blood flew at me. I punched him again.

"Motherfucker!" he roared.

I ducked as he tried to get a punch in. "Yeah, I fucking am! You want to pull the shit you pulled today, this is how I fucking deal with it."

My mind was zeroed in on dealing with Mario, but the sound of glass shattering and yelling from the back of the house grabbed my attention. Nash pushed past me and stalked toward the noise while J stayed with me.

Mario snarled at me. "That bitch isn't worth the shit this will cause, Blade."

We stood glaring at each other, sizing the situation up. Adrenaline pumped through my veins, and the desire to end him quickly overwhelmed me. "What fucking shit will this cause, Mario?"

"People won't like it when I tell them about this. I hope the cunt is worth it."

Mario always had thought more of his standing in the world than what it actually was. I shoved my face in his and grabbed his shirt with both hands. "You're missing something here, Mario."

"What?" His smugness only fuelled my rage.

"The fact you won't be around to tell anyone about this," I growled, and enjoyed watching the smugness slide off his face.

I shoved him away from me. Hard, so he stumbled back into the wall and slumped to the floor. His confidence disappeared, and my darkness surged up as I looked down at him. The demons I forced into hiding most days circled, begging to be let out. Today, they were in luck.

J slammed the front door shut and made sure all the curtains were closed. The house had grown quiet as Ben and the guys dealt with whoever Mario had out the back. "Just you and me now," I spat at him. "Regretting your greed yet, asshole?"

Fear lined his face. He knew how I dealt with problems. "I'll forget the debt, Blade. And I'll leave her alone, whatever you want." He forced his words out in a haste to stop me.

Too late, motherfucker.

My monsters have already been unleashed.

I slid my blade from its sheath attached to my belt and stepped closer to him. Bending to a crouch, I pressed the tip of the knife to his chest. "Your problem, Mario, is that you just don't have the fucking brains for this shit. Takes a smart man to handle the dirty work of this world. Idiots are slowly weeded out, and it looks like your time's up." I cut the top button of his shirt off. The sound of it bouncing on the floor was the only sound to be heard in the quiet of the house.

His chest rose and fell, rapidly, sweat pooling on his face as he fought to breathe through his terror. No words were said, however. He knew we were way past that.

I cut the next button off and slowly worked my way down his shirt until they were all discarded.

J grunted from behind me. "Did you piss yourself, motherfucker?"

He had.

My monsters roared at the smell of fear in the room.

I trailed the knife down his body, from chest to waist, pushing his

98

shirt out of the way as I went. His skin hypnotised me as I imagined sinking the knife in and drawing blood.

Blood.

I hungered for it.

He'll never threaten a woman again.

I pressed the knife into his stomach, just deep enough for blood to pool on his skin. The whimper he emitted touched the edge of my consciousness as I concentrated on my revenge. A moment later, the smell of his blood hit my nostrils, and I fought the urge to lift my arm and bury the knife in his chest.

"Blade."

Ben's voice cut through my fog, and I snapped my head around to look at him. I glared my question at him. *What?*

"We need to take him to the warehouse for this." His voice held urgency.

He was right.

Mario began snivelling as he cowered against the wall.

With one last scowl at him, I stood. Jerking my chin at Ben and the guys, I ordered, "Get him into the back of the van and I'll meet you there."

Ben nodded his understanding, and the three of them moved into action.

Nash looked at his watch. "You good now, brother? Or do you still need us?"

I reached behind me and slid my knife back in its sheath. "We can handle this from here. How many are out the back?"

"Two. They're unconscious." He gave me the information I needed, and I nodded. They wouldn't be a problem as they were only men for hire. Mario had no loyalty in his operation.

Nash slapped me on the back. "Yell out if you need us again. Always happy to help."

J gave me a chin jerk, and I watched them leave. Scott had come through for me today when I'd called and asked for his help. I hadn't wanted to ever ask him for it, but when Layla called, I was dealing with a situation I couldn't leave, and Scott was my best option.

★★★

It was ten o'clock that night before I saw Layla again. She sat in the corner at a table.

My table.

Her head rested on her arms on the table, and, as I approached, I sensed she was asleep. She didn't stir when I sat, so I rested my hand on her shoulder. "Layla," I murmured as I gently nudged her.

Her head shot up, and groggy eyes stared back at me.

"Sorry, didn't mean to scare you," I apologised.

"You okay?" she asked, rubbing her eyes.

I frowned. "Yeah. Why?"

"I never heard from you after you left, so I've been worried."

I'm an asshole.

What the fuck am I doing?

I leaned back in the chair and stretched my back. My muscles were all knotted, and the pain I always felt there had intensified this afternoon. Raking my hand through my hair, I said, "I took care of Mario. You don't need to worry about him anymore."

She stared at me silently. Her quick nod was all she gave me before she stood and walked away.

Fuck.

I dropped my head and squeezed my eyes shut.

She'll never accept your demons.

What the fuck are you doing?

I took a deep breath. Best to face the truth before beginning something. Disappointment washed through me, though. I'd thought the connection had been there. I'd thought she might accept my darkness.

I opened my eyes and lifted my head.

She stood in front of me.

"Thought you could do with a drink," she murmured as she passed me a glass and the bottle of scotch.

Fuck.

You don't deserve her.

"Thank you." I poured a drink and asked, "You want one?"

"No, I've already had a few tonight. I'm so tired that another one might knock me on my ass." She sat down again, her movements sluggish.

I eyed the scarf around her neck. Reaching across the table, I loosened it to reveal the marks I'd left there last night. The asshole in me loved those fucking marks.

Her hand landed on mine and held it there. Our eyes met. The noise in my mind that never shut off quietened. The ache in my chest that clung to me and never gave me a moment's peace ceased.

"Thank you," she whispered.

Fuck, her touch healed, if only for that moment. She knew what I'd done, and she was fucking thanking me for it. She accepted that part of me.

I drank some of my scotch and welcomed its burn.

She let my hand go, tightening her scarf back around her neck. My need to be connected to her was too great to move my hand away. I trailed my finger along her collarbone and then I traced the skin above the v of her t-shirt, letting my finger slip underneath the material every now and then. The gentle rise and fall of her chest turned me on. I loved how I affected her.

I kept feathering my light touch over her skin while I drank the rest of my scotch. Our eyes held each other, and the slow burn of need sizzled through me.

"I need you," I growled.

"I need you, too," she whispered.

Fuck.

I looked at my hand against her chest and the contradiction of what that hand could deliver wasn't lost on me.

The contradiction of me.

I moved my hand and stood. Picking up the scotch and my glass, I waited for her to stand, and then I followed her. I took the scotch upstairs with me. I'd need it tonight.

CHAPTER 11

LAYLA

Donovan's need matched mine, but he fucked me slower tonight. He didn't have the wild, driving desire of last night. Instead, he blessed me with his touch.

It was almost like a spiritual experience.

He sat on the edge of the bed, facing me while I stood, and wordlessly stripped me, eyes focused on my body rather than my face. Once he had me naked, he snaked his hands around me and rested them on my ass. He bent forward and pressed a kiss to my stomach. A growl came from his chest, and he gripped my butt tight, kissing my stomach as if he was kissing my mouth. I dropped my head back and grasped his hair while the pleasure spread through me.

When he'd finished kissing all over my stomach, he moved lower to my pussy. His hand slid down the back of my leg and he lifted it so he could place my foot on the bed. He opened me up to him, and my core clenched as he licked along my slit. He growled again, a deep growl that vibrated against my opening, and I moaned my pleasure.

It was a slow, exquisite torture as he gently moved his tongue and fingers inside me. He would get me close and then back off, leaving me to ride the waves of bliss, and then pant for more. I was desperate for him to drive me over the edge, but I sensed he needed this to go slow tonight, so I took what he was willing to give until he was ready to give more.

Donovan lost himself in me. His slow movements gradually built and his grip on me tightened, bit by bit, until he was roughly grasping me and holding me firm to his mouth. As he finally brought me to my release, my legs trembled and threatened to buckle. Brilliant white lights burst through my mind as every inch of my body felt the orgasm he'd given me.

"Baby," he rasped.

Yes.

I opened my eyes and looked into his. He was sitting on the bed, watching me closely. Waiting for me.

"Yes," I whispered, my mind a hot mess of thoughts after that orgasm.

"Come here." He pulled me onto his lap, and I went willingly.

I crawled onto him and wrapped my legs around him. He was still fully clothed, which irritated me, and my hands went to the bottom of his tee and began lifting it over his head. His arms went up as I pulled it off. I threw it on the floor and put my hands on his chest.

Oh god, I could get used to this man.

His hands travelled up my arms to my neck. A moment later, his gaze shifted to my neck and he bent to lay soft kisses on the marks he'd put there last night. I tilted my head to allow him access and enjoyed the feel of his mouth on me.

"Not gonna mark you tonight," he mumbled in between kisses.

"I don't mind," I confessed. "I love your teeth on me."

His hands curled tighter around my neck, and he slowed his kisses until he was still. His breathing grew ragged and he spoke in a strangled voice. "No, not rough tonight."

I sucked in a breath at the ravaged tone in his voice. It was like he was fractured somehow, not completely himself.

My natural instinct to nurture kicked in, and my hands moved to his face. I held both cheeks and whispered, "Look at me."

His head jerked up, and he stared at me with eyes that made me want to wrap him in my arms and never let go. He didn't utter a word, just waited for me to speak.

I moved one hand to run it gently through his hair while keeping hold of his cheek with my other hand. Moving my face to his, I brushed my lips over his and forced him to kiss me. His mouth opened to let me in and our tongues tangled with the passion consuming us.

When I ended the kiss, I trailed kisses along his jaw and down his neck. I lightly bit him there to test his reaction. His sharp intake of breath and the way he pressed his erection into me told me what I needed to know, and I bit harder and sucked him.

"Fuck," he hissed, his hands moving down to hold my breasts.

I continued what I was doing while he ran his hands all over my body. He worked me into a frenzy with his touch, and I was breathless with need by the time I moved my mouth from his neck. Pulling his face back to mine, I murmured, "You need to fuck me now. Rough, hard, slow, whatever...I don't care how, just do it."

His body tensed and his arms came around me as he stood, holding me to him. God, I loved the strength this man had. My legs were wrapped tight around him, but I had no doubt that, if I was to let go, he'd still be able to hold me up with ease.

Once he was standing, he turned and placed me on the bed. Eyes on me, his hands went to his belt and he stripped. I held his gaze until he was naked. His body was too spectacular not to look at, and I let my eyes roam all over him. My pussy screamed out for his hard cock, and I moved myself up the bed, ready for him.

He rolled a condom on, and then bent his hands to the bed to climb on top of me. Holding himself over me, face to face, he growled, "Fuck, you're beautiful. Haven't wanted a woman as much as I want you in a long fucking time."

Fuck me.

I pulled his face the short distance to mine and kissed him with everything I was feeling. He pressed his cock to my entrance. I was so ready for him and pushed up against him. He growled his pleasure into my mouth, which only made me want him more. I wrapped my legs around him, locked them in place and used my muscles to pull his body closer to mine. At the same time, I pushed my pussy against his cock and thrust up to take him inside.

"Fuck!" he roared, and pulled out so he could thrust back in.

Hard.

Fast.

Rough.

Thank fuck.

He slammed in and out of me, and I clung to him for the ride.

Frantic.

Wild.

Carnal.

I'm never letting go.

He exploded with a load roar, and I came a moment later, screaming his name.

We stilled and let it wash over us, limbs entwined, skin-to-skin. I drifted off into a pleasure-induced fog. His lips on mine snapped me out of it.

"Fuck me," he muttered in between kisses. "Fucking amazing . . ." His voice drifted off as he deepened our kiss. We stayed like that for a long time, him lazily kissing me and not letting go. I could have spent eternity like that.

Eventually, he broke away from my lips and pushed himself up off the bed and left the room. When he returned a moment later, he'd disposed of the condom. Standing at the side of the bed, he let his gaze drift over my body. "Don't ever change," he murmured.

I frowned my confusion. "What?"

As he bent to retrieve the bottle of scotch and glass he'd placed on the floor next to the bed, he said, "You're perfect just the way you are. Inside and out. Don't change that for anyone."

His words went straight to my heart and I felt breathless as I soaked them in.

He sat on the edge of the bed and poured himself a drink before placing the bottle back on the floor. Turning his upper body to look at me, he held the glass out to me. "Do you want some?"

I took the glass and downed half its contents. It burnt going down, but I wanted that.

Anything to counter the intoxicating happiness floating through me.

This is too good to be true.

I handed it back to him and watched as he drank the rest of it. He put the glass on the floor and then moved onto the bed next to me. Lying on his side, he propped himself up on his elbow and placed his hand on my stomach. My belly fluttered at his touch, and I rolled into him to press a kiss to his lips.

When we pulled apart, he whispered, "You're okay with what I did today, aren't you?"

His body grew tense while he waited for my response.

I nodded. "Yes."

He took a long breath, held it for a moment and then expelled it on a, "Fuck."

I cupped my hand to his cheek. "Is that not okay?"

His hand gently smoothed my hair as he stared intently at my forehead, almost like he was avoiding my eyes. Then he gave them to me and said, "You've no idea how okay that is."

I smiled, and said softly, "Good."

He didn't return my smile, just continued to silently watch me.

Eventually, I asked, "Are *you* okay with what you did today?"

Surprise flashed on his face for a split second. "You don't think I am?"

Why's he avoiding the question?

I chose my words carefully. "I think your feelings on it are split down the middle."

Again, he didn't say anything, so I continued. "You strike me as a man who isn't afraid to do whatever it takes to keep people safe. I also think you like the violence, so I'm not sure why you'd have any doubts about it."

This got a response. He moved fast, rolling me onto my back and moving on top of me. One of his hands restrained mine on the bed above my head; the other one traced a line down my face. His breathing was rough and his eyes were flashing something I couldn't quite pick. "I don't do what I do because I *want* to do it. I do it because it's in me and I can't deny it most days," he said bitterly. Pushing an angry breath out, he continued, "As much as I fucking try to keep it caged, it won't fucking leave me alone. And yes, I do fucking like it, but, *fuck*, I don't want to."

He let me go and pushed up off the bed. In one fluid movement, he was up and getting dressed. His face was a mask of fury, and I didn't know what to say or do to calm him down. I figured, if it were me, I'd want to be left alone to deal with it until I felt calmer. So, I let him do what he had to, and a moment later, when he stalked out of the room, I let him go.

Shit.

CHAPTER 12

BLADE

"ASHLEY!"

She couldn't hear me, so I screamed louder. "Ashley!"

Still couldn't hear me.

Fuck.

Why couldn't she hear me?

Her attacker moved his hand between her legs and roughly pulled them apart.

No!

"Ashley!"

I tried to run to her, but my legs were like lead, and I couldn't lift them.

Fuck.

He slipped his hands in her panties, and she screamed until he slapped her.

I tried yelling for her again, but she didn't turn to me.

And then my legs moved, and I ran to her.

As her attacker thrust inside her, I finally got to them, but she still couldn't hear me. And when I stood right in front of her, she looked straight through me as she screamed her horror into the air.

"Ashley!" I begged her to hear me, but she couldn't.

I didn't exist to her.

I sat bolt upright in bed, my skin clammy with the sweat the dream had induced. So much sweat tonight.

Fuck.

I turned to the bedside clock.

Four fucking am.

Jesus fucking Christ.

I threw the bed covers off and stalked into the bathroom.

Deja-fucking-vu.

I'm getting sleeping pills today.

I angrily splashed water on my face and leant my hands on the vanity, staring at myself in the mirror. The exhaustion was getting worse and manifesting in more anger than I usually felt.

Except when you're with Layla.

Yeah, you fucked that up, asshole.

I snatched the towel up and dried my face before throwing it across the room. I slammed my hand down on the vanity and roared, "Fuck!"

Three days without seeing her, and I was losing my shit.

Motherfucking fuck.

★★★

Scott greeted me at his front door four hours later and raised his brows at me. "How many days since you've slept?" he asked as he held the door open for me.

"Too fucking long," I muttered as I entered.

"Yeah, that's pretty obvious."

He led me down the hallway and into the kitchen. "Coffee?" he asked.

I nodded and grabbed a stool at his kitchen bar. "Who else is coming?"

"Nash and J," he said while making the coffee.

"I'll be honest, Scott. I can't fucking find Blue, and I've *never* had that problem."

"Same. I'm beginning to wonder if he even fucking exists."

"The thought had crossed my mind. Wondered if Marcus intentionally led us astray to give him space to do whatever he's got planned while we're busy, off chasing someone who we'll never fucking find."

Scott stared at me. "Our brains run the same way, brother."

I stared back at him. He'd never called me that before, and I wasn't sure what to make of it. I was too tired to process it this morning, though, so I left it alone and moved on with the conversation. "So you guys don't have any more leads on him?" I'd hoped he would have something today. Anything.

He shook his head. "Nothing."

"Fuck."

"Yeah."

He passed me my coffee and I took a long gulp. It was so hot, and it burned my throat, but I couldn't give a fuck. I needed the caffeine.

I eyed him. "How are you and Harlow doing?"

His silence told me a lot, but he did give me an answer. "Not good. She hasn't slept here the last few nights." He scrubbed his hand over his face.

"Fuck, you're as exhausted as I am, aren't you?" I asked, feeling his pain.

"Feels like it. There's too much shit going on lately. I've never had to deal with relationship shit before, and I've gotta say, I'm fucking struggling with it."

"She's coming back, though, yeah?"

His hard stare held the anguish he fought. "I'll make fucking sure of it."

Shit.

We were interrupted by Nash who swore all the way down the hall. By the time he entered the kitchen, we both had eyes trained on him. "That motherfucking cat! I swear, if it fucks with me again, I'm gonna stuff it."

Scott scowled at him. "You go near that cat, and I'll fucking stuff you."

Nash ignored him and announced, "J's not coming."

"Why not?" Scott asked.

"Some shit about Madison and her car not working and a haircut she needed that wasn't worth his balls if he didn't take her." He shrugged. "You fuckin' know women . . . there's always some bullshit to deal with if you want to keep getting your dick sucked."

"Didn't fucking need that visual of my sister, dickhead," Scott muttered.

My head throbbed with a headache I hadn't been able to shake for three day.

It's been three days since I've seen Layla.

I downed the rest of my coffee before interrupting their bullshit conversation. "Ricky Grecian contacted me a few days ago."

That got their attention.

"And?" Scott demanded.

"He doesn't want to share his territory. Threatened me with something if I don't get Marcus to back off."

"What?" Nash asked.

"An old crime that he covered for me."

"He wouldn't hesitate to use that shit, too. You got anything on him?" Scott inquired.

"Yeah, it's all good there. Not that he knows that, of course, but I wanted to give you a heads up. He's coming for Storm."

"Thanks," Scott said, and I heard the honesty of that in his voice.

I nodded. "Yeah," I said, and then added, "Thanks for your help the other day."

"All good, brother," Nash said. "Layla okay now?"

"Yeah."

I have no idea.

I've got eyes on her, just not mine.

★★★

I walked into my office an hour later, dropped into my chair, leaned my head back and shut my eyes. My head ached to the point of desperation. I massaged my temples, praying that would ease it, but it hadn't helped all morning so I wasn't holding my breath.

"Have you still got that headache?"

I opened my eyes to find Merrick standing in my doorway, arms crossed over his chest.

"Yeah."

He uncrossed his arms and walked towards me. "You need to go to the fucking doctor and get that shit sorted."

"You're worse than a wife, you know that?"

"And you're a stubborn motherfucker who needs a fucking wife to kick his ass into gear."

I yanked my desk drawer open looking for aspirin, but there were none to be found. I slammed the drawer shut. "Fuck."

I pushed my chair back and stood before stalking to the floor-to-ceiling window that overlooked the river. Clenching my fists, I took some deep breaths to try and get my shit together.

Merrick interrupted me. "Have you called her?"

I spun around and glared at him. "Fuck, Merrick. I told you I'm

113

not gonna fucking call her. Don't say that shit to me."

His temper almost matched mine. "You need to fucking call her, Blade. It's clear to me there's something there, and it's about fucking time you pulled your head out of your ass."

My chest squeezed tight with the turmoil I was experiencing. "No, I won't taint her with my darkness."

"Did you ever stop to think she might not care? That she might share some of her lightness with you? She might be the best fucking thing to happen to you in a long time, and you're willing to just throw it away before you even find out?" His voice gradually grew louder and he rubbed the back of his neck as he fought his frustration with me.

"And did you stop to think I might be the worst thing to happen to her?" The brutal heaviness in my chest made it hard to breathe.

Fuck.

I clenched my fists again, craving violence. It helped ease the demons.

I need to find another outlet.

You had one, asshole.

"Fuck!" I roared, and turned and smashed my fist into the wall behind me. The pain radiated up my arm, and I welcomed it. I'd learnt to embrace pain rather than fight it. I'd also learnt to inflict it upon myself: the distraction of physical pain calmed the hurt of emotional pain.

Turning back to Merrick, I demanded, "Is she okay?"

He ignored the hole I'd put in the wall. It wasn't the first one I'd ever put there and it probably wouldn't be the last. "Yes. Ben's got some of the guys watching her and has reported no problems. No backlash from Mario's people."

"Good," I murmured.

"You calmed down enough to discuss Phil Deacon?"

"Yeah, what the fuck's he up to now?"

"Ben's been investigating, and has confirmed Phil's definitely putting a bid in for the Hurley job. Ben's also been able to confirm Phil's got you in his sights."

I frowned. "How so?"

"Not sure yet, but he's told his men anything goes."

"Yeah, I bet he has. Keep Ben on him." I stared at him for a moment. "This is gonna be a fucking cock fight, isn't it?"

He grimaced. "Yeah."

Just what we fucking need.

CHAPTER 13

LAYLA

"HAVE YOU HEARD FROM HIM?" JESS ASKED WHILE SHE straightened the bottles of alcohol on the shelf behind the bar.

I watched her from the bar stool I'd sat my ass on fifteen minutes ago. Weariness had claimed me and it was only four in the afternoon. *How the hell was I going to make it through the night?* "No," I answered her and did my best to ignore the ache in my heart.

She jerked her head around to look at me. "Shit, what's it been now? Like, five days?"

"Jess, I know you're obsessively compulsive about those labels facing out but even you've taken this too far. This is the third time you've done it today and the day's hardly even begun," I said, distracting her.

Glaring at me, she muttered, "Shut up. We hardly have any customers and I get all fidgety when I'm not busy. The fucking labels call to me, and I can't shut them up."

I laughed and held up my hands defensively. "The labels are all yours."

"Now answer my question," she said as she finished with the bottles and gave me her full attention.

I sighed. "Yes, five days."

I miss him.

"Why don't you call him? It's not like you to let a man walk all over you."

I sighed. "He's broken somehow."

She shrugged. "So? We all are in our own way, babe."

"Yeah, we are, but he's really struggling with it at the moment I think."

"So push him. If you want to pursue something with him, fucking fight for it."

"I know I should, but . . . "

She cut me off. "No fucking buts, Layla. Either you want him or you don't. It's as simple as that. And really, it surprises me that you haven't confronted him and squeezed his balls till he came to his senses. So unlike you."

I leant against the bar to get closer to her, almost like I was sharing a secret. "You know guys . . . some of them fuck you around with bullshit commitment hang-ups or other shit. Donovan's different. I don't know how to explain it, but he's all fucking man . . . I don't think he has it in him to fuck around with trivial shit like that. The stuff he's dealing with seems bigger than that, and I feel like he just needs some space to sort through it."

She listened to what I said and then moved closer to me. "Okay, I get that, but you should still call him. Let him know you're here for him. Let him know he's not alone if he doesn't want to be."

I stared at her.

Fuck.

I've wasted five days.

I jumped off the stool and pulled my phone out of my pocket.

Eyeing Jess, I said, "Thanks, I needed that pep talk."

She waved me away with her hands. "Go. Make the call and leave me to my labels. I think they might have moved while I had my back to them."

I grinned at her. "I fucking love you, Jess."

She rolled her eyes. "Yeah, yeah, I know, you'd be lost without me, right? You just love me for my OCD that keeps your bar in top shape."

As I dialled Donovan and placed the phone to my ear to wait for him to answer, I poked my tongue at her. "No, I love you for your wonderful, non-sarcastic outlook on life."

She blew me a kiss and I turned to walk out to the back to have this conversation.

The phone rang.

And rang.

And rang.

And then it went to his voicemail.

I pressed end without leaving a message.

Disappointment slapped me in the face.

Maybe he needs more time.

Maybe he's done.

The phone vibrated in my hand.

My heart danced to the sound of its ring.

Caller ID confirmed it.

Donovan.

I pressed it to my ear. "Hello."

Silence.

"Donovan?"

His breathing filled the silence. Ragged. "Are you okay?"

"Yes." I paused for a moment, unsure how to proceed. "Are you?"

Silence.

And then, "Don't worry about me."

His words sliced sorrow through me. "I *do* worry about you. And as much as you might not want me to, I won't stop worrying about you. I've given you space but I'm done. I want you, Donovan. I can't put it into words, but I *feel* you. And I think you feel me. I think you want this as much as I do. So I'm gonna keep pushing you because, fuck it, life's too short not to push for what you want." My heart pulsed, and the apprehension I felt pumped through my veins.

Silence.

And then, "Fuck."

"I'm here for you," I whispered.

"I can't do this, Layla," he rasped.

"Can't or won't?"

"Both."

No.

I should have known better.

Anger took over the sadness careening through me. "That's bullshit, and you know it."

He hissed. "Don't fucking push this. I'm not who you think I am, and I'll never be who you need."

"How the fuck do you know who I need you to be? You don't know me well enough to make that call."

"I know *me.* And no one fucking needs what I have to offer," he said, his torment clear.

I wanted to shred his words and bandage his damaged soul with love. The self-hatred oozing out of his mouth calmed my anger and fed my desire to pull him into my embrace. "Donovan, I know what *I* want. I want you in all your fucked-up glory. I want the chance to get to know what that looks like and decide for myself if I can handle it. What I *don't* want is you making that choice for me."

I heard him suck in a breath and then expel it. "No."

He ended the call, and I stared at my phone.

The first crack hurt like a bitch but I knew, as my heart

completely splintered, it would kill like a motherfucker.

★★★

"Pass me the bottle, bitch."

I squinted my eyes at Jess. "Don't call me names, bish." I sloshed more vodka into my glass before giving her the bottle. Without waiting for her to pour a drink, I raised my glass. "To men who are stubborn assholes and don't know a good thing when it's right in front of them. May they grow some balls and man the fuck up." I tipped the glass to my lips and downed the whole lot in one go.

"Jesus, you need to slow down, boss. You've been at this for two hours now."

She blurred into focus as I tried to look at her. I pushed my glass at her. "Make me some sex," I slurred.

She raised her brows. "Wouldn't it be nice just to be able to make sex like that?"

"Fuck you. You know what I mean."

Shaking her head at me and muttering shit I couldn't understand, she did as I had asked.

"Why are men such hard work?" I asked.

"It's God's way of driving women insane, babe. I'm sure it amuses him to no end."

"Well, it doesn't fucking amuse me. And what amuses me even less is that he finally sends me a man I want, like *really* fucking want, and it turns out the guy's not fucking interested."

She finished making my drink and slid it to me. "Enjoy some sex on the beach, babe. Looks like that's gonna be the only sex you'll get in a while."

I wanted to poke my tongue at her but I couldn't muster the energy. Raising the glass, I said, "To friends who never leave you." I enjoyed the sweet taste as it slid down my throat. Looking at her, I added, "I think I might love you, bish. You love spending time with me, you do what I say, you make me drinks when I want them and you listen to me whinge. The only thing you don't do is put out."

She sipped her vodka. "Bitch, you pay me to spend time with you, you pay me to do what you say, and, usually, you pay me to make you drinks. Just because you're not paying me for making these drinks, don't think tonight means something it doesn't. And fuck, I'm not sleeping with you, even if you pay me. Okay?"

I grinned and raised my drink at her. "Don't try to make out you don't care. I know you love me, too."

She rolled her eyes. "Yeah, yeah." Looking at her watch, she said, "It's nearly four am. You do realise I'm sleeping over, don't you?"

"Is that what you say to all your dates?"

"You're on the couch, babe. I'm taking the bed. Don't get excited."

"Why is it that approximately twelve hours after getting my heart fucked, I feel happy?"

She laughed. "One, you've got me, and you know that makes you a lucky bitch. And two, you've had enough alcohol to drown that hurt. In about five hours, your head and your heart are gonna be screaming at you in pain."

"Shit," I muttered.

Her face grew serious, and she leaned on the bar, and gave me her full attention. "You do know he *is* interested, right?"

My heart raced at the thought. "I know he is, but I don't think he's even close to admitting it to himself."

"Oh no, babe, he's admitted it to himself. I saw that in his face the night I spoke to him about you. But something's holding him back and *that's* what you have to figure out if you're ever going to get him to take the next step."

"I don't know how to do that if he won't see me or even talk to me." I hated feeling like a whiny bitch. I didn't do this shit. If a guy wasn't interested, I moved the fuck on, but Donovan had me all tied up in fucking knots. And he was the only one who could free me.

"For what it's worth, I think it's a matter of sitting back and waiting now. You've let him know how you feel, so he's got all the information he needs to know you'll be here for him when he's ready. He's just got to wade through his shit first."

"Yeah, well, I hope he doesn't take too long to do that."

She winked at me. "You and me both. You're a cranky bitch when you're not getting any."

"Fuck you."

She burst out laughing and I couldn't help but laugh with her.

Thank god for good friends.

CHAPTER 14

BLADE

I STARED AT MY COMPUTER SCREEN, NOT SEEING ANY-
thing as the words all ran together.

Seven days since I've seen her.

I pushed my chair back and stood. The need to escape the
suffocation of my office had taken over, and I couldn't concentrate on
anything. I reached for my car keys, shut the laptop and strode out to
find Merrick.

He looked up from his desk when I entered his office. "You
leaving?" he asked.

"Yeah."

"Your headache back?"

I shook my head. "No, thank fuck. I just need to get out."

"Maybe you should take a couple of days off," he suggested.

*Christ, that was the last thing I needed. Time to think? Fuck
no.*

"No, I'll be back in the morning. Besides, we need to finalise some things on the bid for the Hurley job and I want to get that done tomorrow."

"Okay, I'll see you tomorrow."

I drove straight home even though the pull to Layla's bar had me in its grip. After our phone call two days ago, I'd emptied a bottle of scotch and fought the desire to go to her. She thought she wanted me but if she knew how deep my darkness ran, she'd run a fucking mile. I refused to let her start something that could only end in ruin.

When I pulled into my street, I was surprised to see a woman leaning against a car parked in my driveway. I took in the tight jeans, knee-high black boots, the black singlet with a skull on the front and boobs on display.

Fuck.

Sharon Cole.

This couldn't be good.

I parked my car next to hers and got out. She watched me with trepidation. My gaze shifted to the bruise on her cheek.

Fucking Marcus.

Walking to her, I said, "Sharon."

"Blade."

I opened my palms in question. "We've never spoken. Why now?"

She jerked her head towards the house. "Can we go inside?"

I put my hand out indicating for her to lead the way. As I followed her, I couldn't help but think about the differences between Sharon and my mother. From what I could work out, Marcus had chosen completely different women to spend his life with. Sharon appeared to be a very confident, ballsy woman who didn't mind putting herself on display. My mother, on the other hand, struggled with self-confidence, doubted herself at all turns and hid herself away. Such extremes.

We made it into my lounge room and I asked her the question

again. "What's going on?"

A nervous energy surrounded her. "Is your mother seeing my husband again?"

"Not that I'm aware of."

"I think that either has changed or will change."

I weighed my options before settling on one. "I don't believe it will change, but not because Marcus isn't pushing for it."

My words pierced her. I saw the evidence on her face, and in the way her breathing changed. Fuck, why do these women fall at his fucking feet?

Her hand went to her chest, and she grabbed at her singlet in an anxious manner. "I've suspected it for a while now. Thank you for confirming it."

"Why do you stay with him?"

Her eyes widened. "I love him," she whispered.

My anger flared, and I didn't try to hide it. "How the *fuck* can you love a man who hits you, has cheated on you for years, and who lies to you repeatedly?"

The nervousness slid off her face and she put on the mask I assumed she used when defending her choice of Marcus. "My relationship with Marcus is not one I expect anyone to understand, let alone you."

"You talk a good game, Sharon, but you don't fool me. You need to remember one thing: we're both intimate with the evil of Marcus Cole. If anyone can understand your relationship with him, it's me."

"No one can - "

The headache I'd managed to rid myself of crashed its way back into my skull, and the anger that talking about my father caused collided with the pain in my head. I finally lost my shit. "I fucking can!" I thundered. My skin heated with crazed madness and my heart thumped in my chest. "You think you're the only one who ever wanted to be loved by Marcus? You think you're the only one who craved his presence in their life? Fuck! I fucking *get* it. But he will never love us or anyone the way we want, the way we fucking deserve, because Marcus Cole exists to please only one person. Him-fucking-self."

She stood staring at me with wild eyes, and I watched as the mask tumbled off her face.

We faced each other, two broken and scarred people, fucked up by the same man, and I felt a shift inside me.

Something had cracked.

A realisation.

I'd uttered the truth when I said Marcus would never love us.

A truth I'd never wanted to admit out loud.

I'd buried that truth so fucking deep in my soul and refused to believe it.

There was no more hiding from it now.

"I love him, and I can't stop," she whispered. "I know it makes no sense, but I've always loved him, even through all the shit."

I stared at her and waited for more.

"In the beginning, he wasn't like he is now, not this bad. Then we had Scott, and, at the same time, shit went down at the club. It was a blood bath as they battled a war with Black Deeds and shed members with no loyalty. Marcus changed through all of that, hardened, and became more violent. He also began seeing your mother around that time, and I suspect he took most of his anger out on her because he was leaving me alone back then. My father was still around and kept an eye on him."

"So you knew he was cheating on you?"

"He always had, but I didn't care. I grew up around the club and knew it was just part of the lifestyle."

I stared at her. Stunned a woman would accept that for herself. "Were there other women besides my mother?"

"From what I could work out, one or two, but not really. As his duties at the club increased, he didn't really have the time."

I took a breath and asked the one question I'd always wanted to know the answer to. "Did Marcus abuse your kids?"

"No!"

"Why not? He never hesitated to take to me with his fists if he was in the mood." I didn't believe her.

"Blue helped me. After Dad died, he stepped up and looked out for us. Marcus only began hitting me after Blue left."

Fuck.

Blue.

"Who is Blue?"

"My brother."

Fuck, under our noses all this fucking time.

"Why did he leave?"

"It was after his girlfriend died of a drug overdose. Something happened between him and Marcus. Blue knew something, I don't know what, but it was enough to force Marcus to get the club out of drugs. Blue always hated they were into that."

"Blue blackmailed him?"

"Yes."

"Do you know where he is now?"

"No, he never tells me."

He knows Marcus would kill him if he found him.

"How often do you hear from him?"

She shrugged. "Every couple of months."

"Does Blue know Marcus has pulled Storm back into drugs?"

"I haven't spoken to him for a while now, so unless he's heard it from someone else, I don't think so."

We need to get that information to him somehow.

I stared at her. I struggled to understand what made a woman still want her husband even after she knew all this shit about him. I could grasp her falling for him when she was younger, but how could she still love what he'd become? "Don't you think it's time you started putting yourself first, Sharon?"

She swallowed hard and that anxious look returned to her eyes. "I don't remember how." It was barely a whisper, but it fucking hit me in the chest.

It was like a piece of the puzzle fell into place for me.

My mother doesn't remember how, either.

"The first step is to get him out of your life."

The look on her face told me she had no idea how to do that.

Fuck.

I clenched my fists as the demons reared their ugly heads.

Marcus had infected our lives with his sins for long enough. I may have grown up hating this woman for all she represented, for everything she had that I didn't, but I couldn't bring myself to feel anything other than compassion for her now. She'd done nothing wrong other than falling in love with a man who didn't have the capacity to love her back. He'd taken her love and smashed it into pieces.

He's broken all of us into pieces.

It's time to put the pieces back together.

★★★

I needed to see my mother after Sharon left. She'd stirred so many feelings and thoughts in me, and I had to get some of them off my chest. Thinking of everything Marcus had put us through caused my skin to itch with agitation, and adrenaline surged through me at the thought of leaving all that shit behind.

The first thing I saw when I pulled into Mum's street was Marcus's bike sitting outside her house.

The second thing I saw was him yelling at my mother in her front yard.

The third thing I saw was red.

SLAY

I parked the Jag and stormed towards them. Rage blurred my vision but I managed to land a punch on his face. He stumbled back, holding his face, anger radiating from every inch of him. When he regained his balance, he came at me and punched me in the gut.

Pain.

I embraced it.

This was nothing compared to the pain of my youth.

The torment of my life.

My mother's screams barely registered as he and I fought.

Nothing registered except my inescapable need to inflict pain on my father.

My thirst for his blood.

Every punch was for every moment he hurt us.

For every moment he ignored us.

For every moment he trashed the love we ached to give him.

"Donovan!"

My mother stepped into the fray. She frantically tried to pull me away from the fight, but my rage had taken over.

My anger and hatred owned me.

It ruled me.

It stripped me of the control I'd carefully cultivated in my life.

"Donovan, you'll kill him! Stop!"

I ignored her. I wanted to kill him. His death could not come fast enough.

When he finally went down, I didn't stop. I kept punching. His face was mangled, and every inch of it was covered in blood, but I could still hear his breathing. I wasn't done yet.

"Donovan! I don't want to lose you, too."

Her words filtered through to me, causing me to stop.

Lose me? Why would she lose me?

I turned to her with a questioning glance.

"If you kill him, you'll go to jail." She choked on a sob. "I've given him up...all I have left is you. Please stop . . . "

Fuck.

My mind frantically tried to process everything going on. I looked down at my father. Sprawled unconscious on the ground, bloody, and battered, but still fucking breathing. I looked back at my mother. Distraught, tears streaming down her cheeks, worry and panic clear on her face.

Fuck.

This was going to fucking happen, but not in front of my mother.

I stepped away from him.

"Go inside," I said to her.

"What are you going to do?" she begged to know.

Before I could answer her, the rumble of bikes filled my ears. Turning, I saw three bikes pull up.

What the fuck?

I stalked toward them. "What the fuck do you want?"

They were Storm bikers, and one of them jerked his chin at Marcus. "He asked us to meet him here. You want to tell us what the hell happened."

"No. What I want is for you to fuck off and leave my father and I to deal with family fucking business."

He pulled his gun out as a menacing look crossed his face. "Doesn't look like Marcus is dealing with anything."

I stepped forward so the gun was pressing into my chest. "You use that, and you'll have shit come down on you like you've never fucking known," I snarled.

The air tensed with a standoff none of us wanted to back down from.

"Donovan!"

I jerked my head to look at my mother.

Fuck.

Not in front of my mother.

Turning back to look at the biker, I muttered, "Put the fucking gun away, get your fucking president off my property, and fuck off."

I stepped away from him and waited for him to do as I'd said.

They dragged Marcus out of the yard. He'd regained consciousness and spat blood at my feet as he passed me. "I always knew you were worthless," he sneered.

His words no longer had the power to wound.

This was what freedom felt like.

I ignored him and went to my mother.

"Go inside, I'll be there in a minute," I murmured. I wanted her as far away from him as I could get her.

She nodded and left.

After she was safely inside, I watched as Marcus left. They'd put him on the back of one of their bikes and left his here. Someone would collect it. I could care less.

Pulling my phone out, I dialled a number.

"Hello," he answered.

"I'm out."

"What the fuck?"

"I can't wait any longer. It's time to deal with Marcus now."

"Fuck! That fucks the whole plan, Blade. Scott's not ready yet."

"I don't give a shit anymore. Storm can deal. I need him gone now."

"Motherfucker," he swore, and hung up.

I put my phone away as a sense of peace settled over me.

Finally.

★★★

I cleaned the blood from my body and found some old clothes of mine in the cupboard of Mum's spare bedroom to change into. Once I was clean, I met her in the kitchen. Still shaken from earlier, she

131

looked at me with anguish.

"I hate I've done this to us," she whispered.

I caught her cheek in my hand. "Marcus did this to us."

"Yes, but I let him." She collapsed against my chest and broke down again.

I ran my hand over her hair and placed a kiss to her head. I held her for a long time, letting her get her tears out. When she finally lifted her head to look at me, I said, "There comes a point where we have to forgive ourselves, forgive the mistakes we've made, and make the decision to move forward. You'll be consumed by hate and regret if you don't. I don't want that for you. You've already been through so much shit. I just want you to be happy now."

She stared silently at me before asking, "How do I forgive myself for the pain I've caused in your life?"

"You accept you're not perfect, Mum. We're all flawed and capable of making bad decisions. We start now and move forward from this point in time. Everything in the past stays there."

"I won't take him back, Donovan. I promise you that. And I told him that today."

My heart squeezed in my chest at the words I'd waited my whole life for.

"Thank fuck," I murmured, and pulled her close again.

"I love you," she mumbled into my chest.

"I love you, too, Mum."

★★★

I spent the rest of the day alone.

Thinking.

Planning.

My headache had eased. It was still there, though, and later that night I finally decided to deal with it.

I walked into her bar just before midnight.

She watched me walk towards her and didn't say a word when I stood in front of her a moment later.

We stared at each other until she eventually reached for the scotch bottle and two glasses. She filled them and slid one to me. I watched as she sculled hers, and then I downed mine.

I placed the glass down, and murmured, "I'm fucked up."

She grabbed the glass off me and refilled it. Pushing it back to me, she said, "We're all fucked up, Donovan. It's how you deal with that shit that matters."

Fuck me.

This woman.

"I'm dealing," I said before drinking the second scotch she'd given me.

"Seven days. You pull that shit again, and you can deal on your own."

I nodded. Message received.

Her gaze travelled over my face. "You need sleep." She ignored the cuts and bruises.

"Yeah."

She took in my beaten-up hands and then said, "Go upstairs. I'll be there in a minute."

I did as she said and sat on the edge of her bed, waiting for her. For the first time, I really took in what her room looked like. It wasn't at all what I would have expected of a woman's bedroom, and yet it was all her. Bed, bedside table, dresser, wardrobe and mirror; she had what she needed, no more. A painting on her wall and a rug; she kept the decorations to the minimum. It spoke of a woman who didn't add fuss to her life.

She walked in a couple of minutes later with a bucket of ice, a plastic bag and towel. After she placed them on the bedside table, she indicated for me to stand. And then she put her hands to the bottom of my tee and gently lifted it up over my head.

"Shit," she muttered, as she took in the bruising on my body. "Who did this to you?"

"It's not important," I murmured, not wanting to drag her into my shit.

Her eyes came to mine. "Yes, it is. Tell me."

I stalled.

Fuck.

"My father."

She sucked in a breath. "Fuck."

"It's okay. He couldn't walk once I was finished with him."

Her eyes widened. "Jesus, Donovan."

I placed my hand under her chin and tilted her face to mine. "I like you calling me that," I whispered.

She smiled. "I love your name," she said, and fuck if that didn't hit my sweet spot.

Moving to grab some ice, she placed it in a plastic bag and wrapped it in a towel. She handed it to me. "Lie on the bed and put that on the bruises. I'm gonna get some painkillers."

I did as she said and placed the ice to my ribs. Fuck, the pain was intense. But fucking worth it.

She came back with pills and water.

I didn't take my eyes off her.

She fucking amazed me.

After she had me sorted out with ice and painkillers, she gently moved onto the bed. I was lying on my back with my arms by my side, and I moved one arm out across the pillow so she could rest her head on my shoulder.

She hesitated. "I don't want to hurt you."

"You won't hurt me, baby. Come here."

Something crossed her face.

"What was that?" I asked.

"What?"

"That look on your face just then."

Her eyes came to mine and she held me there. "I like it when you call me baby."

Fuck.

Fucking hell.

"Get here," I growled, desire swirling in my gut.

She didn't hesitate this time and came to me.

My arm went around her, and she curled herself into me.

"You look like you've been to hell and back," she whispered against my skin.

"I'm still dealing with shit, Layla. I'm not gonna be an asshole and walk away again, but I need you to know it could get rough."

"I can handle rough. But you've gotta let me in."

"I'm barely keeping my shit together at the moment, and I have no fucking clue how to let someone in on that. I don't even know if I want you having to deal with it," I admitted, and then added, "Fuck, it's like I'm in a million fucking pieces and I don't even know where the fuck to start to fix it."

She shifted so she was propped up on her elbow. "Donovan, sometimes you have to shatter to find strength, and sometimes you have to let someone in to help you put the pieces back together."

I held my breath for a moment, and as I let it out, I cupped her cheek. "I don't fucking deserve you."

Her hand came up to rest against mine. "Yes, you do. We all deserve someone who sees us, and accepts us for who we are."

I shut my eyes and focused on my breathing.

This is too good to be true.

My body buzzed with a concoction of emotions.

Happiness.

Peace.

Awe.

Fear.

My mind was like a racetrack with the emotions racing through it.

Fighting for recognition.

Fighting for domination.

When will the madness end?

Her warm lips pressed against mine.

A balm to my chaos.

"Open your eyes," she whispered.

I opened them.

Caring eyes stared back at me.

"I'm not going anywhere," she said.

"Not now."

My chest tightened.

"Our parents taught us to expect rejection. We have to unlearn that, baby." She brushed her lips against mine again. "Together," she whispered.

Fuck.

The ghosts of my childhood circled, fighting for their place in my soul. I always let them in, but not tonight. Tonight, I clung to Layla. My lifeline to a new place in the world.

Together.

★★★

"Ashley!"

She fought her attacker. Frantic hands clawed at his face, drawing blood. He grunted and punched her. She fell to the ground.

I struggled to run to her, my legs heavy and unable to move fast enough.

She kicked her attacker, but her frantic efforts were useless. He towered over her and ripped her dress up, panties down.

My heart almost exploded in my chest.

Terror filled me.

I can't get to her.

"Donovan!"

Her scream froze my blood.

Ice slithered down my spine.

She turned her face to me.

Ashley was gone.

The horror of my life pressed hard against me. It crushed me, flattened me, and squeezed me until I could hardly breathe.

I gasped for air.

"Layla!"

No.

I sat bolt upright in bed.

Pain shot through me at the sudden movement, but I pushed through it. I reached across the bed to find Layla. I had to touch her. Had to know she was okay.

"Layla." My hand pushed against her, shaking her awake.

"Donovan . . . what . . . " She sat up and bleary eyes stared back at me. Questioning.

I cupped her cheek.

"Thank fuck," I breathed out on a choppy breath, and laid my forehead against hers.

She reached for me. "What's wrong, baby?"

I roughly pulled her close. Enveloped her in my arms. Didn't even feel the pain as her body connected with my bruises. Layla wasn't capable of inflicting pain on me.

"Just a bad dream," I murmured.

Her arms came around me, and we cradled each other for what seemed an eternity.

I never want to let you go.

I won't ever let the evil take you from me.
Not this time.

CHAPTER 15

LAYLA

THE SMELL OF COFFEE DREW ME AWAY FROM MY BED AND into the kitchen.

Holy shit.

Donovan stood, back to me, in my kitchen, muscles shifting under his skin as he moved his arms.

A happy sight first thing in the morning.

He heard me and turned.

I ignored the bruises on his body.

Smiling at him, I murmured, "Morning."

Heat simmered in his eyes. "Come here," he ordered.

My tummy fluttered.

I did what he said, and he pulled me into his arms and kissed me.

I could get lost in his kisses. Rough to show his passion and need. Soft to show his tenderness and care. And the way he injected rough and soft into the one kiss made my knees weak.

When he ended the kiss, he said, "I didn't know what you like for breakfast but I figured the bacon and eggs I found in the fridge were a sign."

He made me breakfast.

His eyes narrowed.

"What was that look?" he asked.

I grinned and laid a palm to his face. "*That* was happiness. And pure fucking amazement that I finally found a man who knows how to use kitchen utensils."

He returned my grin, and fuck me, there needed to be more of that shit in my life. Smiles from Donovan lit my world. "I'm domesticated, baby. My mother taught me well," he said.

"I look forward to meeting her one day. The wonderful woman who produced a man as good as you."

His eyes widened, and his shoulders tightened.

I pulled his face down to mine to get close. "I don't mean right away. When you're ready," I said softly.

He nodded. "Yeah," he said, gruffly. "She'd like you. She's always asking me when I'm gonna find a woman and settle down."

"She sounds amazing, and I have no doubt she is. I mean, any woman who can teach their son to look after a woman the way you do must be a good woman."

"She *is* a good woman. I just wish she'd met a good man to share that with."

He still seemed a little uncomfortable with this conversation so I reached around and smacked his ass. "I'm hungry. Feed me."

The grin returned to his face, and he gave me another quick kiss before moving into action. He'd found everything he needed and a couple of moments later had food on plates and coffee in mugs.

I eyed all the food he'd cooked. "Are you really hungry?"

"No. I made enough for Annie, too. Wasn't sure if she'd want any, but figured I'd make some in case."

My heart fluttered in my chest. "Thank you," I whispered.

He nodded. "Yeah."

"No."

Confused eyes came to mine. "What?"

I walked to where he was, placed my hand gently on his chest, looked up into his eyes, and said, "No, I'm not thanking you for cooking breakfast. I'm thanking you for being you. For being so good, so kind . . . so thoughtful. I've never had that from a man in my life, not even from my father. I know this thing between us is only new, and what I'm about to say might not be what you're ready to hear . . . fuck, I'm not sure it's what I'm ready to say, but I have to say it. I need you to know it."

He stared at me, waiting for what I had to let him know. I couldn't read his emotion. It didn't matter anyway; this was more for me than for him. He could do whatever he wanted with it.

I took a breath before continuing. "I feel stuff for you I've never felt for a man. And I want you in my life in a way I've never wanted anyone. I don't know what the future holds, but I'm going to fight for this, Donovan."

He stood, unmoving, his breathing rapid. When his hand came to my face, it was firm but gentle. He grasped my cheek, and when he spoke, his voice was rough. "There's only been one woman in my life who meant the fucking world to me, and I've never wanted anyone since. Then I found you, and fuck, baby, you've turned my whole fucking world upside down. I wake up in the morning thinking about you, and you're the last thing on my mind before I go to sleep at night. We're gonna fight for this together."

My heart soared.

I moved into his space, put my arms around his neck, and I kissed him. His lips welcomed mine, and he proved his words with his mouth. Our souls joined in a kiss that began to wipe away the damage of our pasts. A kiss that promised we would meet the future together and fight for the love we both so desperately needed.

★★★

Later that day, Damian burst my happy bubble when he resigned.

"I'm sorry, Layla, but I can't pass up this opportunity."

I couldn't blame him. He'd been offered a job as a lighting technician for a band, and since that was what he'd been trained for, I would say goodbye with happiness.

"You better get me tickets when they come to Brisbane," I said.

He grinned. "Absolutely, boss lady."

"When do you leave?"

"In a week. I can work right up until I leave if you want me to."

"Do you know anyone who wants a job? Who could actually do as good a job as you, I mean?"

He contemplated that. "No, but if I think of anyone, I'll let you know."

"Thanks."

"Have you heard from Dale?"

"No, and I don't think I will. That fucker is long gone." The anger I'd felt towards Dale had shrunk a little. Enough, so that if I saw him again, the first thing I reached for wouldn't be his balls.

"Yeah, I think you're right. I'm sorry he screwed you over."

"He will be, too, if I ever catch up with him again."

He laughed. "I don't fucking doubt it. Lord fucking help him."

"Sounds about right," I said with a smile.

We worked quietly to get the bar ready, and as I walked to the door to open for business, he said, "You seem happier today. Did you sort stuff out with Blade last night?"

I turned and nodded. "Yes."

"I'm glad. You deserve that in your life, Layla."

I opened the door and let the few customers, who were waiting outside, in, and walked back to where Damian was. "I'm gonna miss you, dude."

"Yeah, I'd miss me too," he joked.

I rolled my eyes at him. "I'm not sure how the fuck Jess and I will cope without you. I mean, you spend half your time checking guys out and the other half annoying the crap out of us. It's gonna be so hard to replace you," I said, cocking my head and winking at him.

"Yeah, fuck you, too, boss."

I grinned. "Right, I'll leave you to it for a bit. I want to check on Annie and pay some bills. Call out if you need me, yeah?"

He nodded. "How's Annie doing?"

"She's retreated a little back into herself after doing well to begin with. I need to find ways to draw her out and get her involved in life again. She wouldn't get out of bed this morning, not even for bacon and eggs, which, I've gotta say, I would never say no to."

"Has she started seeing that psychologist?"

"Yeah, she had an appointment last week, and I think it went alright. She's got another one tomorrow afternoon, so fingers crossed it goes well, too."

"I think you're doing all you can, and I also think what you're doing is amazing. I know people who wouldn't do half the shit you're doing, not even for their closest family members. You're good people, Layla."

I shrugged. "I guess my family showed me how *not* to love people."

"Yeah, sad but true. And I guess at least you have one thing to be thankful to them for."

"That's one way to look at it."

I left him and headed upstairs to find Annie. Deep in thought about my shitty family, the ringing of my phone startled me.

Donovan.

"Hey you," I murmured into the phone, my tummy fluttering.

"Hey." His voice was soft, and that caused my tummy to progress from flutters to somersaults.

"How's your day going?" I asked.

"Yeah, getting through stuff. Just wanted to make sure you're okay."

"I was until one of my staff quit on me."

Silence, and then, "You want me to help you find someone new?"

Oh god, could this man get any better?

"Sure, thanks. I don't know anyone I would ask."

"Leave it with me, I'll ask around."

"I owe you. Come over tonight and you can collect." I bit my lip thinking about how I could repay him.

"Fuck, baby," he growled. "It's only lunch time. You can't say that shit to me this early in the day."

Oh, this is gonna be fun.

"Sorry," I said, sweetly. "I guess I also can't tell you that I've been imagining your mouth on my pussy all morning."

"Jesus," he muttered. "How the fuck did I find a woman with such a dirty mouth?"

"Just lucky, I guess."

"Depends how you look at it. I'm sitting here with a fucking hard-on at eleven thirty in the morning and no way for it to be taken care of. Doesn't sound fucking lucky to me."

"Baby, you've got a hand, haven't you?" I breathed into the phone.

"Fuck, Layla, don't fucking tempt me," he rasped.

"Wrap your hand around your cock and imagine it's my hand." My voice was husky with the desire consuming me.

The only sound I heard was his heavy breathing, and then the sound of his zipper in the background. His breathing picked up a second later, and he grunted something unintelligible into the phone.

"That's it, baby. Now shut your eyes and picture my tits, naked in your hands. I'm pumping your dick in my hands while you've got your hands full of me."

"Fuck," he groaned in between ragged breaths.

My pussy clenched, and I walked into my bedroom and closed the door behind me. Leaning against the door, I unzipped my jeans and reached my hand into my panties.

"I'm touching myself. Imagining it's your hands on me," I told him as I fingered myself.

"Tell me how wet you are," he grunted.

Oh fuck.

I ran my finger through my wetness, and squeezed my eyes shut at the intense pleasure I felt. "I'm so fucking wet for you, Donovan. I wish it really were your fingers in me. Wish your mouth was down there, eating me."

"Fuck!" he roared, and I knew he'd come.

My fingers frantically worked to give me the orgasm I craved, and a couple of moments later, I cried out his name as I came.

We were silent except for our heavy breathing. And then he murmured, "Fuck, Layla. I need more."

I do too.

"I'll be there soon. Tell me your address."

He gave it to me, and I ended the call so I could deal with the stuff I had to do. I needed to get to Donovan as fast as possible.

★★★

An hour later, I entered the warehouse at the address Donovan had given me. Looking at it, I realised I didn't even know what Donovan did for a living. Time to fix that.

A beefed-up guy met me at the front door and escorted me up to Donovan's office. We passed lots of offices, but their doors were all shut so I had no clue what they held. When we got to the end of the corridor, the guy knocked on the door. "Blade, Layla's here."

I waited silently.

The door opened and Donovan stood on the other side, a formidable force staring back at us.

At me.

His eyes didn't connect with his staff member's at all; they came straight to mine.

"Thanks," he said to the guy, and stepped aside to let me pass through.

My body brushed against his as I moved past him, and my pussy ached with desire.

I needed him.

Now.

He closed the door and fixed his gaze on me. The intensity rolling off him today was something new. He'd always been fairly intense, but *this*...this was orgasm-inducing.

He wants me.

His eyes flashed hunger.

Need.

Desire.

"Come here," he growled.

Yes.

I walked to where he stood.

"Take your clothes off," he commanded, and I did as he said.

He watched every piece of clothing come off, until I stood naked before him. I didn't say anything, and I didn't move to take his clothes off. I sensed Donovan needed to be in control of this.

After he inspected every inch of my body, he stepped closer to me and curled his hand around my neck and brought his lips to mine in a long, rough kiss. His other hand went straight to my pussy and a demanding finger thrust inside me.

My body jerked. I hadn't been expecting that, but it was so very welcome, and I pushed my pussy into his hand. He pushed another finger inside and rubbed my clit with his thumb. Donovan's expert touch caused a rush of lust to shoot through me.

I placed my hands on his hips and softly moaned into his mouth, "Fuck."

His fingers grew more insistent as he chased an orgasm for me. It wouldn't take long; I was still worked up from our phone sex. Keeping his hand firmly around my neck, he pulled his mouth from mine and moved to take one of my nipples between his lips. His teeth lightly grazed against my breast and I begged for more on a moan.

He growled at my need and worked his fingers harder while he sucked my breast further into his mouth.

Oh fuck me.

I cried out as the orgasm tore through me. My hands moved to his head at my breasts, and I threaded my fingers through his hair and roughly pulled.

That set him off, and he let my breast go and pulled his fingers out of me. Feral eyes looked at me, and I gulped for a breath at the sight of his wild need. Donovan's carnal hunger for me was something I'd never experienced from a man before. It unleashed my matching hunger and we lost ourselves as we fought for what we needed from each other.

"I want you on your hands and knees," he growled, and waited for me to do as he'd ordered.

I did as he said and he grunted his pleasure. Then he stripped his clothes off while I waited on my hands and knees for him. I was turned on just knowing he stood above me. I knew he wouldn't be able to tear his eyes from me.

I heard the crinkle of foil and I squeezed my legs together, knowing he was closer to being inside me. His body pressed against mine, and he leaned over me to speak in my ear, "I haven't been able to think of anything other than your fucking pussy for the last hour, baby. You shouldn't get me this fucking worked up. It's gonna be hard and fast."

I moaned, and he thrust his cock inside me. His loud grunt echoed around us, and I bit my lip as the pleasure gripped me. Fuck, I loved this man's dick and his talent at using it.

We fucked like fucking animals.

Raw.

Rough.

He gave me everything I needed, and I devoured it and begged for more.

As he drove me closer, he grunted, "You close, baby?"

I squeezed his cock as he slammed into me again. "Yes," I panted. My orgasm surrounded me, and I could reach out and touch it, but I struggled to catch it. It teased me, and I cried out for it.

He kept going, fucking me harder and deeper. I knew he was barely holding his release in by his grunts and ragged breathing. "Fuck, Layla, not gonna last much longer . . . "

I worked harder.

Fuck, I needed this.

Sweat slicked our skin as we moved together, and my hair stuck to my face. The feel of his body against mine, and the feral sounds surrounding us as we both fought for it, collided in my mind to create a brilliant explosion of light and bliss. Pleasure scattered throughout my body, hitting every single nerve ending. The sensations were so intense, so fucking pleasurable, and I tumbled into an abyss of ecstasy.

"Fuck!" he roared and came.

He thrust one last time and then stilled, his body tense against mine as his own pleasure consumed him.

I dropped my head and concentrated on getting my breathing under control. My heart beat wildly in my chest and the last jewels of pleasure fluttered through me. I sagged under him, but he moved one arm to hold me up.

"You okay, baby?" His gravelly voice was tinged with the softness I loved from him.

"Yes."

His strong arm around me caused my brain to scramble again. I loved his arms, and I especially loved being held in them.

He moved so he could lay kisses softly along my spine, and a shiver ran down my back.

Oh god. No more. I can't handle any more pleasure today.

He pulled out of me, and pulled me up with him. When we were standing, he cradled my face in his hands and kissed me. "I'll be back in a minute," he promised.

I nodded, and he walked into what I figured was a bathroom. He didn't waste time and came back to me a moment later. I could hear water running and gave him a questioning look. He jerked his head towards the bathroom. "I'm gonna clean you up."

I shook my head. "Fuck no. I think I might explode from the pleasure if you come anywhere near me in the next few hours."

He grinned and held his hand out to coax me. "I promise not to touch you inappropriately."

I raised my brows. "Jesus, Donovan. Every time you touch me, it's inappropriate. Every time you look at me, it's fucking inappropriate. You don't know any other way."

Heat flared in his eyes. "Okay, baby, you clean yourself up. I'll keep my hands and eyes away from you for a bit, but I'm warning you now, I'm only giving you a few hours. After that, you're fair game again."

"Shit. We need to add to my earlier statement, that every time you talk to me, it's inappropriate."

He nodded at the bathroom. "Go," he growled.

I left him and spent the next fifteen minutes enjoying the heat of the water on my muscles. Sex with Donovan was almost an athletic experience, and my muscles already ached. I wouldn't have it any other way, though.

When I re-entered his office, I found him dressed and on the phone. He looked up at me and let his gaze roam over my body. I loved the desire in his eyes that he didn't ever try to hide from me. His gaze got stuck on my breasts and I bit my lip as he abruptly ended his call and stalked to where I stood.

"Fuck, Layla, I fucking want you again," he muttered as his hand came to my breast.

Oh god.

I took a step back so that his hand fell from my body. "You said a few hours, and I'm holding you to that."

A scowl fixed itself on his face. "No, I'm holding *you* to it, baby." He checked the time on his clock. "I'm coming to you at five o'clock and you're going to let me fuck you."

Fuck.

I didn't respond. My tongue was tied in my mouth at his dirty words.

"Tell me you understand," he demanded.

I nodded. "Yes."

"Good."

As I stood there, my bossy man ordering me around, and my body in a state of bliss, I decided I'd never been happier in my life.

CHAPTER 16

BLADE

AFTER LAYLA LEFT, I SPENT THE AFTERNOON DEALING with shit Merrick kept dumping on my desk. Construction jobs we were in the middle of needed issues dealt with, and jobs we were considering bidding for needed some details sorted out. The security side of our operation required my attention at the moment as well. Ben's job was to keep an eye on our competition and ensure our business was clear of threats. The construction game was a ruthless business to be in and dirty tricks were common. He'd recently come across some things that needed to be further investigated.

At three thirty, Merrick stepped into my office, and Ben followed after him. Fuck, this couldn't be good. I closed my laptop and stood. "What?" I demanded.

"We've had a mass walk-off on the job we're doing in the City at the moment," Ben informed me. "Union officials convinced the workers to strike, and although we're working to fix it, I think we're in for a rough ride with this one."

I raked my hand through my hair. "Fuck. Phil Deacon's behind this, isn't he?"

The motherfucker had a reputation for bribing union officials into shit like this.

Ben nodded. "I suspect that, yes."

"Jesus," Merrick muttered. "If that job isn't completed on time, we stand to lose a lot of fucking money."

I eyed Ben. "What do they want?"

"New negotiations on Enterprise Bargaining Agreements."

"Fuck, if that goes through, it pushes the final cost up at least thirty percent."

"Yeah," Ben said.

Tension smashed through me. Phil fucking Deacon had been a thorn in my side for far too long. "It's time to teach that motherfucker a lesson," I declared.

I knew I'd made the right decision when both Ben and Merrick gave me their agreement without hesitation.

Pointing at Ben, I said, "Get the guys together. This shit goes down tonight. I'll let you know the details."

"Will do," he agreed, and left Merrick and me to it.

"We should have dealt with Deacon years ago," Merrick mused.

"Yeah, well, he's about to wish he'd never fucked with me."

"Good. I always thought you were too soft on him."

He was right; I had let Phil get away with a fuck load more than other people. We'd had a good relationship once, and with loyalty being one of my strong points, I'd struggled to deal with him once he'd started pulling away from me.

"I have," I agreed. "I won't make that mistake again."

My phone rang, interrupting our conversation, and Merrick left me alone to take the conversation.

Scott.

"Hi," I answered it.

"I had a missed call from you." He cut straight to the chase. Pure Scott.

"I know who Blue is."

"Fuck. Who?"

"Your uncle."

Silence. And then, "What the fuck?"

"Had a visit from your mother, and she mentioned his name during our chat. Blue is her brother. I got out of her that he has something over Marcus from years ago. He used that to blackmail Marcus into pulling Storm out of drugs, and then he left. Went into hiding from what I can make out."

"Fuck," Scott muttered. "Uncle Dan. Haven't seen him in ten years."

"How the hell did you not know he was Blue?"

"I never called him that growing up. Must be Mum's nickname for him. Red hair and all." He paused before adding, "Why are you telling me this? I heard you were out, brother."

Brother.

"I was, but I've reconsidered."

"Thank fuck, Blade. Shit's going down in the club at the moment with divided loyalties. We need to expose Marcus and get that support back before we take him out."

"Is he still spreading shit about you?"

"Yeah, but at least some of the guys have a fucking brain and can see through him. Just need to get the rest of them to see it."

"What's the split at the moment?"

"About sixty to forty, I'd say."

"Fuck."

"Yeah," he muttered.

"We need to find Blue and get him to come back. I'll protect him until we sort Marcus out."

"I saw the results of your run-in with Marcus. Good job, brother, but thank fuck you stopped."

We talked a bit more and then ended the call, and I contemplated what had been said.

It was the longest conversation I'd ever had with my brother.

★★★

At exactly five o'clock, I walked through the front door to Layla's. She was at the bar serving customers. I looked around and realised she had about double the number of customers in here that she usually had. Narrowing my eyes on the far corner, I also took in the band she had playing. Live music.

As I walked to her, she looked up, and I caught her eye. I also caught the rapid rise of her chest when she saw me. And the bite of her lip.

I waited at the other end from where she was serving, and once she'd finished with her customers, she came to me. Leaning across the bar, she pressed a quick kiss to my lips.

I shook my head when she pulled away.

"What?" she asked.

"I didn't come for a kiss," I said, my eyes firmly on hers.

Her heated gaze told me she'd been waiting for five o'clock. "I know," she breathed out, "but I'm too busy to leave the bar."

She was right, but fuck, I was a greedy bastard. I needed to find her a lot more fucking staff members. "Go back to your customers. I'll be waiting."

"Do you want to wait upstairs?"

"Yeah."

I pushed off from the bar and headed upstairs after one last look at her. She was wearing a short denim skirt tonight. I'd never seen her in a skirt, and fuck, I never wanted to see her in anything but a fucking skirt from now on.

I climbed the stairs slowly. Exhaustion still owned me, and my dreams still hadn't left me alone. I intended to lie down on Layla's bed to wait for her, but Annie smiled at me from the couch and I stopped to say hi. We hadn't spoken much, and I wanted to change that. I wanted to spend time not only with Layla, but also with the people who meant something to her.

"Hi," I murmured as I approached her.

"Hi Donovan."

She spoke in such a timid voice. I fucking hated her father for what he'd done to her, and the fact Layla had taken to him with a knife pleased me to no fucking end.

That's my girl.

"Can I sit with you?" I asked, respectful of her choice to be on her own if that was what she preferred.

Wide eyes stared up at me, and I thought for sure she would say no, but she surprised me when she said yes.

"How's your day been?" I asked, trying to break the ice.

"Good. I helped Layla for a few hours in the bar this afternoon, so I think she's happy with me."

Fuck.

"Annie, Layla loves you and is always happy with you. Helping her in the bar doesn't make her happier with you. She just wants *you* to be happy."

"I'm happy when she's happy."

Jesus, we've got a lot of work to do here.

"So, tell me, what kinds of things do you like to do in your spare time?"

She thought about it, and after a couple of moments of silence, I thought she had nothing, but then she said, "I used to like ice skating, and Layla and I used to do it all the time until Julian hurt her."

Annie had my full attention now. "Who is Julian?"

"He was Layla's boyfriend. The one she met while we still lived on the streets. He was the one who saved us."

"When did you live on the streets?"

Her face became a mask and she shut down. "I shouldn't be telling you this stuff," she said, and turned away from me. The way she huddled into herself told me I'd really hit a nerve with this conversation.

"I'm sorry, Annie. I didn't mean to upset you."

She didn't respond and we sat in silence for a while. Eventually, I got up and made my way into Layla's bedroom. I lay down on the bed and closed my eyes for a minute. A quick rest before Layla came up wouldn't hurt.

★★★

"Donovan."

A hand touched my shoulder and gently rocked me, waking me up. I cracked an eye open to find Layla staring down at me.

I opened both eyes. "Shit, sorry," I muttered as I got my bearings. "How long have I been asleep?"

"A couple of hours. I came up and you wouldn't stir so I left you to sleep, but your phone's been ringing nonstop so I thought I should wake you in case it's important."

Fuck, Ben and Merrick were waiting for me.

I sat up and took my phone off her. "Thanks, I've gotta check this."

"No worries." She smiled at me as I left the bed and exited the room.

I headed downstairs and outside to make the call to Merrick.

"Where the fuck have you been, Blade?"

"I fucking fell asleep."

"Ben's got Phil. They're at his house."

"Okay, I'm heading over now."

I hung up and jogged upstairs to say goodbye to Layla. She was waiting for me on her bed. Naked.

"Jesus," I muttered as my eyes feasted on her beauty.

She smiled up at me as I walked to the edge of the bed, but as the realisation I wasn't staying dawned on her, the smile slid off her face. "You're leaving?"

Nodding, I said, "Sorry, baby, I've got something I have to take care of right away. It can't wait."

Fuck, I hated to do this to her.

I ran my hand along her jaw before I let it drop to her collarbone where I traced a line down to her breast. Her hand met mine, and she grasped my wrist and pulled my hand away from her body.

Angry eyes glared at me. "Don't fucking start something you're not going to finish."

"I am going to finish it, just not now. I'll be back in a couple of hours for that."

She shook her head. "No, I'll be asleep. Don't come back tonight."

Annoyance shot through me. "Don't do this, Layla. I have to take care of this but trust me when I say I'd rather stay here with you."

Her glare challenged me. "Well, stay. It's your choice, Donovan."

"No, it's not."

We stared silently at each other, neither willing to back down.

Eventually, I said, "I have to go. I'll call you when I'm done."

She didn't say anything and I left. I had to. I couldn't put it off any longer.

But I couldn't put her glare and her silence out of my mind.

And it fucked with my concentration.

★★★

As I entered Phil's home a little while later, my demons roared to life at the sight of him tied to a chair with dried blood painted on his face. The wild look on his face as he watched me approach also pleased me.

"Thanks for fitting us in to your busy schedule, Deacon," I said.

Ben had gagged him, so he couldn't form a reply but he grunted his displeasure.

I pulled up a chair and sat next to him. "It seems we have a problem that only you can help us solve." I paused and then continued, "As you know, we had a couple of hundred men walk offsite today due to some fucked up union representative's encouragement. And now we need you to fix that."

He grunted, and I decided I'd had enough of his silence. I pulled my knife out and cut the gag from his mouth. The fear in his eyes at the sight of my knife encouraged me. I stood and grabbed his hair. Shoving my face closer to his, I pushed his head back to expose his neck. I ran my blade across it, light enough not to draw blood, but heavy enough to induce more fear.

"What do you say, Deacon? You gonna fix that shit for us?"

"Fuck you, Blade," he spat.

Anger roared in my ears, forcing the blood in my veins to pump furiously through me. "What the fuck did you just say?" I thundered, pressing the knife harder against his throat.

As the first drop of blood kissed my blade, he answered me, "I said, fuck you, motherfucker."

I pushed his head hard so it snapped back before bouncing forward again. My body moved fast as I kicked my chair out of the way, cut his restraints off, dropped my knife on the table next to us, and yanked him out of the chair. Gripping him by his shirt, I shoved him hard against the wall, and immediately punched him in the face. Blood spurted onto my shirt but I ignored it. My only focus was Phil.

And Layla.

Fuck.

I couldn't get her angry glare and words out of my head.

Shit, I needed to concentrate on Phil.

In that momentary lapse of concentration, he punched me twice. I stumbled back, shocked at this turn of events. No one ever distracted me when I was dealing with shit like this.

"Fuck," Merrick swore, and he and Ben fought to restrain Phil again. Merrick eventually held Phil back by his arms and scowled at me. "Get your fucking head in the game, Blade."

I glared at him. "It fucking is."

"No, it's fucking not, asshole."

Ben interrupted us. "Ladies, let's just get this done and then you two can bicker as much as you want. Yeah?"

We both scowled at him. "Fuck you, Ben," Merrick muttered.

"Enough!" I roared, and punched Phil hard in the gut. "Tell me you're gonna fix this shit, Phil. I've let you off every other fucking time you've screwed us over, even that time you had the shit beaten out of my men, but this time I'm not letting shit slide."

And there was the look I was searching for. The one that told me he would do what I wanted. It was the look of terror mixed with resignation, and it usually meant my opponent just needed one last bit of encouragement before they gave in.

I looked at Ben. "Call Onyx and get him over here. I think he and Phil need to have a little chat." Onyx was the guy you called when you needed shit taken care of. People thought I was a crazy motherfucker. I had nothing on Onyx.

Phil's eyes started blinking and I could have sworn he shit himself. "No! I'll fix it, Blade."

I shook my head. "Call him," I said to Ben.

Looking at Merrick, I said, "Restrain him until Onyx gets here." I picked up my knife and started to head for the front door.

"What the fuck, Blade? You're leaving?" Merrick asked.

"Yeah, I've got shit to get back to," I answered him without

looking back. I was focused on one thing only.
Getting back to Layla.

CHAPTER 17

LAYLA

I TOOK THE NIGHT OFF.

After Donovan left to take care of his shit, anger consumed me, and I knew I wouldn't be able to focus on work. So I locked myself away upstairs and stewed on it.

Annie had retreated into her bedroom so I sat alone. Never a good thing when you're angry. But I craved it tonight. I *wanted* to be angry. Kind of like when you're sad and all you want is to lose yourself in sad songs.

Donovan leaving me when I thought we were spending the night together had brought up old feelings of rejection by my parents. Stupid, I knew, especially after I'd told Donovan only last night we had to unlearn the expectation of rejection. It seemed this would be harder than I thought if my reaction tonight was anything to go by.

I ignored his five phone calls.

He'd been gone an hour and a half when the first call came. They'd continued to come every five minutes or so, with the last one over ten minutes ago. I guessed he'd given up, and that began a new round of anger.

God, could I be any more fucked up? I didn't want him to call, and yet, when he stopped trying, I wanted him to keep trying. I drove myself mad with my crazy behaviour.

Fuck, this was a good reason to stay single. It had to be a better option than sending yourself mad with stupid expectations. Expectations you knew you shouldn't have but that you couldn't fight.

"Layla!"

Donovan.

I stood and watched as he stalked into my lounge room with a look of fury on his face. He stopped a little over two feet from me, his eyes boring into mine. "I've been calling you."

"I know."

"Why didn't you answer?"

"I didn't want to."

He exhaled sharply. "Fucking hell," he muttered, pushing his fingers through his hair.

We stood sizing each other and the situation up in silence.

"I'm mad at you," I blurted out, stating the fucking obvious.

"I can see that," he said in a tight voice.

"I want you to leave."

"No."

"Yes, please go. I need to think."

He came toward me with that intense look of his I knew well. Before I could stop him, he slid his hand around my waist and yanked me the rest of the way to him. Bending his face to mine, he growled, "No, you don't need to think. You need to feel."

His spare hand pressed against my stomach and then slid down into the shorts I was wearing. I sucked in a breath when his hand slipped inside my panties and he held my pussy in his hand and gripped tight. He moved so he could whisper in my ear, "Feel that,

162

baby. Feel my fucking need for you." Then his hand around my waist moved to my ass and pushed me into him, into his erection. "Feel how hard my dick is for you."

"I feel you, Donovan, but it doesn't take my anger away."

His lips crushed to mine in a brutal kiss. We both poured our anger and passion into it. Lips, tongues and teeth collided. My body pulsed with pleasure, and my mind raced to process the mixed emotions assaulting it. I kissed him, but at the same time, I fought him. My hands tried to push him off me, but his strength wouldn't allow it. His hold on me was too hard to fight. And when he pushed his fingers inside my pussy, I jerked from the explosion of sensations that shot through me.

I moaned into his mouth. I couldn't stop it.

He pulled away from the kiss to stare at me. "You feel it, don't you?" he demanded as his fingers continued to pleasure me.

"Yes," I said, and pulled his face back to mine. Our lips met in another excruciating kiss.

Oh god. This man could be my saviour and my downfall all rolled into one if I wasn't careful.

His fingers worked me into a frenzy, until I was a panting mess in his arms. As I came, he rasped, "I fucking love watching you come."

I opened my eyes and focused on him. His need was written all over his face, and my core clenched at that. My need still warred with my anger, but need would always win out. I grasped his face in my hands and begged him, "Fuck me, Donovan."

A growl rumbled out of his chest, and he lifted me into his arms. My arms and legs wrapped around him, and he carried me into my bedroom depositing me on the bed. He tore his clothes off, not taking his eyes off me while I frantically stripped, too. I was sprawled across the bed, and he spread my legs before moving on top of me. As he did that, I wrapped my legs around him and held on tight, ready for him to take me. His cock pressed against my entrance but he didn't push in yet.

Staring down at me, he asked, "You gonna stay mad for long?"

"Just fuck me." My eyes pleaded with his.

He teased me with his cock, pushing it against me and then pulling away. "No," he grunted, "tell me."

I moved my hands to his head and pulled hard on his hair. "I don't know."

He buried his face in my neck and bit me hard before sucking and licking me.

Fuck, yes.

I tilted my hips, trying to push myself into his cock, but he moved his hips up, thwarting me.

"Fuck me!" I demanded, and his head reared up, angry eyes coming to mine.

"Feel me!" he yelled back.

"I am fucking feeling you."

"No, you're not!" He pushed up off me, and although I had my legs tight around him, his strength was too much for me to fight and he pushed through my hold and stood. Standing at the edge of the bed, body straining with anger and passion, he demanded, "Put all that shit out of your head, and feel it here." He pounded on his chest before continuing. "Life's too fucking short to let that other shit get in the way of what we feel, and I'm not going to fucking lose it again."

I watched his breathing grow ragged and took in the ravaged look on his face. There was something else going on here, and my anger eased enough to let him in. I moved off the bed and into his space. Placing my hand on his chest, I asked softly, "What won't you lose again, baby?"

His chest heaved, and he took a moment to answer me. "You. I won't fucking lose you."

He wasn't making sense; he'd never lost me before. "I'm not going anywhere, Donovan. I'm just mad, but I'll get over it."

"Now," he forced out, "You need to get over it now. I'm not doing this again . . ."

He still wasn't making any sense. I grabbed his face with both my hands and begged, "Tell me what you're not doing again."

The despair on his face pierced my heart. My strong man struggled with so much, and all I wanted to do in that moment was wrap him in my arms and never let go. I wanted to soothe his hurt and take it all away from him. But that wasn't how life worked, and he had to move through it before he could escape from its clutches.

I waited, but he didn't say anything.

"Baby," I whispered, "I feel you. I feel the pain that lives in you, the pain that has shredded you and left scars all over your soul. I feel the passion you feel. I feel the anger you have at life. And I feel your struggle with the darkness."

His breaths were coming hard and fast as he stood staring at me, taking in my words. I stepped even closer to him, skin to skin, and pressed a soft kiss to his lips. My hands went to his chest and I slid them up and around his neck. Pulling his face down to mine, I kept kissing him until he opened his mouth and let me in. This kiss was unlike any we'd ever shared. Gentle and loving, there was none of the roughness we usually preferred. I moaned into his mouth as the sensations washed over me. The pleasure Donovan never failed to give me.

He fell into the kiss and his hands went around me and slid over my ass to cup my cheeks. I ground myself against him, and he lifted me into his arms. As my legs locked around him, he turned and walked us to the wall.

He broke the kiss and brought his hand to my neck. Rubbing his thumb over me, his gaze focused on my neck as he murmured, "How the fuck . . ." His voice trailed off, leaving me confused again.

"How the fuck, what?" I asked him, puzzled.

His eyes flicked to mine. "How the fuck did I find you?"

I held my breath for a moment as the intensity in the air settled over me. "How the fuck did we find each other?"

He felt what I said; what the spaces in between my words held. I saw it written all over his face. "Fuck," he muttered, and then his lips gave me the roughness I craved from him.

Our mouths and bodies moved together as we forgot the stuff holding our minds back and simply let what we felt in our hearts consume us. I clung to him and when he thrust inside me, I squeezed my legs tighter around him and moved my hips with his. He fucked me with the raw, animalistic passion that was Donovan.

That was us.

As he brought me to orgasm, I moaned and dug my nails into his back. And then he came, too, roaring out his release.

As he stilled, his head dropped, and he grunted words I couldn't make out. He seemed to be lost somewhere within himself. I simply held him and gave him the space to work through whatever was running through his mind. Eventually, he lifted his head and looked at me. I stared back at him, waiting.

"Never again, baby," he said, his voice hoarse.

My brows pulled together. "What?"

"If you're angry at me, we work that shit out before I leave. Not gonna be away from you again when you're mad at me."

My stomach fluttered. "Okay," I whispered.

"And in the future I won't leave if we've got plans."

This time my heart fluttered. "Good."

We stayed like that for a couple more moments.

Silent.

And then he muttered, "Fuck."

"What?"

He pulled out of me and let me down. "I fucked you without a condom."

"I'm clean and on the pill." I tried to reassure him.

"I'm clean, too." He still seemed annoyed, though.

"It felt good, baby."

"Yeah," he agreed, gruffly. "But I won't lose control like that again, I promise."

I grabbed his arm and pulled him to me. "It's okay to lose control, Donovan. You're wound so tight with that control. Let it go, baby."

He didn't say anything, and then he left me to walk out of the room. I watched with a heavy heart. Something held him back, kept a part of him locked away from me, and I wanted to know what it was.

CHAPTER 18

BLADE

"Baby, stop."

A hand landed on my arm and gently shook me awake. I sat bolt upright, my heart beating wildly in my chest, my breathing hard to get under control.

"Donovan," Layla's voice penetrated my thoughts, and I turned to look at her.

"Sorry," I murmured as I scrubbed my hand over my face.

Fuck.

"Don't apologise. You were having a bad dream."

Fuck.

I pushed the bed covers off, moved off the bed and headed into the bathroom. Staring at my reflection in the mirror, I flicked the tap on and splashed water on my face. Jesus, I looked like shit today. When the fuck would this madness end?

I walked back into Layla's room and picked up my clothes. As I began dressing, she left the bed and came to me.

"Are you leaving?" The disappointment in her voice was unmistakable.

I kept dressing and said, "Yeah, I've got stuff to take care of this morning."

"Who's Ashley?"

I froze.

My heart thumped in my chest.

I struggled for breath.

My eyes met hers, and my focus went in and out as I struggled to see through the haze.

"Fuck." The word came from my mouth, but I heard it as if someone in the distance uttered it.

My past collided with my future and the torment I'd lived with for so long came rushing to the surface.

"Talk to me," Layla whispered, and I heard the plea in her voice.

"She was my fiancé."

Her eyes widened but she didn't say anything.

"She died three years ago." I forced the words out, hating the sound of them on my lips and the feel of them on my skin.

She still didn't say anything. Just watched and waited.

"She was raped and murdered." More filthy words out of my mouth.

"You've been dreaming about her, haven't you?"

"Yes."

"Bad dreams?" Her voice was soft, coaxing.

"Yes."

"Oh, baby," she murmured as her arms came around me, and pulled me to her.

I let her hold me, but my arms stayed by my side. I was unable to hold Layla while talking about Ashley.

Fuck.

She let me go and said, "Tell me about her."

I stared at her.

I can't do this.

I rubbed my hand over my face. "I've gotta get to work," I muttered, trying desperately to fight through the haze.

"Don't do this, please, " she begged on a whisper.

"I can't . . . " My voice was a strangled mess as I fought the emotions pressing against me.

Fuck.

I finished dressing and sat on the bed to put my boots on.

I didn't look at her.

I couldn't.

I stood, and walked to the door. Pausing, I said, "I'll call you."

And then I left without waiting for her response and without a backwards glance.

★★★

"Onyx took care of Phil," Merrick advised me an hour later.

I sat in my office chair, staring out the window at the river, a million thoughts racing through my mind. Turning to him, I said, "Good."

"Said he would have preferred for it to be more than just a chat."

I nodded. "Yeah, there's no love lost between those two, but we need Phil alive so he can sort this shit out for us."

"I'm sure we could have come up with an alternative plan."

I threw my pen down on the desk. "Fuck, Merrick, when does the fucking blood end?"

He stared at me in shock. "What?"

"Do you ever get sick of the shit we do? Of the bloody battlefield it feels like some days?"

"You know I do, Blade, but you also know as well as I do that we can't walk away from that fucking battlefield. We made the decision years ago to help those girls, and we've worked fucking hard to keep that good in the world. There's no turning back now, unless you're willing to throw them to the wolves again."

"Fuck!" I roared, and shoved my chair back.

"What the hell has gotten into you, Blade?" Merrick stood as well, his forehead creased with worry.

"Every-fucking-thing. I'm fucking stuck, and I don't know how to escape it."

He watched me silently. "Shit."

I clenched my fists at my side. "Yeah. Shit."

"She's gotten to you, hasn't she?" he asked, quietly.

All the thoughts racing in my mind came to a halt. "Yes."

"But you're holding back from her, aren't you?"

"Fuck, Merrick, how the hell do you read my fucking mind like that?"

"Blade, we've known each other since we were fucking kids. Twenty years of friendship will do that shit to you. You're an unpredictable bastard to most people, but, to me, you're like the back of my fucking hand."

I glared at him. "So tell me, how the fuck do I get my shit back under control?"

He smiled. "You let it all go."

"What?"

"Go to her, and let yourself go. Give yourself to her. If she's half the woman I suspect she is, she'll take that shit and put you back together."

The chaos of my mind eased as I considered what he'd said.

Maybe he was right.

Maybe the way forward was to revisit the past and deal with that shit once and for all.

★★★

I didn't go to Layla.

I drove around for hours before finally going home.

And I slept.

For hours.

I woke to my phone ringing in the darkness.

Two am.

Layla.

I answered it but struggled to form words so remained silent.

"Donovan?" Her voice was soft, hesitant. I hated that I'd caused that.

Asshole.

"I'm here, baby."

"I'm at your front door. Can you let me in?"

Shit.

My thoughts shifted to how she knew my address, but I knew without even thinking about it that Merrick was involved in this somehow. I headed to the front door, and pulled it open to find her waiting patiently for me.

"Why are you on my doorstep at this time of the morning?" I asked as I let her in.

"Your friend rang me."

"Merrick?"

"Yes." She grasped my face with both hands. "He's concerned about you. Told me you need me and gave me your address."

"Fuck."

She squeezed my face. "He told me you had stuff to tell me, and that I wasn't to leave until you'd told me everything."

"Jesus," I muttered.

"He told me I had to make you tell me about Leroy, Ashley and the women."

Her voice dropped to a whisper as she mentioned the women. She thought it was something it wasn't.

Shit.

That motherfucker.

I pulled away from her hold, and stalked down my hallway, into the kitchen. I pulled the bottle of scotch from the cupboard and two glasses. Filling them, I slid one across the counter to her. Lifting my glass to my lips, I said, "Drink up, baby. None of this shit is pretty. You're gonna need that."

I slammed the drink down and poured another one, downing that one as well.

I took a deep breath, looked her in the eyes, and started at the beginning.

This would either be the end of us or the beginning of something I knew deep in my heart I wanted.

"I began selling drugs when I was twelve. My mother worked two jobs and yet we still never had everything we needed. My father didn't give two shits if our cupboards were empty. Leroy roped me into his gang and taught me how to make money. He also taught me how to channel the anger that was burning holes in my soul. Up until that point, I directed my anger at myself. I fucking hated myself. My father resented my existence, and so did I. Leroy taught me how to fight and used me to take care of his shit. It was bad shit and as much as I hate some of what I did, it forced the anger out of me. Forced me to stop bottling it all up." I took another breath and watched her reaction.

She poured us another drink, and as she gave it to me, said, "Keep going, baby."

Fuck.

The softness in her voice fucking slayed me.

Perhaps Merrick was right.

Perhaps she would cope with this shit and accept me.

"I was seventeen the first time I killed someone. That's how I got my name, Blade. I killed him with a knife. I did it for Leroy. He had us all under his control to the point where we did whatever he said. Even my mother couldn't break the control he had over me. God knows she tried. Leroy ran drugs and women, but I was pretty much only tied up with the drugs side of his organisation. I only learnt more about the prostitution when I met Ashley. I was twenty-five by then, and she opened my eyes to the evil in Leroy that I'd been unable to see before. He was forcing women into his brothels by getting them hooked on his fucking drugs, and when they owed him so much money they'd have no way of paying it back, he'd force them to work for him. Ashley was different; she didn't owe him money, her brother did. Leroy tried to force her to pay off her brother's debt when she attempted to negotiate the payment of the debt with him. Our paths crossed the day she went to see him and she told me everything. I didn't want to believe her, but hearing her story made me go to the brothels, and I talked with the women there. After some persuasion, they confirmed everything."

I stopped talking. My heart pumped furiously in my chest as the memories assaulted me, and I took a couple of deep breaths, trying to get my breathing under control. Layla placed her hand on my back and began rubbing it. My eyes found hers and I saw only kindness and concern there.

"Do you want more?" she asked, jerking her chin at the scotch.

I shook my head. "No."

"Okay, baby." She kept massaging my back, her touch reaching my soul.

"Thank you," I whispered.

She nodded and waited for me to continue, her hand never leaving me.

"Merrick and I came up with a plan to deal with Leroy. I'd known Merrick since I was about fourteen. He'd been recruited by Leroy to sell drugs as well, and he'd had enough of all the shit we were involved in. I killed Leroy, and we split his organisation in half.

One of the other gang members took the drugs, and we took the women. We shut the brothels down, but then we had the problem that they needed to earn money, and most of them were junkies by that point and all they knew was prostitution. Merrick found a clothing manufacturing business for sale so we bought that with the profit Leroy had made, and the women worked there instead."

I paused and she asked, "So that's what you do?"

I realised I'd never spoken about my work with her. "It's not my main business. We don't make any profit on that side of our organisation. In fact, that business runs at a loss because we employ more women in it than we actually need. Some of the women who've been with us since we split from Leroy now spend their time helping prostitutes, and if any of them want out of the game, we take them on and help them change their lives. We put a lot of money into rehab because most of them are addicted to drugs when they come to us."

"How do you make money, then?" she asked, looking puzzled.

"Construction. When we pulled the girls from the brothels, I discovered they were living in shit conditions, so we bought a rundown building and renovated it for them to live in. After we took care of Leroy, some of the gang members came with us, and I put all of us to work on the renovation because we couldn't afford to hire someone to do it. Merrick and I saw an opportunity there; we had the manpower to do that kind of work so we started off small and we've worked our way up in the construction industry. We now employ hundreds of guys and have multiple jobs going at once. It's a dirty industry, though, and we deal with a lot of shit."

I poured us both a drink. I'd need it for the next part of the story.

Layla drank it silently and waited for me to continue.

After I drank mine, I said, "Ashley helped me become a better man. She helped us push all those changes through and she helped the women change their lives. We moved in together and were planning our wedding when she was murdered." The pain sliced through my heart, but I pushed on. "She was out with friends one night and her drink was spiked, and . . . they took her. Fucking gang raped her and slit her throat."

I fought to catch my breath again and forced the rising bile back down. Layla kept massaging my back, soothing me with her touch, but this pain couldn't be soothed away completely. Not when it was my fault.

I stared at her, preparing to tell her the worst part.

"What else?" she whispered, knowing there was more.

"She tried to call me that night. Her message said she needed a lift home. I didn't take her call, though, because I was angry at her. We'd been fighting on and off all week and had a huge argument before she went out. It was over fucking trivial shit, but I was a stubborn bastard and didn't want to talk to her when she rang. She was supposed to be staying at a friend's house after they finished at the club. I didn't know she wanted me to come and get her . . . didn't know she'd walk the streets trying to find a fucking taxi . . ."

"Oh god," she said, her eyes wide. "I'm so sorry, baby, no wonder you were upset last night."

I rested my hands on the edge of the kitchen counter, curled my fingers under the edge of it and squeezed hard. I tried to squeeze the agony out of me. It was fucking torture, and after living with it for years, I just wanted it gone. I craved silence in my mind.

I pushed off from the counter. "Fuck!" I yelled into the silence of the night. My body screamed at me, and the anger coursing through me took over. I turned and punched the wall behind me. And then I doubled over, my arms going around my body. I clawed at myself as the emotions tangled together in one big mess.

I can't do this any longer.

I'm going insane.

And then Layla turned me back around to face her, and wrapped me in her arms. She held tight and didn't let me go. My arms went around her, and I clung to her.

"Shhh, it's okay to let it out. Don't fight it anymore. Holding onto it is hurting you more."

I took her words in and tried to process them, but after years of fighting this, I knew no other way.

"It's not your fault, Donovan," she whispered in my ear.

I stilled and tightened my hold on her, but remained silent.

"We all say and do shit in life we wish we could take back. But what people choose to do with that stuff is up to them. We can't control their actions, and we sure as shit can't foresee the future. We also can't control what other people are going to do to the people we love. *You* didn't cause those men to do what they did to Ashley. That's on them, not you. Baby, you've spent long enough beating yourself up for this. It's time to forgive yourself for whatever you think you've done wrong. It's time to move out of the shadows of the past and start living your life again."

I buried my head in her neck and let her words wash over me. She held me close and ran her fingers through my hair. Her touch felt so good. After years of denying myself the chance to find love again, Layla's caresses moved through me, reaching deep into my soul. I had no idea how to even begin to forgive myself, but I figured letting her in was a good place to start.

Lifting my head, I looked into her eyes and said, "Thank you."

Her smile shone light over me. "Always," she whispered.

Always.

I needed her skin.

Needed to hold her.

I grabbed her hand and led her to my bedroom.

She let me strip her, and once we were both naked, I took her face in my hands and slowly kissed her. When I ended the kiss, I murmured, "I need you in my arms, baby."

"I know," she said, and crawled onto the bed.

I followed her and settled her in my arms. She placed her hand on my chest and traced the skin there. Her body was pressed against mine, our arms and legs entwined, and I wanted nothing more than what she'd already given me.

Tonight, I just needed to hold her.

CHAPTER 19

LAYLA

"ANNIE!" I CALLED UP THE STAIRS.

No reply.

"Shit," I muttered under my breath. We were going to be late if she didn't hurry up.

"I'm coming," she yelled out, and I blew out a breath.

Thank fuck.

A couple of minutes later, she joined me downstairs and I smiled at her choice of outfit. "You look beautiful," I said, meaning every word I'd said. Annie was a stunning woman, but with the confidence of a child, she didn't see it.

A blush spread across her cheeks. "Thank you."

I smiled and reached for her hand so I could join our arms together to walk out to the car. "Okay, chick, let's get you to your new job."

She walked with me, and I felt her body tense. "I'm so nervous," she admitted.

"I know you are, but Donovan will be there the whole time, and he'll make sure you're okay."

Just thinking about him caused my heart to dance. It'd been three days since he'd cracked and opened up to me. Three days since he'd finally let me all the way in.

"I can't believe he offered me this job," Annie cut into my thoughts.

I stopped her and turned so we were facing each other. "He offered you this job because he knows you're capable of it, Annie. You have so much to offer the world and yet you hide yourself away. I really wish you could see you the way I see you."

Donovan had asked me about Annie and when he'd suggested she go to work for him in administration, I'd been stunned. I wanted to keep her close to me, so I could keep an eye on her and make sure she was okay, but he suggested she needed to spread her wings a little more and learn to be more independent rather than relying on me so much.

"I love you, Layla. I know I don't tell you that very much, but you've done so much for me. And I know, I annoy you with my lack of confidence, but I'm trying to change."

Her words almost broke my heart. "That means the world to me, but do it for *you*, not for me. It's time for you to make yourself happy, Annie, rather than always trying to make everyone else happy."

Her psychologist had spoken to her about her need to please everyone at our last session. Annie always insisted on me attending the appointments with her, and I'd actually gotten a lot out of them. I'd gained a better understanding of where her behaviour stemmed from.

"I know," she whispered. "And I am working on it, I promise."

I squeezed her hand. "Good."

We drove to Donovan's warehouse in silence. I sensed Annie's nervousness and fought my instinct to try to take it away for her. She had to learn to cope with it herself. *God, being a real mother must be so damn hard; fighting that need to make it all better for your child would do my head in.*

One of Donovan's men met us at the door and took us up to him. When we arrived at his office, he was on the phone and had his back to us as he stared out the window. I let my gaze roam over his body. He wore his signature jeans, black t-shirt and heavy boots. As he spoke, he waved his hand in the air and I watched his arm and back muscles flex while he did that.

Oh god.

He'd left my bed at seven this morning after fucking me for an hour, and I needed him again.

He turned and caught me checking him out. Grinning at me, he ended his call and walked to where I was. He reached for me and pulled me close so he could press a kiss to my lips. "Fuck, I need you again," he growled in my ear.

"God, baby, don't say that to me when you can't do anything about it," I complained, pulling away from him.

He let me go, but I suspected it would have been a different story if Annie hadn't been in the room. Turning, he gave her a smile. "You all ready?" he asked. I loved the way he was with her; soft and caring. It was like he knew she needed that rather than the harshness the rest of the world showed her.

Nodding, she said softly, "Yes."

He turned his attention back to me for a moment. "Stay here, okay? I've got something to tell you when I come back." His voice was gravelly, and I figured he didn't have something to tell me as much as he had something to give me.

I raised my brows at him. "Where else would I go, baby?" I asked, sweetly, in the way I knew drove him wild.

Desire flashed in his eyes, and he gave me a quick shake of his head before leading Annie out of the office.

I waited for him on the couch in his office. He'd worn me out the last few nights with his marathon sex sessions, and my body craved sleep. I curled up on the couch and rested my head on the arm. Donovan woke me with a gentle kiss. My eyes flew open to find him crouched down in front of me, a smile on his face.

"Tired?" he asked, as he ran his hand over my waist.

"Yeah, someone keeps me up all hours."

He lifted his brows in that sexy way of his. "I bet he's worth it, though. Bet he knows what he's doing."

"I'm still not sure. I think he needs some more time to prove himself."

His hand gripped me hard around the waist, and he stole a rough kiss. "He'd be happy to work on that now."

Yes.

I pulled his face back to mine and kissed him again. When I ended it, I asked, "Did you really have something to tell me?"

"Yeah. I've found someone to replace Damian if you're still looking."

"Absolutely. Who is it?"

"My father's wife."

Confused, I asked, "What?" Surely, I couldn't have heard that right.

"Marcus's wife, Sharon, is looking for a job, and I think she'd fit right in at your place; besides, she's had plenty of experience working a bar and dealing with assholes. She came to see me a little while ago, and we've been in touch since. I think she's finally thinking about leaving him, and I'm encouraging her in that."

My man amazed me. "Do you have any idea how fucking wonderful you are, Donovan?"

He scowled. "No, I'm not. I'm just trying to help a woman who has no fucking idea how to help herself."

I smiled and kissed him. "And that's what makes you wonderful.

Now, shut up and fuck me."

He didn't have to be told twice.

★★★

The next day, Sharon Cole walked into my bar, and I knew Donovan had been right. She was going to be a valuable addition to my team. I spent a couple of hours talking her through how we ran the place, and when I had to step out the back to take a call, I wasn't the slightest bit concerned she could handle the bar by herself.

Jess arrived at work later that afternoon, and we headed outside so I could catch her up on things while she had a smoke. "How's Sharon doing?" she asked.

"I think she's going to work out."

"Thank fuck, I was worried when Damian said he was leaving. Just when we had a good thing going with the three of us."

"I hear ya, babe."

"And how did Annie do on her first day yesterday?"

"She didn't say a lot, but she went back today without any complaints so I'm hoping that's a good sign. Donovan said she didn't have any problems that he knows of."

Her eyes lit up at the sound of his name. Jess had a tiny crush on my man. "Bitch, how the hell did you get so lucky finding a guy like him?"

"I've been through my share of shit, don't you worry."

She narrowed her eyes on me. "Mmm, one day you'll have to tell me about that." She stubbed out her cigarette and we headed back inside.

Sharon was deep in conversation with a woman at the bar while another woman stood listening. They all appeared to know each other, and when I took a closer look, I wondered if she was Sharon's daughter because I could see the similarities in them. Which meant she was possibly Donovan's half sister.

I made my way to the bar, and Sharon smiled at me. "Layla, this is my daughter, Madison," she said. Then she indicated to the other woman and introduced us. "And this is Velvet."

Madison gave me a huge smile. "Hi Layla, I've been dying to meet you."

"Really?" She was nothing like I'd imagined. I'd figured the daughter of a biker president would possibly be a nasty bitch, so her friendliness surprised the hell out of me.

"Of course. The woman who tamed my brother . . . but he's been so damn secretive."

I laughed. "Tame Donovan? I don't think any woman could do that."

"You call him Donovan . . . I love that," she murmured.

Velvet joined in the conversation. "I don't think I even knew what his real name was."

Before I could say anything, Madison said, "I'm having a BBQ next weekend. I'd love for you and Blade to come."

"I'd love to, but I have to work."

"I'll work for you, Layla, if you want to go," Sharon offered.

I frowned. "Won't you be at the BBQ?"

"I don't mind not going so you and Blade can go."

Madison didn't hide her excitement. "Fantastic! Not this Sunday, but the next at five o'clock. I'll see you then."

They said their goodbyes and left. I looked at Sharon. "Is Madison always that excited?"

She grinned. "When it comes to Blade, yes. Those two have a special bond I can't even begin to understand. I think it's perhaps because she gave him her love without any conditions when they finally met, and that wasn't something he'd ever had before."

It sounded like it could be true. Donovan craved love and

acceptance after his shitty childhood. I just hoped he would continue to let us all in.

CHAPTER 20

BLADE

I LISTENED TO MERRICK GO ON ABOUT THE ISSUES WE HAD with the Hurley bid, but my mind kept drifting to Layla and thoughts of fucking her this morning. It had been nearly two weeks since the night I'd shared my shit with her, and she'd been nothing but fucking amazing since.

"Blade, are you listening?" Merrick cut into my thoughts.

"Yeah. Tell me where we are with the union."

"Whatever Onyx said to Phil worked because the union negotiations are almost finished and didn't hurt us too much. Phil obviously talked to his buddies there."

I snorted at his choice of words. Phil Deacon didn't 'talk' to anyone, he used force.

"Thank fuck," I muttered.

"I've still got Ben watching him, though. I don't trust him not to fuck with us again."

I raised my brows. "Surely not. I would have thought, after our last encounter, he'd realise that's not a good idea."

"You were too soft on him. You know he's a fucking loose cannon."

I scowled at him. "We'll see."

Shaking his head, he muttered something I didn't quite catch.

Ignoring him, I asked, "Have you heard anything on the street about Ricky and what he's up to with regards to Storm?"

"No. Scott hasn't kept you updated?"

I stood. "No, I haven't spoken to him for over a week. It's about time I set up a meet with him. I want an update on Ricky and also on Blue."

"Today, yeah?"

"Yeah."

I grabbed my keys and phone and walked towards the door. "I won't be back in today," I said.

He grinned. "Fucking pussy-whipped."

I headed out into the fresh air, my thoughts drifting back to Layla.

Her back arched, head thrown back, hair splayed across the bed.

Her hands gripping the sheet as she screamed out my name.

Her eyes as they focused on mine after her orgasm.

He's right.

I'm fucking pussy-whipped.

I forced her out of my mind and called Scott.

"Blade," he answered.

"We need to meet and go over where we're at."

"Today?"

"Yeah. Can you guys do it now?"

"Pretty sure we can both make it. I'll let you know if there are any problems. Usual place?"

"Good. I'll see you then," I said and hung up.

It was time to move this fucking plan along. And it looked like

Ricky Grecian just might be the key to make that happen.

★★★

I arrived at the meeting place an hour later. It was a hidden picnic area in a national park far away from Storm's clubhouse, and it was the place we met when the three of us needed to talk without having any prying eyes or ears on us. I watched as they walked towards me, thinking the day we put this plan into motion was a turning point in my relationship with Scott. Griff had come up with the plan so he could get closer to Marcus and find out insider information that would help Scott boot Marcus out.

"Scott, VP," I greeted them with a chin lift.

Scott chuckled because he knew how much Griff hated it when I called him that.

"Fuck off," Griff muttered.

I smirked. "Griff, it's too fucking easy to shit you."

"Yeah, well, you'd be the same if you had a mind full of shit and people in your fucking ear all the time about bullshit club business." He looked at Scott. "I don't know how the fuck you managed to do this job and not lose your shit."

"Which is why we need to move this along," I said. "The sooner we get rid of Marcus, the sooner you can restore some order in the club."

"We still haven't located Blue," Scott said.

"I think it's time we gave up on that," I suggested. "We can use Ricky instead."

Griff furrowed his brows. "How so?"

"We need to flush him out, make him show his hand where Storm is concerned. He wants you guys to back off his territory, and if you push him, he'll come for you."

They contemplated it, and then Scott said, "So, he fucks with us which will hurt Marcus and cause his supporters to think twice, yeah?"

"Yeah, you just need to make them doubt him so that once he's gone, they're more receptive to you stepping into his shoes. Up until now, he's had too much support for that to have much impact but there's so much disorder in the club now, I think this has a shot at working."

Griff nodded. "I like it."

"You know Ricky well, Blade, so what do you suggest is the best way to piss him off?" Scott asked.

"Contact him and tell him you have no intention of stepping away, and then flood his territory straight away." I looked at Griff. "It will be up to you to get that timing right with Marcus and to get him to flood it more than whatever he has planned.

Griff nodded. "Yeah, I can do that."

"And what's his reaction likely to be?" Scott inquired.

This was the part of the plan they wouldn't like. "Ricky's unpredictable, which is his strength. Leroy taught us that. He'll likely come for you at the clubhouse, try and take as many of you out at once as he can. Bring you to your knees that way. So you'll need to up your security there. I can give you manpower, but the tricky thing will be trying to explain that to Marcus."

"Okay, so we work that out, and then I'm assuming we'll need to also take Ricky out at the same time as we deal with Marcus, yeah?"

"Yes," I answered.

Scott raked his hand through his hair. "Fuck, Blade, this is a fucking risky plan."

I gave him a hard stare. "Do you think I got where I am today without risk? You can keep doing what you're doing, and you'll likely still be pissing in the wind in a year's time. I know what I'd rather fucking do."

Griff looked at Scott. "He's got a point. I'm sick to fucking death of the way the club is now."

"Okay, let's do it," Scott agreed.

"Thank fuck," I muttered.

★★★

I walked into Layla's bar with a ready-to-go hard-on just after four that afternoon. Usually that was a quiet time for her, but it was just my fucking luck that wasn't the case today. Based on the number of customers vying for her attention, she'd be at least an hour away from taking care of my dick. And that was as long as no new customers arrived.

Fuck.

She saw me and nodded her head towards my table, holding a glass up with a questioning look.

I nodded back to indicate I wanted a drink and took a seat at the table in the corner. It was the table I'd occupied every time I visited her bar over the last year, so she referred to it as my table these days.

I watched as she, Sharon and Jess handled the customers. It seemed Sharon was a good addition to the team, and Layla seemed happy with her. My hope was still that Sharon would walk away from Marcus. *Mind you, we'd be taking care of that problem for her soon enough.*

Fifteen minutes later, Layla brought me a drink. I admired her body as she walked towards me. She knew I loved her in a skirt and she didn't disappoint today. The tiniest scrap of denim covered her ass, and her tits were barely encased in a tight singlet top. When she placed my drink in front of me, I grabbed her wrist to stop her.

Heat flashed in her eyes as she looked down at me. "Hey, baby," she murmured as she placed her free hand on my cheek.

"That skirt doesn't cover much," I said.

I let her wrist go and moved my hand to her leg. Her eyes

widened when I ran my hand up her inner leg under her skirt. She stepped closer to me, and when my fingers pushed her panties to the side, she sucked in a breath.

"Donovan," she moaned, "I have to get back to work, baby."

I ignored her and pushed a finger inside her pussy while I savoured the way she bit her lip and squeezed her eyes shut while I did it. My other hand moved to her ass so I could tilt her forward, closer to me.

"Layla!" Jess called from the bar.

Her eyes flew open, and she stepped away from me. "Fuck," she muttered. "You're turning me into a fucking hussy, Donovan Brookes. Letting you finger me in fucking public."

I stood and roughly pulled her to me. "Baby, if I wanted to fuck you in public, there'd be nothing you could do to stop me," I growled before I crushed my lips to hers in a rough kiss.

Her lips were swollen by the time I was finished with her, and she had that glazed look in her eyes that told me she was mine.

Mine.

I let her go, turned her around, and smacked her on the ass as I rasped in her ear, "Hurry those customers along. I've got a dick as hard as fucking steel that needs taking care of."

She returned to her customers, and I downed the scotch she'd given me. As I did so, I recalled Merrick's words from earlier. I didn't give a fuck how hung up on Layla I was, this was the fucking happiest I'd been in years.

CHAPTER 21

LAYLA

"OH...GOD..." I MOANED AS I RODE DONOVAN'S COCK. I'D waited all night for this, and he didn't disappoint.

"Baby, you gonna cut to the chase soon?" He sat on the bed cross-legged while I sat in his lap. It had to be one of my favourite positions. His impatient tone, though, was *not* a favourite of mine.

I opened my eyes and glared at him. "What the hell?"

He smirked. "You've been teasing the fuck out of me all night. I just want you to screw me and put me out of my misery."

"I *am* fucking screwing you."

His eyes flared with desire. "You need to hurry the fuck up because I've been aching to get my mouth on your pussy all day."

Shit, my pussy loved his dirty talk. "Well, why didn't you do that first?"

He moved his face closer to mine and growled, "Because you were dead-set on taking charge tonight and I didn't want to ruin your party."

I grinned at him as I squeezed his dick with my pussy. "You're such a thoughtful man, aren't you?"

"Too fucking thoughtful sometimes," he muttered.

I ran my fingernails down his back and enjoyed the hiss that came from his mouth and the way his hands gripped my ass harder. "Okay, baby, let's pick the pace up," I whispered in his ear.

He made a face as if he was thanking God and murmured, "I'm all yours, sweetheart."

Sweetheart.

My lips found his and I deepened our kiss while I fucked him harder and we rode out our release. After hours of build-up to this orgasm, it gripped me hard and we came together. I screamed out Donovan's name and after he'd come, he moved his mouth to my neck and marked me there.

When he lifted his head, his eyes held his need, and he said, "My turn now."

"Baby, I hate to break this to you, but we need to take a breather in-between, otherwise you might send me and my pussy insane from all the pleasure."

He raised his brows. "Really? And what do I get in return?"

I grinned, loving the playful nature he didn't show too often. Nibbling along his bottom lip, I murmured, "Sex anywhere, any way you want it tomorrow."

"Fuck," he said. "How the hell can a man say no to that?"

"He can't."

Smacking my ass, he said, "Okay, get off. I need a drink to deal with this setback."

I crawled off him and settled myself against the headboard so I could watch him move. His muscles never failed to turn me on. I could stare at them all day. Being the woman he'd chosen to share them with made me very happy.

When he returned five minutes later, he had a bottle of scotch and two glasses from downstairs with him.

"You stealing from my bar, baby?" I asked. "'Cause if you are, I'll have to think of ways to punish you."

His nostrils flared and his breathing picked up. His face was a wild mask of desire as he growled, "If anyone's doing the punishing, it'll be me, sweetheart."

Oh, fuck.

My powerful man had no idea how much he affected me.

Everything about him affected me.

His words.

His body.

His beautiful soul.

Everything.

We stayed in that moment for a while.

Eyes never leaving each other.

Our breathing all over the place from the desire surrounding us.

Donovan eventually broke the spell and poured our drinks. He passed me mine, and surprised me with a change in conversation. "Who's Julian?"

Shit, a name I hadn't heard in forever.

A man I hadn't thought of in nearly as long.

A person I didn't want to think of.

My heart rate picked up as the memories flooded my mind. I gulped my scotch and turned my gaze back to Donovan. "Julian was a motherfucker I should have known better than to get involved with." I gulped more scotch. Fuck, I hated dredging up memories.

He sat on the edge of the bed, his concerned eyes focused on mine. I loved the way he looked at me when he was worried about me. Sometimes, his eyes could be so soft for such a hard man. "Tell me about him," he murmured.

I tipped the rest of the scotch down my throat, took a deep breath, and shared the darkest moment of my life with him.

"After Annie and I left home, we had nowhere to go, so we had to stay with friends for awhile. I had no work experience at all. I mean, I never had to work while I was at school because my parents gave me whatever I wanted. So, I struggled to find a job, which meant we couldn't afford rent. Like I said, some friends did let us stay but we wore out our welcome eventually and ended up living on the streets. I met Julian at a café one day when I was applying for a job, and he took us under his wing and helped us get back on our feet. He found me a job with a bartender friend of his and he gave us a place to stay." I stopped to take a breath and put my glass out for a refill.

Donovan filled my glass again before saying, "I'm not gonna like this story, am I?"

I shook my head. "No."

He poured himself another drink and drank half of it straight away. "Fuck." His features had hardened, and I wished we'd never started this conversation.

"We eventually started something. To me, it was just sex, not a relationship. Julian was the third guy I'd ever slept with and he showed me a whole other world of sex. He liked it rough, and I discovered I did, too, so we were a good match. Julian made it clear he wanted to keep sleeping with other women, and I had no issues with that. I was young and wanted to see what was out there. I thought him sleeping around meant I could, too. Turns out I was wrong." I stopped again to drink some more scotch. My chest had tightened and a chill ran through me thinking about this. I raised my eyes to Donovan's and let the care I found there help me get the rest of the words out. "He'd been getting rougher with the sex, inflicting a lot of pain, and I had started to pull away a little. I can handle rough, but only when there's some emotion involved. With Julian, there was nothing. It was just fucking and pain while he got off. One night, I was at work and a guy I'd never met flirted with me. Julian saw it, and when we got home, he let me know just how unhappy he was that another guy had shown interest in me." My voice caught in my throat. "He beat me so badly I ended up in hospital for days . . . He tried to kill me, but Annie saved me . . . she hit him over the head with the baseball bat he kept in his bedroom and got me out of there." My heart beat fast in my chest and my mind swam with the bad memories. I wanted to squeeze my eyes shut and pretend none of this was true. I'd never told anyone this story; Annie was the only person who knew about this.

Donovan moved fast. He shifted to take me in his arms, and I let him hold me.

I needed that.

I needed him.

He didn't say anything, and I needed that, too; the silence where our actions spoke louder than anything either of us could say.

We simply clung to each other.

Eventually, he moved us so I lay in his arms. And then he whispered, "There's a lot of bad shit in this world, sweetheart, but you've got me now. I won't let anyone or any-fucking-thing get to you again."

I spread my arm across his chest and let my hand curl all the way around and under his side. Holding him tight, I whispered back, "Thank fuck you like crappy little bars in the backstreets . . . thank fuck you found me."

★★★

We fell asleep, and I woke up a while later to his hand on my pussy, his mouth on mine. Before I was even fully awake, my instincts took over, and I opened my mouth and my legs to let him take whatever he wanted.

He can have anything he wants.

His leg shifted over mine and pushed it further apart from my other one at the same time that his hand slid from my pussy to cup my ass. He lifted my ass slightly off the bed and demanded to know, "Your pussy ready for my mouth?"

Oh, god, I was *more* than ready.

"Yes," I managed to get out.

He let me go, moving down my body until his head was situated between my legs. It was still dark, and I couldn't see his face clearly, but I could *see* his hunger.

My man needs me.

I shut my eyes and held onto the sheets as he flicked his tongue against my clit.

Fuck.

He used his tongue to get me wet, and then he pushed it inside me while he brought his finger to my clit. Rubbing me with his finger and exploring me with his tongue, he brought me close to orgasm, and then he backed off, pulling his face away from me.

Fuck.

I reached down to grab his hair, showing him how desperate I was for his mouth.

He placed his hand on my stomach, splaying his fingers out before roughly dragging his hand down to hold my pussy. "Jesus," he murmured. "I can't fucking get enough of you, baby."

I moved my hand to cover his hand on my pussy, and our eyes met as I said, "I can't get enough of you, either."

My eyes had adjusted to the darkness now, and I watched as he stared at me with heat. "Fuck," he said, before shifting our hands off me, and lowering his mouth back to me.

He gave me his tongue and his teeth, and, this time, brought me to orgasm. As the sensations shot through me, my heart constricted, and I knew this was the moment. The moment my feelings for Donovan took the leap off the cliff: a leap of complete faith that this man would hold my heart in his hands and cherish it forever.

CHAPTER 22

LAYLA

"LAYLA, WE NEED TO GO," DONOVAN SAID IN HIS IMPATIENT voice.

My head snapped up from what I was doing, and I glared at him. "Don't use that voice on me."

His brows quirked. "Which voice?"

"Your hurry-the-fuck-up voice," I muttered, and looked back down at the table where I was in the middle of fighting with plastic wrap to cover the salads I'd made. Plastic wrap and I were not friends, and I was just about to throw it out of the fucking window.

Donovan moved towards me and stilled my hand by placing his over it. His warm breath whispered across my cheek when he murmured, "Let me do it."

I turned my head slightly to look into his eyes. "How do you manage to piss me off and then make it all better in the space of two minutes?"

His lips brushed mine. "Just talented, I guess."

SLAY

I shook my head at his cockiness. "Okay, Mr Talented, hurry up, because we're already running late and I don't want to annoy your sister."

He finished wrapping the salads. "Something tells me Madison is gonna love you regardless," he said as he picked up both the salads.

"How do you figure that?"

As he began ushering me down the stairs to go to the car, he said, "My sister has been giving me grief for a while to start dating again. So you should probably expect an interrogation."

I followed him to his car and waited while he opened the door for me. "Oh, God."

His hand rested on my arm, stopping me. "Are you worried about this?"

There was no point lying to him, even though I would have preferred not to be this open so soon in our relationship. "Not worried so much as feeling a little anxious." I held back the rest, hoping he'd let me off.

"Why?"

My eyes struggled to meet his, but he cupped my cheek and tilted my face up so I had no option but to look him in the eye. "I want your family to like me, and I've never had that feeling before. I've never given a shit if people liked me, so I'm a little rattled by it."

His eyes glazed with the desire for me that was never far away. When he spoke, his voice had that growly tone to it I liked, but at the same time, there was softness there. "It means something to you that my family likes you?"

Butterflies fluttered in my tummy. "Yes," I whispered.

"Fuck, you're something else," he murmured. "They're gonna like you, and if they don't, I couldn't give a fuck."

"Thank you."

He kissed me and then asked, "We good now?"

I smiled. "Yes."

He settled me in my seat, put the salads on my lap, and then drove us to Madison's house. It was a good twenty-minute drive, and when we pulled up outside her home, I'd completely calmed down. Donovan's words had eased my nerves, and I was glad I'd been honest with him.

I fell in love with Madison's home the minute I saw it from the outside. A brick lowset, she'd landscaped the front yard with lots of colourful flowers and a water feature. I sucked at identifying flowers, so I had no clue what kind they were, but there was such a mix of colours it reminded me of a beautiful painting. It turned out she loved colour. She'd filled her home with it: on the walls, in the decorations and with more flowers scattered throughout. I got the impression Madison loved decorating.

We walked through her home, down the hallway and ended up in her kitchen. Donovan placed the salads on the counter and smiled at Madison who was getting steaks ready for the barbeque. It wasn't often he smiled, so I knew straight away they were pretty close.

"Blade!" She greeted him by flinging her arms around him in a welcoming hug.

I watched in interest as he let her hug him. His arms didn't go around her but he did place his hands to her arms and hold her there. Donovan didn't seem to be a touchy-feely man. Except where I was concerned, and then it seemed he had no problem with touching me in any way he chose.

Madison let him go and turned her attention to me. Her face lit up with delight before she pulled me into a hug, too. "I'm so glad you could come today, Layla. Blade's been very quiet about you, so I know nothing about how the two of you met." She let me go and gave her brother a dirty look.

Donovan scowled and turned to look at J who was walking towards us. Jerking his chin at him, he said, "J."

J gave him a chin lift in return and said, "Blade." He moved into

Madison's space and slipped his arm around her waist. She sunk into him, nestling her head against his chest, placing her hand on his stomach. I noticed the ring on her finger: J was her husband.

"J, this is Layla, Blade's girlfriend," Madison introduced me. *Girlfriend.*

"We've met," J said, flashing me a breathtaking smile. His smile was enough to melt the panties off any woman in close proximity.

I returned his smile. "Hi, J."

Before anyone could say anything else, another guy came down the hallway towards us. Jesus, another fucking panty-melting dude. This guy didn't look so friendly, though.

"Scott," Madison greeted him quietly. She gave him a questioning look and when he shook his head, she asked, "She's not coming, is she?"

He flinched, and his whole body tensed at her words. As I looked closer at him, I noticed his exhaustion. He scrubbed a hand over his face. "No."

Madison looked crushed. "Shit, I spoke to her last night and she said she'd think about it."

Scott blew out a long breath. "Yeah, I thought she would."

"What are you going to do?"

"Keep fighting for her. I won't give up on her or on us. Whatever she needs to get through this, I'll make happen," he said with determination.

She gave me an apologetic look. "Sorry, Layla, meet my brother, Scott."

We exchanged greetings, and then he left us to go out to the back yard.

Donovan watched him go, and then turned to Madison. "Is he okay?" he asked.

Sighing, she went back to preparing the steaks and said, "I honestly don't know. He won't talk to me about it. You know what he's like, bottling everything up."

"Maybe you should just leave him be, baby," J suggested, earning a frown from Madison.

"No, we need to get him to talk about it."

Donovan bent to whisper in my ear, "You okay in here if I go out and talk to Scott?"

I looked up at him and nodded. "Yeah, you go and talk to your brother. Seems like he might need that."

He brushed his lips over mine and left us. I watched him go and then looked back to Madison who stood staring at me with a look of wonder on her face.

At my questioning look, she said, "I've never seen Blade like that before."

"Like what?"

She pointed at me. "Like he just was with you. Affectionate. He's usually so tightly wound and doesn't do displays of affection. I love that he's like that with you."

I thought back to the Donovan who came to my bar for a year before talking to me. "Yeah, he's a very intense man, that's for sure."

"I'm so glad he found you," she said, softly, before finishing up her steaks.

J had started rearranging food in the fridge so he could put the salads I'd brought in there. He pulled sausages out, and took them and the steak outside to the barbeque. Madison smacked his ass as he left and grinned at me when he muttered something about not revving him up when he couldn't do anything about it.

"So tell me, how did you meet Blade?" she asked once we were alone.

"He'd been coming to my bar for a long time but never really spoke to any of us. He just sat in the corner and kept to himself, but one night recently, he stepped in and helped me sort out a problem with a debt collector who came to the bar looking for my business partner. It just progressed from there."

"He'll look after you. You know that, right? I've known him for a year now, and I've never seen him date before. Blade's the kind of man who is either all in or all out, and something tells me he's all in here."

I smiled at her. "I'm pretty sure we're both serious about this. He's given me that impression, and even though we've only been seeing each other a short time, and have still got a lot to get to know about each other, I feel like I've known him forever." I dropped my voice. It felt odd to admit this stuff to a stranger. "Do you ever feel like that with people?"

The look on her face told me everything I needed to know. Madison totally got where I was coming from. She squeezed my arm. "Yes, I know exactly what you mean. I've met people like that before."

I breathed a sigh of relief. "Thank God. I've never met anyone like that, so I thought perhaps I was going crazy."

She grinned. "Only the best of us go crazy, honey. Welcome to the loony bin. Besides, if you weren't crazy, these guys would send you there soon enough with the crazy shit they get involved in."

"She's right, darlin'. You should think twice about getting involved with any of us." I turned to find Nash standing in the hallway watching us, a cheeky look on his face.

Madison rolled her eyes. "Don't listen to anything Nash says. He mostly speaks shit." The affectionate look she gave him told me she liked him anyway.

Nash moved to the side and let the woman standing behind him move next to him. Putting his arm around her, he introduced us. "Layla, this is Velvet."

I smiled at her, and then said to Nash, "We've met."

Velvet was stunning with her long dark hair, olive skin and trim body. She wore a fitted dress that showed off her curves, and killer heels that drew attention to legs any woman would die for. Probably any man, too. But it was the smile she gave me, and her kind words that showed her true beauty. "Hi Layla. I'm so glad you could make it today. I've been looking forward to spending time with the woman who has stolen Blade's attention. That man so needs a good woman."

"I have to agree," I murmured.

I loved how his family and friends cared for him, and wondered if he realised the love they had for him.

Nash joined the guys outside, leaving us girls alone in the kitchen.

Velvet turned to me. "I think we might have to organise a girls night out at your bar."

"Absolutely!" Madison agreed. "We should do it soon. Harlow needs a night out with us. Serena will be in, too. She was disappointed she had to work today and couldn't come."

Velvet frowned. "What's going on with Harlow? I've left a couple of messages and she hasn't gotten back to me, and she cancelled her last hair appointment at the salon so I didn't get to catch up with her then, either."

"She and Scott are going through some stuff. I'll let her tell you in her own time, but she really does need us at the moment. She's trying to withdraw, I think, so I just keep pushing myself on her."

"I haven't been to Indigo for a while, either. Is she still working there?"

Madison nodded. "Yeah, but she's had some time off over the last couple of weeks. I think she'll start back next week."

"Okay, I will drop by and force myself on her, too," Velvet promised.

"Indigo is the strip club the MC own. Harlow works the bar there," Madison informed me.

"And she's Scott's girlfriend," Velvet added.

The pieces were all falling into place. "Gotcha," I said.

"Madison, the meat will be ready soon. Do you want to bring

everything else out?" J yelled to her from the yard.

"Sure, baby," she replied, and we gathered everything up and headed outside.

★★★

During lunch, I sat back and watched everyone interacting and couldn't help but think this was like a family. Although they weren't related, they seemed like one big family.

I loved that.

Madison caught my eye and smiled at me. "I spoke to my Mum the other day and she said she loves working at your bar, Layla. Thank you for giving her a job. I can see a change in her since she started working there."

I returned her smile before looking at Donovan. "You should thank Donovan because he put me onto your Mum. I had no idea who to hire until he suggested Sharon. The customers love her which is great and she's doing a wonderful job so I couldn't ask for more than that."

She smiled at Donovan but didn't say anything further about Sharon. I figured they'd already spoken about it.

Velvet changed the subject. "What's everyone doing for Christmas?"

J groaned. "Fuck, don't get Madison started on that."

Madison glared at him and smacked him lightly on the chest. Looking at me, she said, "Just ignore, J, he gets grumpy around Christmas time."

"Only because you go on and fucking on about Christmas for weeks, babe," he muttered.

Nash grinned a cheeky grin. "I vote we have a Christmas party here."

The look J hit him with could have killed, but Madison's face lit up with a huge smile. "I love that idea, Nash."

"Thought you might, babe," he said, grinning at J.

"Fuck you, asshole," J directed at Nash.

Velvet slid her arm across Nash's shoulders and pulled him to her so she could say, "You're a devious man, Nash Walker. I like it."

He turned his face to hers and kissed her. "I know you do, sweet thing. I keep that shit up just for you."

As they continued bantering back and forth, I watched Scott. He'd hardly engaged in the conversation today and sat staring into space. It was pretty clear he wasn't interested in what was being said and I wondered again what was troubling him.

"Will you come to the Christmas party, Layla?" Madison asked, interrupting my thoughts.

I dragged my attention from Scott to look at her. "If I can get someone to work the bar, I will."

"We could lend you some staff from Indigo if you need it," Nash offered.

"Thanks," I said.

J nodded. "Yeah, we've got some good staff there who won't let you down."

I was amazed at their generosity. They hardly knew me and yet they were offering to help me out and it wasn't the first time they'd done that. It wasn't often I'd come across such giving people in my life.

Donovan whispered in my ear, "You okay?"

I turned to him. "Yeah, I'm more than okay," I said with a smile.

He nodded, and turned back to the conversation. Looking at Madison, he asked, "So, what date are you doing this?"

J groaned again, and I had to laugh.

Warmth spread throughout me.

This was what family was.

SLAY

★★★

Donovan's hand rested on my leg underneath the table, and while I did my best to keep up with the conversation, his touch distracted me, forcing my thoughts to wander off in his direction. Thinking about his hands all over me was not the thing to be doing while sitting across from his sister, so I pushed his hand away.

He turned to me as he moved his hand back to my leg. I glared at him and pushed him away again. He shook his head slightly, slid his arm around my shoulders, and pulled me close so he could whisper in my ear, "Don't fight me, baby. You tell me no, the more I'll push."

Shit, his words shot straight to my core, and I squeezed my legs together as the desire moved through me. "Not in front of your family, Donovan," I whispered back. The lunch had been going so well, and I'd felt completely welcomed by everyone. I didn't want to risk ruining that.

"It's time to leave then." Without waiting for my response, he directed his attention to Madison and said, "We have to go."

She nodded although she did seem disappointed. Looking at me, she said, "Thank you for coming. It was so good to meet you. And we'll definitely have to do the girls night out thing at your bar soon."

"I'd love that," I said, as Donovan stood, dragging me up with him.

He quickly said his goodbyes to everyone, and we left.

"I really like your sister," I said as he drove us back to my place.

"Yeah, she's special."

"Scott seems quite moody, or is it just because of his girlfriend problems?"

"He is a moody bastard. For a long time, he wouldn't have anything to do with me, but over the last few months we've been

207

working together on something and it's brought us closer. I don't think we're going to suddenly be great friends or anything, but he has changed a lot."

"That's nice. What's Harlow like?"

He gave me a smile. Interesting, he must like her. "She's the perfect woman for Scott. Kind, caring, and she has a beautiful soul. I have a lot of time for Harlow."

"Well, I hope they can sort their stuff out because she sounds amazing."

"Did you have a good time today?" he asked.

"I did. Everyone was so welcoming and I was stunned when J and Nash offered to lend me staff for the bar so I could go to their Christmas party."

"So you'll come to the party?"

"Of course," I answered.

"Good," he murmured.

I turned to look at him. "Did you think I wouldn't?"

He kept staring ahead, watching where he was driving. Giving me a quick glance, he said, "I wasn't sure if today might have overwhelmed you. Madison can be pretty full on, as can the guys when they all get together."

"No, I loved it," I said, softly. "Coming from the shitty family I did, I craved that kind of get together because we never did that kind of thing. And even when they were arguing, you could still see the affection they had for each other."

"Yeah, I never had that growing up either." His voice said everything his words didn't. Donovan craved family as much as I did.

I reached across and ran my hand over his shoulders. "I think you and Madison are lucky to have each other now."

He gave me a quick smile before placing his hand on my leg and tracing a pattern. His touch was gentle and soft. We remained silent for a while before he finally said, "I'm lucky to have *you*, sweetheart.

I've never felt this kind of connection before."

I stilled, unsure of what to say. I was fairly sure I knew what he meant, but I struggled to believe it. His fiancé had meant a lot to him, so I wasn't convinced he actually meant he felt more with me. Before I could question him, his phone rang and he gave me an apologetic look before answering it.

I'd question him another time.

CHAPTER 23

BLADE

I LEANT BACK IN MY CHAIR, DISTRACTED FROM MY WORK.

Layla.

It had been four days since the barbeque at Madison's house. Four days since I'd admitted to her I felt more for her than I'd ever felt for another woman. Four days since she'd pulled away from me a little. Nothing too noticeable, but I *felt* it. It was in the way she didn't say everything she was feeling, in the way she didn't touch me quite as much as she had before, and in the way she fucked me. Up until four days ago, she'd abandoned herself during sex. She'd shut her mind off and gone with it. Now, I could almost hear her mind ticking over. It caused her to hold back, to not give herself to me completely.

I need to fix that.

My phone rang, breaking into my thoughts.

Scott.

"What's up?" I answered it.

"Just wanted to keep you up-to-date with the Ricky situation. Griffs advised me the drug shipment has been delayed. Seems the cops in New South Wales busted them on the way, so now we have to wait for another lot to come through. It could be a week or more, though, because they've got too much heat at the moment."

"Shit."

"Yeah, brother, that's one way to put it."

"Okay, let me know when you know more so I can get the guys ready."

"Will do," he said before hanging up.

I stood up and walked to the window. As I stared out at the river, I thought about how things had changed in my life over the last few months. Between my relationship with Scott improving, and my new relationship with Layla, things had changed a lot. For the better. Even my relationship with my mother had shifted, and the changes she was making in her life were for the better. Finishing off Marcus would be the end of a lot of things, as well as the beginning of so many more.

We need to make this happen soon.

"Donovan!"

I turned to find Layla stalking through my office door, followed by Merrick, with an angry look on her face. She was wearing denim shorts and a fitted singlet that accentuated her breasts. I was instantly hard, but when she began talking, that was quickly forgotten.

"I've just had an altercation with a man called Phil Deacon, and I'm fucked the way off. He said that you know him, and I'm guessing, from what he said, you're definitely *not* friends, but I want to know where to find the bastard so I can go and give him a piece of my fucking mind."

Fuck.

"Calm down, sweetheart, and tell me what the hell happened."

She took a deep breath. "I was sitting in my car at the shopping centre when the asshole got in and sat in my passenger seat. He introduced himself and said he was a buddy of yours in the construction industry, but that you'd pissed him off, and he wanted me to talk to you about it. Said that he bet I had sway over you, and that I could convince you to walk away from some job he wanted. And then the fucker ran his finger across my neck and said something about him hating it if you had to deal with two lost women in your life."

"Fuck!" I thundered, anger bursting through my mind.

Merrick cut into the conversation. "Fucking hell, Blade! I knew we should have taken care of him when we had the chance."

I flashed him a warning with my eyes. "Leave it, Merrick."

"No, you've gone soft, and it's time you fixed that shit."

We glared at each other until Layla interrupted. "Well, I want a word with him before you fix shit," she said, her angry eyes showing me how worked-up she was.

"No, you need to stay out of it," I barked, a little more forcefully than I meant to.

Her eyes widened. "You don't get to decide that, Donovan."

Fuck, I'd pissed her off even more, but my mind was closing in on me with worry over her safety, and I struggled to control my emotions. "Yes, I do," I dictated.

As Layla and I stood locked in a battle over her actions, Merrick muttered something under his breath and left my office. I waited for her reply, not confident she would back down. I'd wanted a strong, independent woman, but, fuck, in situations like this, I wished my preferences lay with women who didn't have that streak in them.

Eventually, she huffed out a breath and said, "I'm coming with you when you go to see him."

I raked my hand through my hair. "Fuck, Layla, you don't understand what's going on here. Phil's not a man to underestimate, and I won't have you anywhere near him."

She raised her eyebrows. "You *won't*? What makes you think you can control me?"

"I don't want to control you. I just want to keep you safe, and the only way to do that is to keep you away from him."

Her phone rang, cutting through the tension between us. I watched her answer it and frown. She turned and walked away from me, speaking in a hushed tone. I left her to go to find Merrick. He was in his office on the phone. Looking up, he motioned for me to come in, and as he ended the call, he said, "Ben's finding Phil, and then you and I are going to fix this fucking situation up."

"Yeah, we are. Once and for fucking all."

"Thank fuck," he murmured, relief clear in his voice. He stood and made to say something, but his eyes shifted to something behind me. "Layla," he called out.

I spun around to find her walking towards the stairs to leave. She didn't respond to Merrick, so I stalked after her and called out, "Layla!"

She stopped and looked at us. Fuck, anger still painted her face. "What?" she snapped.

"Where are you going?" I asked, catching up to her.

"I've got stuff to do at work."

There was a divide between us, slight, but there. I didn't like it, but neither of us had the time to discuss it at the moment, so I let her go. Once she'd disappeared from my sight, I pulled my phone out and dialled Ben.

"What's up?" he asked when he answered.

"Put some eyes on Layla until we deal with Phil."

"Already organised."

"Good."

Thank fuck.

★★★

Eight hours later, I parked my car outside Layla's bar. The afternoon had been futile in our search for Phil. He'd disappeared, and no one on the street was talking. I hadn't managed to catch Layla on the phone, so I had to wonder if she was avoiding me on purpose. Exiting the car, I searched the street for my boys and found them parked a little down the road. The relief I felt at their presence was immense. The thought of something happening to Layla almost paralysed me with fear.

I entered the bar, scanning for her as I walked. Unable to see her, I headed toward Jess who was just finishing up serving. Her gaze shifted to me as her customer walked away. "Hi Donovan," she greeted me.

"Layla in?"

"She's upstairs."

I lifted my chin at her. "Thanks."

Without waiting for her to say anything else, I made my way upstairs. I found Annie in the lounge room watching television, and she smiled at me. "Layla's in the shower."

"Thanks," I said, and headed towards the bathroom in Layla's bedroom. Annie was still guarded with me, and while I'd usually take some time to talk with her, tonight I just needed to find out what was running through Layla's mind.

I couldn't hear the water running, so I figured she must be finished in the shower. The door to her bathroom was open, and I stood in the doorway and watched as she dried herself. Her side was to me, and when she sensed my presence, she turned her head to look at me.

"Have you been here long?" she asked, as she wrapped the towel around her and turned to face me completely.

"No, just arrived."

She didn't say anything, just nodded and then turned back to face her mirror again, beginning to brush her teeth.

Fuck.

What the hell was going on?

I walked to where she was and stood behind her. We watched each other in the mirror, and I took in the closed-off look on her face. "Why have you shut down on me?" I asked softly.

She stared at me for a few moments before spitting out her toothpaste and rinsing her mouth. Finally, she lifted her head, and, still watching me in the mirror, she said, "I'm annoyed at you for trying to boss me around today."

I nodded. "I know that, but that's not why you've shut down."

"You pissed me off, Donovan. I won't ever be the type of woman you can control like that, so if that's what you're looking for, it's best to walk away now."

What the fuck?

I slid one hand around her waist, and the other around her neck. Gripping both hands tightly around her, I bent my face to her ear and growled, "I'm not going anywhere, sweetheart, so you need to tell me what the fuck has gotten into you over the last few days. You've pulled away from me, and we need to fix that. Tonight."

I felt her suck in a breath, and watched in the mirror as her eyes widened. When she didn't say anything, I spoke again, "*Feel* it, Layla. Stop thinking so hard, and just tell me what you feel."

As we stared at each other in the mirror, the only sound in the room was our uneven breathing. We were both feeling this, I was sure of it.

"I feel like I'm falling so deep into this with you, Donovan, and I think you feel the same way, but then I don't want to believe it..." Her voice trailed off.

"Why?" I held my breath, waiting for her answer.

She hesitated for a moment. "Because if it's not true, it will kill

215

me when you walk away," she whispered.

The brokenness in her voice hit me in the chest, and I pulled her into me, my arms wrapping tight around her. "I'm in deep, baby, with no intention of walking away. I told you I've never felt it like this before, and I meant that. I fucking *need* you, Layla, like I've never needed anyone."

She stared at me, and I knew her brain had kicked in again. When she didn't speak, I squeezed her, and demanded, "*Say it.* Whatever it is, say it."

Her eyes shut for a couple of moments, and when she opened them, I could see the change. "I worry you're not over Ashley, that one day you'll realise I can never be her . . ."

I cut her off, "I don't want you to be her." I let her go and spun her around. "I want *you.* You accept me in ways she never could, and you've never once tried to change me. I fucking needed that because I was buried so far down in my own self-hatred it was suffocating me. For the first time in years, I feel like I can breathe again, and that's because of you."

Her eyes searched mine, and she brought her hand up to my face, gently resting it on my cheek. "I'll never want you to change," she whispered. "I want you, flaws and all, Donovan, because you've been there for me in ways no one in my life ever has. And you might not want to hear this so soon, but I'm fairly sure I'm falling in love with you."

Fuck.

I pulled her into my arms and kissed her. This woman fucking owned me, and she had no idea. I used my mouth and my body to show her just how much I wanted to hear what she'd just said to me. And I knew she felt it when her arms wrapped around me, and she sunk into my embrace. It was like the barrier she'd erected between us four days ago came crashing down, and she let me back in.

Reaching my hands down to cup her ass, I lifted her into my arms and carried her to the bed. After I deposited her there, I stripped out of my clothes, and enjoyed the feeling of her eyes on my body. Layla never hid her hunger for me, and that turned me on more than anything. I watched as she removed her towel and revealed her body to me. Fuck, she was beautiful.

I moved to position myself over her and bent my face to kiss her again. She opened her mouth to me, and our tongues danced as we lost ourselves to the kiss. Her hands were urgent on me, pulling me closer. I didn't need encouraging, though. I fucking wanted her as much as she wanted me, and when her legs wrapped tightly around me, I knew this wouldn't last long. Our needs demanded to be satisfied quickly.

As she rocked herself against me, I thrust inside her. Hard enough that she cried out and clawed my back. I pulled out and thrust in again.

"Fuck," she yelled out as her head arched back against the pillow.

I worked us up into a relentless pace, and as I felt my orgasm hit, I thrust hard one last time before burying my face in her neck, marking her. I'd never wanted to sink my teeth into a woman as much as I did with Layla. It was as if some primitive desire came over me that I was helpless to control.

Her pussy squeezed around my dick, and she gripped me tighter as she let her orgasm take over.

She eventually let me go, unwrapping her arms and legs so I could shift to lie next to her on the bed. I put my arm out and pulled her against me so her head rested on my shoulder. She entwined her leg with mine and whispered, "Maybe I should tell you I'm falling in love with you more often."

I squeezed her against me. "Maybe you should."

I could hear the smile in her voice when she said, "I like it when your voice goes like that."

"Like what, sweetheart?"

She shifted so she was looking up at me. "All growly and hot. You should talk to me like that more often, cause you'd get laid more."

"Fuck, Layla, I get laid plenty. You've got demands on my dick morning and night as it is."

She grinned. "Stop your grumbling. Any man would love to have that problem. I'm thinking of adding in a lunch time session, too."

Fuck me.

I moved fast so I had her on her back, and I was on top of her again. Possessed by desire I growled, "If that's what you want, it can be arranged. You just say the word, baby, and my dick is all yours."

A soft smile spread across her face. "Is that your way of telling me you're falling in love with me, too?"

I heard the hesitation in her voice, the vulnerability behind her words. Bending my face closer to hers, I whispered, "No, this is: I'm falling in love with you, sweetheart, and there's not a damn thing you can do to keep me away."

I didn't miss the slight intake of breath or the rapid rise and fall of her chest as her breathing picked up. And I sure as hell didn't miss the way her body pressed up into mine as she murmured, "Fucking hell, Donovan, why did we waste all that time?"

My thoughts exactly, but fuck, life was a mysterious bitch and worked her shit out in her own good time. Thank fuck we got here in the end.

CHAPTER 24

LAYLA

I STOOD IN THE MORNING SUNSHINE AND LOOKED UP INTO Donovan's eyes as he murmured his goodbye. Wrapping my arms around him, I grumbled, "I don't know why you can't take the day off and spend it with me?" Last night had been amazing, and I just wanted to spend the day in bed with him. I didn't want to let him go.

Trying to extricate himself from me, he said, "Baby, we've been over this. You're not safe until I deal with Phil, and I need to do that today."

I pouted. So unlike me, but he brought all kinds of weird behaviour out in me. Fuck, was that what they meant when they said women did crazy shit when they were in love? I'd never really loved a man before, but I knew what I felt for Donovan was off the charts crazy. "Send him to me and I'll deal with him, and then you and I can get back to what we do best."

His heated gaze shot more desire through me. God, this man was too much. When his hand slid around me a second later and yanked me to him, I wanted to climb up into his arms and force him to change his plans.

With his hand planted firmly on my ass, he growled into my ear, "Get ready, sweetheart, 'cause once I've sorted this shit out, I'm coming back here to fuck you until you can't walk properly."

My legs swayed under me at his promise. I grasped his face and said, "You don't play fair."

"You wanna tease me like you just did, you'll have to learn to play my way," he growled again.

Oh fuck, I wanted more than anything to learn to play his way.

With one last long stare, he let me go and walked to his car. He opened the door, looked back at me, slid his aviators on and then got in. As he drove off, I decided today would suck while I waited for him to return.

★★★

Four hours later, Sharon and I were knee-deep in shit while we dealt with crappy customers, missing stock deliveries, and an air conditioner that had decided to pack it in. I'd just finished a phone call with one of our suppliers when she turned to me and said, "Jesus, some of these customers need a swift kick up the ass."

I totally felt her. I sagged against the bar and wiped the sweat from my forehead. It was a miserably hot day today, and with one air conditioner down, the heat had filled the room to the point of irritation. Nodding at her, I said, "Some of them need more than that."

She grinned at me and poured us both a glass of water. Passing it to me, she said, "Regardless of shitty customers, I'm so thankful to you for giving me this job."

I gulped some of the water down and considered what she'd said. "Donovan hasn't told me much about you, but he has told me a lot about his father. I got the impression he thinks you might leave him."

She stared at me, and I wasn't sure if I'd overstepped a boundary or not. Sharon was a hard woman to read and held her cards close to her chest, but I'd sensed a vulnerability in her that led me to think she might need someone to talk to. "I am going to leave him. I told him this morning I was done."

"Good for you, babe." I'd really grown to like Sharon while she'd been working here, and this piece of news pleased me to no end. Marcus Cole didn't deserve the love of a woman like Sharon.

She blew out a long breath. "God, that was a hard decision to finally make. After all these years together, it's hard to walk away from someone you love even though you know you shouldn't."

"Why do we do that?"

She frowned. "Do what?"

"Love men who don't deserve it? I watch women do it all the time, and it baffles me."

"I think, for me, Marcus was my first love. I've never known anyone else, never had anything to compare him to. And then you add in two kids, a lifetime of memories and everything in my life connected to him . . . that's hard to walk away from. Especially at my age, where you wonder if you're too old to find someone else."

"I don't think you're ever too old, and I also believe a woman is better off on her own than letting a man treat her like shit."

"Yeah, I can see that now, but you've got to remember, I grew up in the club lifestyle and all I've ever known is women who put up with this kind of shit."

"So, does your son treat his girlfriend like that? And does Madison's husband treat her like that?"

She shook her head. "No, Madison would never stand for that. Hell, she would cut J's balls off if he so much as looked at another woman. And although Scott has a wild temper, he'd never treat Harlow the same way his father treats women."

NINA LEVINE

"Thank fuck for that. I thought Madison seemed to have J under control."

She laughed and drank more of her water. "Yeah, you could say that, although I think it goes both ways for them. He's got just as much control over her."

"A good match by the sound of it," I mused.

She looked at me thoughtfully. "I'm relieved Marcus's sons didn't turn out anything like him insofar as the way he treats women. You've got a good man there in Blade. I've never had a lot to do with him, but I can tell he's special."

"He really is," I agreed.

A customer interrupted us, and Sharon turned away to serve him. I left her so I could go wipe down tables and clean up empty glasses. When I came back to the bar, she was deep in conversation with a man who didn't look happy with her.

Fuck, he looks like Donovan.

I took in Sharon's tense body language and decided to step in to make sure she was okay. As I approached, the man turned angry eyes on me and I noticed the faded bruises on his face. "What the fuck do you want?"

"I take it you're Marcus," I said, standing my ground. I wouldn't let this fucker intimidate me.

"And what's it to you?"

"This is my bar, and Sharon's working, so you need to leave."

He'd been leaning across the bar and now straightened. "I'm here for a drink, that's all."

I raised my brows. "Really?"

"Yeah." He turned back to Sharon. "I'll have a beer, babe."

I watched her flinch at his term of endearment, but she quickly grabbed him a beer. Placing it on the bar, she said, "You can sit at a table away from the bar, Marcus. I've got work to do."

Surprisingly, he did as she said and left us to go and sit at a table.

"Are you okay?" I asked her once we were alone. "Do you want me to call Jess in so you can go home?"

"No, I won't let him win. This is just the beginning, Layla, and he needs to know I'm serious about this being over."

I admired her determination. "Good. I'm with you on this so whatever you need, you just let me know, okay?"

"Thank you," she said softly, and I knew in that moment, Sharon didn't have a lot of friends offering to be there for her.

"Sharon, did you leave the house or did you ask him to leave?"

"I told him he had to go. I'm not leaving it."

"Did he go?" I had a feeling Marcus would be hard to get rid of.

"I don't know, because I had to come to work. I told him to be gone by the time I got home this afternoon."

"Have you told Scott and Madison yet?"

Sadness crossed her face. "I'm not close to Scott at the moment, and Madison and I are still on shaky ground, so I haven't told either of them. I will, though."

"Today?"

She grimaced. "I don't want to drag them into it, Layla. I need to do this on my own, and then begin to rebuild my relationships with them. But...I've got to find myself first, you know?"

I nodded. "Yeah, I get that, but I'm concerned you might need at least Scott's help on this. If Marcus won't take no for an answer, it could pay to have Scott behind you."

"I'll think about it. Please don't tell anyone yet."

I could read between the lines. She didn't want me to tell Donovan.

Nodding, I said, "Okay, it's your call, but I really want you to think about it."

"I will," she promised.

I turned to look at Marcus and found him staring at us while he drank his beer. Fuck, this afternoon was about to go to complete shit. I was sure of it.

CHAPTER 25

BLADE

I CLOSED MY EYES AND SENT A PRAYER OF THANKS TO THE universe. I'd given up believing in God a long time ago, but my belief in the forces of good was slowly being restored.

When I opened my eyes, I found my mother smiling up at me. "It's good news, right?" she asked.

"Yeah, it's good news. When do you start?"

"Next week. Thank you for helping me get this job. I think it's just what I need."

I had no doubt. I'd watched Sharon Cole working at Layla's bar, and saw the change in her, so I'd put the feelers out with my contacts regarding a job for my mother. I kicked myself for not thinking of it sooner, but perhaps she wouldn't have been ready for it until now.

"Has Marcus been around?" I held my breath, waiting for her answer.

"No, I haven't seen him since the day of your fight."

Thank fuck.

My phone vibrated in my pocket. Pulling it out, I saw Layla's name on the screen. Holding it up at Mum, I indicated I needed to take this. She smiled and left me to it. "What's up, baby?" I asked, answering the call.

"How far away from the bar are you?" Her tone put me on high alert.

"About fifteen minutes. Why?" I went in search of Mum while Layla kept talking.

"Marcus is here, and it's not pretty between him and Sharon. I'm concerned."

Fuck.

"I'm on my way, but until I get there, I've got some guys watching your bar so I'll send them in to watch him."

"Thanks," she said, ending the call.

I found Mum in the kitchen. "I've gotta go, but I'll call you later and check in."

She nodded and gave me a hug. "Love you, baby," she said as she let me go.

"Love you, too," I said and headed out to the car. Layla's voice over the phone had told me everything I needed to know. Marcus was going to be a problem, and I needed to get there as fast as I could.

On the way, I called Scott and asked him to get over there as soon as possible. Better to have both of us there to deal with Marcus.

The traffic was a bitch and it took me longer to get there than I thought it would. By the time I parked the Jag, my head felt like it would explode from the anxiety tearing through me. Worry about Layla getting hurt filled me, and I bolted out of the car and into the bar.

Thank fuck three o'clock was a quiet time for the place. Layla stood at the bar serving the one customer she currently had. Sharon and Marcus were nowhere to be seen. I walked to her and raised my eyebrows in question.

After she finished with her customer, she pointed towards the back of the bar. "They're outside in the back alley. Marcus has had a bit to drink, Donovan. When he started getting angry with her, she took him outside. Your guys followed them, so, hopefully, that means she's okay." Her worry was clear, but I was simply glad she hadn't been hurt.

"I'll go see what's going on. You stay here, yeah? Don't come out there, because if Marcus hurts you, he won't be leaving here in anything but a fucking body bag," I said, and, at her nod, I left to go out to the alley.

Angry voices filtered through as I pushed the back door open. I took a step outside and came face to face with Sharon yelling at Marcus. "I should never have married you! You couldn't keep your dick to yourself before we got married, and you still can't keep it to yourself. If you thought I didn't know about your new piece on the side, you're a fucking idiot. She's welcome to you."

No fucking surprise there.

Marcus took a step closer to her, anger rolling off him. "She means fucking nothing to me, babe. None of them have." His gaze flicked to me, and, while staring at me, he added, "Not even Stella."

Blood roared in my ears, and I clenched my fists. As the craving for his blood threatened to take over, I forced myself to remember Storm needed him alive. Killing him would only cause them more problems, and that could possibly have an impact on Madison.

Fuck.

Sharon slapped him. "You think that makes it okay, asshole? You're a fucking pig to women."

He grabbed her hand, pulling her to him. "You think you can walk away from me that easily? Fucking try it and see what happens," he threatened her.

My guys had been hanging back but they both took a step

forward. I held up my hand to halt them and walked toward Marcus. "Let her go," I demanded.

Training his filthy gaze on me, he snarled, "This is between me and my wife, Blade, so you can fuck off and leave us to sort it out ourselves."

I kept walking. "No way am I leaving, and there's no fucking way you're beating your wife up again."

He shoved her away and came at me. His fist tried to connect with my face, but I blocked it and punched him in the gut. As he stumbled, I punched him hard in the face. Bone crunched and blood spurted. My demons roared to life at the sight of that blood, and in that instant, I succumbed to the darkness. I let it pull me under and take over my soul.

My father was as good as dead.

For every punch I got in, I recalled a childhood hurt.

For every punch he got in, I remembered why his time was up.

My father would *never* hurt another human being again.

Every emotion I'd experienced at my father's hands bubbled up as I kept punching. Blindly, madly punching. I was a crazed man. My father had made me this way, and this was his reckoning.

His sins were finally coming back to haunt him.

I blocked out the world as I fought to end his life, so it wasn't until strong hands pulled me off him that I heard someone yelling out my name.

Scott.

"Blade! Fuck, don't kill him," he thundered, while fighting to pull me away.

I tried to punch Scott so he'd let me go, but he'd anticipated that and punched me first.

Motherfucker.

The pain roared through me, but I breathed through it, raising my arm to take aim again. However, another set of arms grabbed me.

Griff.

They held me back, and Marcus staggered forward, his mouth twisted in a sneer. Blood dripped down his face as he threatened me. "That's the last fucking time that happens, you worthless piece of shit! I should have made your mother fucking abort you all those years ago."

His words didn't hit their mark. Not anymore. He'd shredded me for too long now, and I'd finally realised his words were as meaningless as he was.

Bang!

The shot rang out loud and clear, and the bullet that hit Marcus sent him reeling back. My head snapped around to find the perpetrator, and I was stunned to find Sharon staring at him with a gun in her hand. She began walking toward him, her intent to shoot him again evident. Scott let me go so he could halt her progress, but Sharon was lost in some kind of crazed state, too, and Scott struggled to stop her. Griff let me go, moving quickly trying to help Scott.

I didn't give them my attention at all. It was focused completely on Marcus, and on the pain he was in. He deserved that pain and so much more for everything bad he'd ever done in his life. My demons took over again, and I pulled my knife from its sheath.

My father lay on the ground, staring up at me with a look of sheer terror as I approached.

Yeah, motherfucker.

My head pounded as the rage took over.

The rage I'd lived with my whole life.

The rage I'd done my best to deny and keep locked deep in my soul.

It swirled up through me, and my chest threatened to explode as it desperately fought to be let out.

And then...

I stopped fighting it.

I let it consume me.

I let it shatter around me, and, in that moment, I met the darkness I'd hidden even from myself.

My darkest moment.

The first time the blade sliced through his flesh, satisfaction like I'd never experienced before rushed through me.

The second slice produced a strong sense of justice.

The third slice, however, brought with it all the anger I'd bottled up my entire life.

I lost track after that as I stabbed my father to death.

CHAPTER 26

LAYLA

I LAY ON THE BED NEXT TO DONOVAN AND HELD HIM while he slept. It had been about five hours since he'd fallen asleep, and it was the most peaceful I'd ever seen him. Usually, he thrashed about in his sleep and called out Ashley's name. Tonight, he hadn't moved, except to curl closer to me. He now lay with his head on my chest and his arm across my body, holding me.

He'd killed his father this afternoon. I didn't have a clue what was happening in the back alley until Griff came in and asked me to close the bar so they could ensure complete privacy while dealing with it. I'd immediately done what he'd asked and gone to find Donovan. Pain had pierced my heart when I'd found him on his knees on the ground out the back, covered in his father's blood. When I'd knelt next to him, he'd looked at me with such a haunted expression on his face. I'd never seen someone so broken in my entire life, and the need to make it all better had overwhelmed me.

Nothing would make this all better for him, though.

I'd eventually managed to get him to stand, and Scott had helped me get him upstairs to the bathroom where I stripped his clothes off and put him under the shower. Scott had left us so he and Griff could take care of Marcus's body and the mess in the alley. They also had to take care of Sharon who had fallen apart, too.

That had been about six hours ago. Once I'd cleaned Donovan up, I'd gotten him into bed, but he hadn't fallen asleep straight away. He'd spent a long time staring into space before finally succumbing to sleep.

I'd hated seeing him like that. It wasn't the strong, powerful man I knew. And I hated his father even more for it. As far as I was concerned, his father had deserved everything he'd got today.

After Donovan fell asleep, I stayed awake as my mind processed it all. I was beginning to feel sleepy now, and just as my eyes closed, he shifted again and murmured something in his sleep. My eyes flew open to find him watching me with a look I didn't recognise from him.

"Hey," I whispered.

His arm tightened across my body as he whispered back, "Hey."

I sensed he didn't need me making small talk, so I remained silent, waiting for him to take the lead here. We lay there watching each other quietly for what felt like ages, until he finally asked, "You okay?"

I nodded. "Yeah. Don't worry about me."

"I'll always worry about you."

I reached my hand out to lightly trace his cheek. "You're an amazing man, Donovan Brookes," I murmured.

He stared at me. "I'm amazed you're still here. I thought you'd be long gone."

I frowned. "What?"

He moved so he was propped up on the bed, looking down at me. "I killed my father today. It wasn't pretty, and yet, here you are, still watching over me. Still making sure I'm okay. That's not something I'd expect from any woman."

"I'm not just any woman, Donovan. I'm *your* woman, and I don't desert the ones I care about in their hour of need."

His eyes searched mine, and then he muttered, "Fuck, I don't know what I ever did to deserve you."

I held his face. "You're a good man. Don't ever underestimate that or doubt it, okay?"

He didn't answer me, so I reiterated it. "Okay?"

"Okay, sweetheart," he said softly.

"Good. Now, come back here and let me hold you. You need more sleep," I said, bossing him around. And, for once, he let me.

My strong man needed me. He needed to know he was accepted for who he was, no matter what he did. And I was determined to give him that.

★★★

The next morning, I woke to find Donovan pacing the room while talking on his phone. I didn't want to eavesdrop on his conversation so I got out of bed and headed into the kitchen to make coffee. He came out just as I'd finished, and I slid his mug across the counter to him.

Eyeing his clothes, I said, "It's a good thing I like to buy you clothes."

He smirked. "Yeah, baby."

Donovan had once made fun of my clothes shopping addiction. It was pretty much my only girly trait and I'd bought him quite a few pieces, which he'd left here. Thank god, because they came in handy now.

We drank our coffee in silence until he murmured, "I don't understand where Sharon got the gun from."

233

"She came back into the bar while you were outside with Marcus. I was busy with customers, but managed to get out of her that you and he were fighting. I got distracted and didn't realise she'd gotten the gun out of her bag."

"Fuck, after all those years, she finally got rid of him. Mind you, he may not have died from the gunshot wound."

"Probably a good thing you finished the job then," I mused.

"Why?"

"Would he have retaliated against her if he'd lived?"

He thought about that and slowly nodded. "Yeah, I reckon he would have."

I sipped my coffee and kept quiet. It was up to Donovan now to decide if he wanted to talk about it or not.

He surprised me when he did speak. "I don't know what I feel."

"Maybe it's too soon, too fresh for you to know."

"I've thought about doing this for a long time, and I thought I'd feel a sense of immense satisfaction."

"And you don't?"

"It's odd. I don't regret it for a minute, and I would do it again, but it's not this overwhelming feeling of anything. It's like I feel . . . nothing about it." He raked his hand through his hair. "Fuck, that doesn't even make fucking sense." He paused for a moment, and then added, "After I did it, I felt a sense of justice . . . relief that he couldn't hurt anyone ever again, but now, there's just nothing."

I reached across the kitchen counter and placed my palm on his chest. "Stop thinking, baby. Just let it be what it is."

He covered my hand with his. "You *do* listen to me," he said, his lips twitching.

I smiled. "Yeah, most of the time."

He finished his coffee and rinsed his mug before coming back to me. "I've got a lot of stuff to take care of today, so I'm not sure what time I'll see you later."

"It's all good. You take care of what you need to, and I'll be here whenever you get back."

He bent his face to kiss me and then asked, "Do you have any idea how much I need you in my life?"

"Probably as much as I need you in mine."

I watched him leave and decided I'd never let him go.

Ever.

Donovan Brookes was *it* for me.

CHAPTER 27

BLADE

I STEPPED THROUGH THE FRONT DOOR OF MY MOTHER'S house with trepidation. The news I had to break to her would either gut her or help her move on. I wasn't sure which.

"Hey, baby," she greeted me with a smile as she wiped down the kitchen counters.

"I've got something to tell you," I said, getting straight to the point. I didn't have it in me to drag this shit out.

She stopped what she was doing and turned to give me her full attention. "What is it?"

I took a deep breath. "Marcus is dead."

Her eyes widened, and her whole body stilled.

I waited.

"How?" she asked eventually, her voice shaky.

I was never one to beat around the bush, so I didn't start now. "I killed him."

Her hand flew to her mouth. "Oh, God."

SLAY

Still unable to tell if she was upset or just in shock, I waited to see what she would say next.

She grasped the chair at the kitchen table and collapsed into it, but didn't say another word.

I sat next to her. "I'm not sorry I did it, and I would do it again, but I'm sorry if it hurts you. I never wanted that for you."

Reaching out for me, she cupped my chin. "Donovan, it hurts but mostly because my son had such a bad father he felt it necessary to kill him." Her voice cracked as she continued. "I did that to you, and for that I am sorry."

I shook my head. "No, I don't blame you for that, Mum."

We sat together quietly, lost in our own thoughts, and I realised something. It's easy to blame yourself for shit in your life and in the lives of those you love, but it just holds you back. Mum had blamed herself for Marcus for far too long, and I'd blamed myself for Ashley for too long as well, and both of us had stopped living our lives fully.

"We have to stop this shit," I muttered, standing.

Looking up at me with a frown, she asked, "What?"

"All this blame. It gets us nowhere. Shit happened, and we survived it. We're still breathing, but we're not living. We need to stop blaming ourselves and get on with life."

She stood, too. "When did you get so smart, baby?" she asked, softly.

"I don't know, but I'm running with it."

"Yeah, you're right, it's time to move forward." She said the words, but I could hear the doubt in her voice. This was going to take her some time to deal with. Understandable seeing as Marcus had been a presence in her life for so long.

I embraced her, and when I let her go, I said, "I've got someone I want you to meet."

A small smile brightened her face. "I thought you might."

"How?"

"You've changed lately, and I'm pretty sure those kinds of changes are usually inspired by a good woman. You better bring her over soon, because I want to meet the woman who has helped you."

"I'll do that," I promised.

I knew she would love Layla, and I was fairly confident Layla would love her, too.

A man was lucky if he had one good woman in his life.

I had two.

★★★

I left Mum's house and drove to see Madison. She had the day off from work, so I was headed to her house. I'd spoken with her on the phone about Marcus, and even though she said she was okay with it, I wanted to watch her face while she spoke the words. That would tell me the truth.

She answered the door with a mixing bowl in her arms and flour all over her face. Smiling at me, she said, "Just in time, big brother, we've just put some cookies in the oven."

"We?" I asked as I walked inside. The fact she was cooking concerned me. Was it a distraction from thinking about Marcus's death?

"Me and Harlow."

I kept walking as she talked and ended up in the kitchen where Harlow was washing up dishes. She turned to look at me, and I was stunned to see her haggard appearance. She'd lost weight since I'd last seen her, and exhaustion marred her features.

"Hi Blade," she murmured.

I lifted my chin at her. "Harlow."

She gave me a small smile before turning back to her dishes. I turned to Madison and widened my eyes questioningly. She shook her head at me; it was her way of saying she'd tell me later. I let it go.

We had other things to discuss.

"Talk to me," I said to Madison as I grabbed a stool at her breakfast bar.

She sighed. "I don't know. I hated him in the end, Blade. You know that. I've already grieved the loss of my father. But to think he's gone, and I'll never see him again, I feel kinda sad even though I don't want to." Her voice cracked at the end, and I reached for her hand to pull her to me. I put my arms around her and held her.

"I think it would be weird for you not to feel sad, babe. You grew up with a different father to me, and it's only recently you've seen that other side to him, so you're mourning a completely different man to the one I knew. It's okay to be sad, and it's also okay to be conflicted about it. There's no right way to feel."

"You have this way, you know that?" she said, softly.

"What way?"

She pulled out of my embrace. "This way of saying just the right thing whenever I need to hear it. Thank you."

Harlow turned around and chimed in. "She's right, Blade. You're a special man."

I stared at Harlow, uncomfortable with this conversation now. Neither of them knew I had killed Marcus, and while I didn't think they would care, it weighed on my mind. I'd spoken with Scott this morning, and we'd agreed upon who would be made aware of what really happened yesterday. That list included those who were present as well as Nash and J. Scott had advised Sharon not to utter a word of it, either. Griff and Scott had dumped Marcus's body and tipped the cops off as to where it was. They needed his death to be made public so they could move forward with club business.

"Have you spoken to your Mum?" I asked, changing the subject.

"She came over this morning and it was the first time in ages we sat and talked about stuff so freely. It'll take her some time to sort her head out, but I think she's gonna be okay."

"And Scott? How's he handling it?"

I was surprised that Harlow answered me. "He was in a bit of shock, but he was okay."

Watching her closely, I said, "I know you and Scott are going through something, Harlow. Are you doing okay?"

A sad look crossed her face. "Not really," she admitted softly. She took a deep breath before opening up. "I was pregnant and lost the baby. Scott's been amazing but I'm so lost and I don't know how to move past it. I need some time but he just wants to fix everything . . . You know what men are like, they see a problem and try to come up with ways to make it better, but this can't be fixed."

Fuck.

Harlow went back to her dishes before I could say anything. It seemed like she needed some space so I left it. My phone rang a moment later and I held it up, and said, "I'm gonna get going, babe. Just wanted to stop in and make sure you were alright."

She came to me with a hug. "Thank you for coming over," she murmured.

"I'll talk to you soon," I promised, and then left them to it.

As I answered my phone, my mind was preoccupied with thoughts of Scott and all the shit he had to deal with at the moment. I hoped he was up to it, because with Marcus out of the picture, he had a lot to take on.

It was Merrick on the phone. "Hi Boss," he said after I'd answered, "got an update for you."

My mind ran blank. "What for?" I asked, getting in my car.

"On Phil Deacon."

"Phil fucking Deacon," I muttered. "What's the update?"

"Turns out the reason we can't find him is because he's dead."

"What the fuck?"

"Yeah, the day he threatened Layla, he also threatened Onyx's woman, and Onyx wasn't too pleased about that so he took care of him."

I chuckled. "So Onyx the fucker finally got his wish to do more than just talk to Phil."

I could hear Merrick's grin in his voice. "Would seem so. Where are you?"

"I'm sitting outside Madison's house and am just about to pay a visit to the Storm clubhouse."

"Fuck, that's gonna be a shit fight over there."

"Yeah, you're telling me."

"Good luck with that," he said, and we ended the call.

God knew what would happen with Storm now.

The mood was grim at the clubhouse. The guys who had still looked up to Marcus were sitting around the bar, discussing revenge on whoever did it.

Scott greeted me in the bar and quickly took me into the office where Griff was. As the current Vice President, he'd had to assume control for the moment, and he appeared to be struggling with it.

"How's the mood in the club?" I asked once we were behind closed doors.

"Not good," Scott answered. It was obvious from his body language and tone, he wasn't happy with me.

Griff threw the pen he was holding down on the table and leaned back in his chair. "We got word this morning that Marcus sent a shitload of drugs into Ricky's territory yesterday morning."

"I thought we'd put that plan on hold for the moment," I said.

"We had," Griff said pointedly.

"Fuck," I muttered. "That screws with everything. We're not ready for that yet."

"You're fucking telling us," Scott threw in, clearly stressed.

I grabbed my phone. "I'll get Merrick to round up some of the boys to come over and set up watch. You're gonna need eyes on this club, and I'd be putting some on your homes, too."

"We also need to get to Ricky," Scott said.

"For what it's worth, Scott, I didn't intend to kill Marcus yesterday. I couldn't control it, though, and for that I'm sorry. But only because of the impact it will have on Storm. I'm not fucking sorry I killed him."

Scott pushed out a long, tired breath. "Yeah, brother, I'm not sorry you did, either. And we'll get through this shit like we always do."

Brother.

It was still there.

"I spoke to Harlow this morning."

He stared at me for a long moment. "She told you?"

I nodded. "Yeah. Sorry, man. I get the impression she's not coping well with the loss."

He raked a hand through his hair. "No, she's not, and as much as I try to figure it all out, she keeps pushing me away. She won't open up to me and let me help her."

"Maybe this isn't something you can figure out. Perhaps it's something you just have to live through while making sure you're there for each other."

"Yeah," he murmured.

"Jesus, Scott. Sorry, man," Griff said.

I didn't say anything, but rather simply watched him and took in everything I figured he must be feeling. Losing a child would be hard enough, but for the woman you loved to shut down on you at the same time would make it even harder.

Sensing Scott's reluctance to talk about this any further, I changed the subject. "What's the plan with the club now?"

"I've called Church for this afternoon and we'll vote in a new

242

President," Griff said.

"Scott?" I asked.

Griff glanced at Scott and then back at me. "That was always the plan, but due to the way shit went down, fuck knows if he'll get the votes needed."

"J and Nash are doing the rounds, working out where everyone stands," Scott said.

"Okay, keep me updated. I'll call Merrick now and organise manpower for you."

Griff nodded. "Thanks, man. Appreciate it."

As I left, I realised that although I'd fucked with their plan, Scott hadn't shut down on me. If anything, Marcus's death was bringing us together in ways I'd never seen coming.

CHAPTER 28

LAYLA

"ARE YOU OKAY?" I ASKED SHARON. SHE LOOKED EXHAU-sted and already had dark circles under her eyes.

She wiped the counter and looked at me. "I honestly don't know, Layla. I killed my husband yesterday so I'm not sure how a wife is supposed to feel after that."

"You didn't kill him," I reminded her.

"I might as well have." She stopped cleaning and sighed. "I don't know what came over me when I got the gun. All the hurt and humiliation came at me, and I couldn't stand it any longer . . . " Her voice cracked and although no tears fell, I knew that if she were a weaker woman, she'd be bawling by now. Sharon Cole was keeping her shit together, but only just.

I had been going to ask her if she wanted time off, but my gut feeling was she didn't, so I'd put her to work. We'd had a quiet afternoon so we'd spent it cleaning the bar. It had just turned six o'clock and the after-work rush was beginning to trickle in.

Jess had just had her break and wandered back in. "Have you heard from Donovan today?" she asked.

"He phoned earlier to check on us and said he'd be busy all day so I'm not expecting him until late."

"That's a good man you've got there," Sharon said. "Hold onto him tight and don't let go."

I smiled. She was damn right I had a good man.

"Go and take your break, babe. Jess and I will manage while you're gone."

"Thanks, I won't be long," she said, leaving us to it.

A customer distracted me and when I'd finished serving him, Jess asked, "Is Sharon really okay? She's putting on a brave face, but her husband just died so I'm wondering how she's managing that?"

Jess didn't know the full story, and Donovan had given Sharon and me strict instructions not to share the truth with anyone. I knew he'd done this for more reasons than to cover himself. He'd vaguely mentioned something about the motorcycle club being at risk if the truth came out, and I knew he never exaggerated anything, so I kept tight-lipped.

"Sharon's a tough woman, Jess. She could be breaking on the inside and I doubt she'd ever show the world. I'm just gonna go with the flow with her and take it as it comes."

"I can see that about her, but if she does crack and can't come into work, I'm happy to pull extra shifts to cover her. I just wanted you to know that."

I smiled at her. "So you do love me," I teased.

She rolled her eyes before grinning at me. "Don't let it go to your head. I'm doing it more for me than you because you can be a bitch if you have to work too much."

I laughed. "Yeah, yeah, that's just your excuse to cover your real reason."

She shook her head at me and turned to take care of the

customers who had just arrived. I helped serve them and couldn't stop thinking how lucky I was to have her.

★★★

We ended up having a busy night, which was great, but by the end of it, I was exhausted. At eleven o'clock Donovan wandered in, looking even more exhausted than me. I was wiping tables down and he came straight to me and pulled me into his embrace. He placed a kiss to my forehead before murmuring, "I missed you today, baby."

As he let me go, I looked up at him and said, "Me too. How was your day?"

"Let's just say I'm glad it's over."

His voice told me everything I needed to know and I grabbed his hand and led him towards the stairs. As we passed the bar, I said to Jess, "Call me if you girls need me, okay?"

Her gaze landed on Donovan and she nodded. Shifting her eyes back to mine, she said, "Sure thing, boss."

I mouthed thank you at her, and led my man upstairs. I knew he needed me tonight and it was confirmed when we entered my bedroom and he shut the door and pulled me into his arms.

I looked up into his face as I wrapped my arms around him. "If you need to talk, I'm here for you but if that's the last thing you want, I understand that, too."

He brushed his lips over mine before saying, "A man could only hope to find a woman like you. I do want to talk but there's no fucking way I can stay away from you a minute longer, sweetheart." His hunger blazed in his eyes and caused me to shiver with anticipation.

Yes.

My hand moved to the bottom of his tee and I pulled it up and off him. At the same time, he removed his jeans and then his boxers. My gaze moved over his body and my heart beat faster at the sight of his muscles. He was so powerful and strong. And yet, on the inside he was so very vulnerable and broken. I didn't like that life had done that to him, but I knew it had made him the amazing man he was.

My amazing man.

His hand came to my chin and he tilted it so our eyes met. "Baby, are you gonna stop fucking me with your eyes for long enough to get your clothes off?" he asked gruffly.

"There's nothing stopping you from taking my clothes off while I continue what I'm doing."

His brows rose, and his lips twitched. As his hands moved to the button on my jeans, he murmured, "You're lucky I like a woman with some fucking balls."

Oh god, I really am.

My body lit up with desire at his words and I tried to help him as he roughly stripped me. We needed to hurry this process along because my need for him had intensified. When I stood naked in front of him, he slowed his movements and let his gaze roam over my body. I waited for as long as I could, but he made it near impossible to drag this out for too long. Donovan Brookes was not a man any woman could resist, and I was so far gone on him that he had me ready to go with just a look.

"Donovan, I need you to -"

He cut me off by placing his fingers to my lips and silencing me. His other hand curled around my waist and pulled me closer to him. He bent his face to mine and whispered in my ear, "*I* need my mouth on your pussy. You good with that?"

I was sure I almost came with all the sensations screaming through me.

Fuck.

He can do that with just his words.

I nodded, and he pushed me backwards against the wall. As he

247

dropped to his knees, I had to wonder what I'd ever done to be rewarded with a man who loved my pussy as much as he did. A moment later, his mouth found me, and I sagged against the wall and closed my eyes, letting him give me pleasure in his favourite way.

His hands gripped my ass and his tongue worked its magic. He'd already gotten me started with his words, though, so it didn't take him long to make me come. I threaded my fingers through his hair and held tight as the orgasm surged through me.

Donovan moved quickly once I came, and he had me on the bed under him in a matter of moments. His intense stare looked down at me as his cock pushed against my pussy, but he didn't say anything.

Oh god, he's gonna fuck me into a state of complete bliss.

Our hunger charged the air around us as we silently watched each other.

This was going to be fast.

Hard.

Shit, I couldn't wait any longer.

I tilted my hips so his cock slid through my wetness. He hissed and thrust inside me.

Yes.

My arms clung to him as he pulled out and thrust back in, over and over. I shut my eyes and let my body take over as I gave myself to him completely. Donovan could have me to do whatever he wanted with. He owned me, body and soul, and as he fucked me, I savoured the delicious sensations spreading throughout me.

I knew he was chasing something tonight. A release, yes, but there was something else there, too. Usually, he connected with me during sex, with his eyes or his lips. Tonight, there was none of that as he fucked me. He dropped his head next to mine and grunted with each thrust, his movements growing wilder the closer he moved towards his orgasm.

I came, but he kept going, nowhere near coming. Something

held him back, and as he kept pushing for it, I opened my eyes and whispered in his ear, "*Feel* it, baby. Stop thinking."

I knew he heard me because he grunted louder on the next thrust, and he must have processed it because a couple of thrusts later, he slammed into me and stilled, his body tensing as he roared out his release.

I held onto him until he finally looked up at me. His eyes held all his secrets, and tonight they were telling me how much he was struggling. I laid a hand gently against his cheek and murmured, "Talk to me."

He stared at me for a moment before rolling off me. Positioning himself on his back with one arm resting under his head, he said, "I killed the man who murdered Ashley, and I thought it would give me peace. I killed my father and thought the same thing." He stopped talking and turned to look at me. Drawing a ragged breath, he said, "I'm not feeling any kind of fucking peace."

The fact my man had killed people should have affected me in other ways, but all I could think was he'd rid the world of people who didn't deserve to be here. But what did affect me was the way he wrestled with every bad thing in his life. It caused him anguish and I wished more than anything that I could take it away for him.

But I couldn't.

I rolled onto my side and nestled myself against him. I laid my arm across his body, hugging him. We didn't say anything, but there wasn't much else to be said. I stayed there with him for a while, but eventually I let him go so I could go to the bathroom and clean up. I pressed a kiss to his lips and murmured, "I'll be back in a minute."

His hand ran up and down my back as he said, "Okay, baby."

I only left him for a few minutes but when I returned, his eyes were closed and I knew he was asleep by the rise and fall of his chest and his steady breathing.

My man needed a break from the unrelenting demons of his life.

★★★

"Who is he?" I asked Annie the next morning when she broke the news to me she didn't need a lift to work because a man was going to take her.

We were sitting at the table having breakfast with Donovan when she broke the news to me, and he watched me carefully as Annie and I had this conversation. Trepidation filled me at this news but I forced myself to remain calm for her sake. Who knew? Maybe this guy would be the one good guy she needed to meet.

"His name's Brett. Brett Moody," she shared, a smile on her face. Oh god, I knew that look. She was all-in already.

Donovan interrupted. "My Brett?"

"Huh? Your Brett?" I asked, confused.

Annie nodded, ignoring me. "Yes, Brett from work."

Stunned, I looked to Donovan, hoping he would give me some indication of what this man was like.

He smiled. "Brett's a good guy," he murmured thoughtfully. "He'll do right by you, Annie."

Relief coursed through me.

Thank fuck.

Her phone rang, and a moment later, her face lit up when she heard the voice on the other end. "I'll be down in a second," she said before hanging up.

As she stood, I said, "Don't forget we've got your appointment with the psychologist this afternoon."

She smiled at me again. "I think I'm ready to go on my own now, Layla."

She'd stunned me again. "Oh, okay. Are you sure?" I struggled to let her go, and I imagined this must be kind of what it was like for a parent not wanting to let their child out into the big, wide world. Fuck, the anxiety her statement had caused in me was enough to make me reconsider ever having kids. I doubted I could cope with it repeatedly like parents must.

Nodding, she said, "Yes." She grabbed her bag and started walking away from the table. As she got closer to the stairs, she turned and said, "I'll see you tonight. Brett will bring me home."

And then she was gone.

I turned to Donovan. He was watching me with a mixture of concern and amusement.

"What?" I demanded.

"I love how you love Annie, but it's time to let her fly, sweetheart."

Shit.

I knew he was right, but fuck it was hard. I sighed. "Yeah, I know."

"She's doing well at work, and she's found a good guy. Hopefully, those things will help her find herself."

I leant towards him and whispered, "Some days I wonder what I ever did before I found you."

My words affected him, and as he took a deep breath, he said, "Me, too."

We stayed in that moment for a couple of beats, and then he pushed his chair back and stood up. He bent his face to kiss me. "I'll call you later, okay?"

I nodded. "Sounds good," I said softly and watched as he left.

He'd been a little better this morning, but I knew it would take time for him to work through his thoughts and feelings about his father's death.

I'd be there for him however he needed me.

CHAPTER 29

BLADE

I ENDED THE CALL WITH MY MOTHER AND PLACED MY phone back in my pocket. She seemed to be okay which caused me great relief. I hadn't been sure how she'd take Marcus's death but I was fairly sure that while she was upset about it, she wasn't devastated by it. I had every reason to believe she'd continue moving forward in her life like she'd planned.

"Blade, we got word on the Hurley job," Merrick said as he strode into my office.

"What's the verdict?"

"We got it," he said, his words laced with the victory he deserved to feel. He'd worked damn hard on this one.

"Good."

He raised his brows. "Is that all you've got? Good?"

I grinned at him. "Fucking good?"

"Jesus Christ, Blade cracks a fucking joke," he muttered.

"Fuck you."

He chuckled and turned to leave, but he'd only taken a couple of steps when he turned back to me. "Forgot to tell you, Ben located Layla's business partner."

"And?" If that fucker came back here, I'd take care of him for her. *Fuck, she'd take care of him herself.*

"He's long gone. Ben doesn't think he'll be back anytime soon."

"What makes him think that?"

"The asshole has shacked up with some rich bitch in Western Australia, and she's funding his new lifestyle."

I was annoyed and relieved at the same time. Relief won out in the end. "Good."

Merrick raised his brows at me again.

Oh, for fuck's sake. "Fucking good, asshole," I muttered before waving him away. "Fuck off and let me do some work."

He gave me one last grin and then left me to it. The heaviness I'd been feeling last night had shifted. It hadn't completely left, but I knew it was easing.

Layla and Merrick did that.

I had people in my life who cared for me.

I'd always known it, but now I let myself feel it.

It felt fucking good.

★★★

"Scott," I said as I answered his call.

"I'm just keeping you up-to-date with where Storm is at," he said, his tired voice telling me a lot about how he was doing. "I was voted in as President yesterday, but only just. Griff is still VP."

I waited for him to say more, and when he didn't, I prompted him. "And?"

I heard him push out a breath. "The club's in fucking chaos. Marcus trashed my name with a lot of members so there's no trust or loyalty there. I don't know how the fuck this is all gonna end up."

"Anything from Ricky yet?"

"No, nothing, which is fucking odd."

"Not for Ricky, it isn't," I muttered.

"What does that mean?"

"You remember I said he likes to play with you a bit before he screws you over? Well, this is Ricky playing with you."

"Fuck. If I wasn't trying to deal with shit here, I'd already be putting plans together to take him out."

"What else are you dealing with?" I asked, confused.

"Turns out Nash and J are pissed off about our plan with Griff so there's tension there. And then I've got some of the club members convinced our Sydney chapter are to blame for Marcus's death and are planning retribution on them. It's a fucking shit-fight over here, brother."

And on top of that, he's dealing with Harlow.

"Do you want me to help with the Ricky issue?"

He remained silent for moment. "No, Storm needs to do it. Maybe it will be the thing to unite us again."

He was right. "Okay, well, yell out if you need something."

"Thanks. Will do," he said and then ended the call.

It felt like a chain of events they would struggle to recover from had been unleashed.

Where Storm would end up, no one fucking knew.

★★★

That night, I took Layla back to my house. We hadn't spent much time there, and I needed to be here at the moment. Needed that secure familiarity, which she seemed to understand.

After we'd finished the dinner she'd cooked for us, I asked her if she wanted to watch a movie.

254

She gave me an odd look but agreed.

"What was that look?" I asked, puzzled.

"You surprised me, that's all."

"Why?"

She moved into my space and wrapped her arms around me. Looking up into my eyes, she said, "I'm surprised you're choosing a movie over taking me to bed. It's good, though."

Her arms around me felt so good.

Loving.

Caring.

Safe.

I put mine around her and let them settle on her ass. "Trust me, sweetheart, I'll be taking you to bed later, but for now, I want to watch a movie with you. I want to just be with you."

Her eyes softened. "I'd like that," she whispered.

I kissed her, and then said, "I don't think you have any idea how much being with you helps me."

She smiled and held me tighter. "I think I might, Donovan, because it's the same for me."

Fuck.

My luck really had changed.

I bent to kiss her again. Quicker this time, because I had something else to say to her. "I'm taking you to meet my mother tomorrow."

Fuck.

The smile that spread across her face lit my whole fucking world.

CHAPTER 30

BLADE

I SAT BACK AND SMILED WHILE I WATCHED MY MOTHER and Layla talk. We'd arrived at Mum's house half an hour ago and she'd promptly monopolised Layla's attention. I'd hardly gotten a word in. Hell, I wasn't complaining, though. I fucking loved watching the two women in my life getting on this well.

"What are you grinning at?" Layla asked, a smile on her face.

"Was I?" I hadn't realised I had been.

"Yeah, you were, baby."

The affection in her voice fucking did things to me, and I felt the familiar tightening in my gut. Fuck, I wanted her, which was not exactly a good thing at this very moment, seeing as we were sitting in my mother's lounge room and about to have lunch.

Layla didn't miss it, and her smile turned into a grin. She placed her hand on my leg and squeezed it. "You were definitely grinning at something."

I pushed her hand off my leg and sat up straighter. Changing the subject, I asked, "Do you need help getting lunch ready, Mum?"

She stood up and said, "No, it's all ready. You two stay there while I get it out." The look of pure happiness she gave me caused my heart to constrict. My mother had missed out on so much in her life. Seeing me happy with someone had been one of those things. To be able to give her that now made me even more determined to make this relationship with Layla work.

As she left us to go to get lunch, Layla leaned into me and said, "I like your Mum."

I smiled at her. "I can tell."

"Thank you," she said softly.

I frowned. "What for, sweetheart?"

"For this . . . For letting me into your family. I know I've only just met your Mum today, but I can already tell she's special and different to my family. And because I've never had that, it means even more to me. It's the best gift you could ever give me."

Fuck.

I curled my hand around her neck and pulled her to me. Pressing my lips to hers, I whispered, "I love you." As the words left my lips, calmness descended on me.

Peace.

Fuck, that elusive fucking feeling I'd been searching years for.

It was right here.

It was Layla's gift to me.

"I love you, too," she said, and fuck if that didn't hit me right in the chest.

We sat staring at each other for a while before I finally said, "You know I'm fucking kicking myself for wasting a year, don't you?"

She smiled that smile of hers that pressed all my buttons. "Yeah, baby, but maybe we both needed that extra year. Life happens in her own good time. Our job is just to be open to it so that when it

257

happens, we can catch it and not let it pass us by."

Fuck.

She amazed me.

I was going to crack myself wide fucking open so I didn't miss a damn thing this woman was offering me. Life wasn't going to pass me by anymore. And although I had a lot of demons still to put to bed, I knew she'd be there right by my side, helping me.

I brushed my lips over hers again. Tightening my grip on her neck, I said, "Thank you for the gift you've given me."

Confusion flickered on her face. "What gift?"

"You accepted me for who I am. Unconditionally. And you've stuck by me, even when most women wouldn't."

She placed her hand against my cheek and whispered, "I love you, flaws and all, Donovan Brookes, and don't you ever forget it."

EPILOGUE

BLADE

"Blade!" Ashley called out to me.

I turned to see her running towards me with a smile on her face.

I stopped and waited for her to catch up to me.

She held something out to me and said, "You forgot this."

I looked down at what was in her hand. A key. "What is it for?"

As she put it in my hand, she whispered, "It's the key to your heart."

I had no idea what she meant so I waited for her to explain.

She pressed her hand to my chest. "You locked your heart and threw the key away when I died. You've found someone to love you now, but you need to open your heart to her completely." She nodded at the key in my hand. "You'll need that."

Fuck.

Stepping closer to me, she brought her hands to my face and held it. Her lips lightly dusted mine, and then she said, "I'll always love you, Blade, and I know you'll always love me, but you need her now."

She let my face go and took a step backwards. "Goodbye."

I watched as she disappeared right in front of me.

I waited for the pain to slice through me.

It never came.

I sat bolt upright in bed and turned to the bedside clock.

Seven am.

Layla's arm reached for me. "Baby, what's wrong?" she asked, sitting up next to me.

I looked at her.

Fuck, she was beautiful. Even with messy hair and that first-thing-in-the-morning look.

"Nothing's wrong, sweetheart," I murmured. "Go back to sleep."

Everything was right.

She shook her head. "No, we've got a huge day today and I want to be ready for it."

I chuckled. "It's hardly a huge day."

She gave me a dirty look and rubbed her eyes. "Don't you give me grief, Donovan Brookes. If I say it's a huge day, it's a huge fucking day." She pushed the bed sheet back and got out of bed.

As she padded into the bathroom, I said, "Okay, you win, it's a huge fucking day."

Stopping, she turned back to look at me. This time she hit me with a grin. "Baby, when will you understand that I always win?"

I shook my head and muttered, "Oh, I fucking understand that, don't you worry."

Her grin grew, if that was possible, and she left me alone.

Today we were going to lunch at Madison's house.

My mother was also coming.

Madison had pushed for it, and Layla had encouraged me to agree.

It had been nearly a month since Marcus's death, and we were all moving forward, leaving the past behind us. Bringing my mother and half-sister together seemed like it could be a mistake, but everyone was looking forward to it.

Everyone except me. I still felt apprehension.

Layla came back to the bedroom and threw a t-shirt at me. I looked at it and chuckled when I realised it was a new one. "Have you been shopping again, baby?"

"I'm ignoring that," she said as she began rummaging in her drawer for clothes. Once she'd found what she was looking for, she looked back at me and said, "I'm going to have a shower. Don't come in there and disturb me. I need time today to get ready."

I raised my brows. "When have I ever disturbed you?"

Her eyes widened. "When the fuck have you *not* disturbed me? You can't keep your hands to yourself."

I moved fast, and a moment later I had her in my arms. Bending my mouth to her ear, I growled, "That's not disturbing you, sweetheart. That's giving you what you want. If you'd like me to show you what disturbing you is, I'd be happy to do that at any time."

Her breathing picked up and she attempted to push out of my hold, but I tightened it instead.

"Are you going to keep me trapped or can I go have a shower?" she asked, feigning annoyance.

"I'm going to let you go, but I need your answer first."

"My answer to what?"

"Your answer to whether or not you'd like me to show you what disturbing you is."

Her eyes widened again, but in a completely different way than before. This time, they flashed her desire for me. *Her desire for me to disturb her.* "Yes," she whispered, clearly affected.

"Yes what?" I demanded, moving my hand to her neck, gripping her firmly there.

"Yes, I want you to disturb me," she said, her voice all breathy.

I let her neck go, trailing my hand down her chest and over one of her breasts. Her chest rose and fell rapidly, and when my hand slipped down the front of her top to take hold of her breast, she let out a whimper. "Good, baby. Tonight," I promised, and then let her go. I smacked her lightly on the ass and said, "Now go and get ready. I promise to leave you alone."

As she walked out of the bedroom, I thought about everything we'd been through over the past month.

Layla had remained patient with me while I got my shit together concerning my father's death. I was still dealing with it, and I knew I would be for a long time still, but I'd moved past those initial hollow feelings. Since then, I'd reconciled the events of that day in my mind and was okay with Marcus's death. My only regret was that it had affected Storm. They were still dealing with the fallout of his death, and fuck knew how that was all going to play out.

"Donovan!"

I turned to look at Layla standing in the doorway. "What?" I asked.

"I was calling you," she said, clearly frustrated.

"What's up?"

Her face softened a little. "I changed my mind. You can come and disturb me now."

Fuck.

I strode to where she stood, grabbed her hand and led her to the bathroom. "Clothes off," I ordered as I began peeling mine off.

The look on her face gave her thoughts away. Layla fucking loved being bossed around, and I had no doubt she was going to fucking love being disturbed by me.

Four hours later, we collected my mother from her house on the way to Madison and J's home. I sensed her nerves, and Layla and I did our best to put her at ease before we got there. As I listened to Layla talk to Mum, I realised she could talk her way into anything.

She never failed to convince me of anything, and she singlehandedly convinced my mother that she had nothing to worry about where Madison was concerned.

When Madison threw her front door open and greeted us with a warm smile, I figured things might go smoothly. And when she reached for my mother's hand and welcomed her into her house, I watched my mother's worry fall away, and I knew everything was going to be okay.

My fractured family was slowly being put back together.

I watched the three most important people in my life chatting, enjoying themselves, and realised I was a fucking lucky bastard.

ACKNOWLEDGEMENTS

I suck at writing these! I am sure to forget someone important. Please forgive me if I do.

I always have to thank my beautiful daughter. She gave me so much space to write this book that she must almost feel like a neglected child. It's a good thing I've raised her to be a fairly independent person. She helped keep our home running while I locked myself away in the cave. I love you, baby. You'll never know just how much.

I also must thank my family and friends who let me write. I love you all. Kathleen, love you long time, dude. You'll always be my DBFFF xx

To my beta readers - Melanie, Paula, Christina, Amanda, Lauren, Sammi, Elle, Becca and Malia. Thank you so much for all your help on Slay. I truly couldn't have done it without you, and I really appreciate all your feedback and suggestions.

To my editor, Karen. I loved working with you on Slay and look forward to working with you again. I love that you loved Layla and Blade as much as I do. Thank you for being so patient with me when I missed deadlines.

To my PA, Melanie Sassymum. Baaaabbbbe. I love you, chick. Thank you for everything you do for me, and for your amazing support. You are an amazing lady, and I am lucky to work with you and also to call you my friend.

To my cover designer, Louisa. Lovely, your covers are amazing! Thank you for making my books look so damn good!!

To all the bloggers who share and read my books. *sigh* I

would be lost without you all! LOST. Thank you for your support not only on Slay, but for the last year. It was you who got my name out there and I will always be grateful for that. Thank you, thank you, thank you xxx

To my Stormchasers! OHMYGOSH I love you chicks hard!!! Did you see the part in Slay that was just for you girls?? I bet you laughed your ass off when you read it ;) Seriously, thank you doesn't begin to cover it. But, THANK YOU <3

To my TGNAFN girls! I thank god for you chicks every single day. You're a bunch of kick ass women who I love working with!!

Jani Kay, thank you for all your words of encouragement and support while I was writing Slay. You've been so busy this year and yet you always had time for me. I treasure our friendship and also love working with you. You're such an amazing woman, and I can't wait for what 2015 will bring!

Chelle "Gandy" Bliss, I am so glad we became friends. Your friendship means a lot to me and I am so looking forward to meeting you in person. And I fucking love your sense of humour, woman! LMAO. Gandy Schmandy... you haven't sent me a pic of our man for awhile now, babe. I'm having withdrawals ;)

River Savage, bitch, who would have thought this time last year when we met for the first time that this is where we would be now?? FARK. How life changes, dude! I love seeing your face pop up in messenger, and the "Dude", "OMG", "Fuck"...that you always send me. LOL! Oh yeah, and the "BAHAHAHA". Seriously, you make my day some days. You always make me laugh. SO looking forward to 2015, babe!! Thanks for being an amazing friend xx

Lyra Parish & Lilliana Anderson, you two are such special ladies. They don't make them like you very often anymore. We worked together recently on the Owned Anthology and I got to know you both a little better, and I have to say that I am so glad Jani and I asked you both to be part of that anthology because otherwise I may never have discovered just how special you are. Thank you for being my friend and for being so giving. Xx

TO MY READERS

From the bottom of my heart, I want to thank you for buying and reading my books. You've changed my life in ways you'll never know and I am so grateful to you for this. The last year has been the best year of my life. I've never worked harder but I've never loved my work as much. I love that you love my Storm men as much as I do. Thank you for all your amazing emails and messages. Some mornings, I wake up to the most amazing messages and I feel so blessed to be able to have this awesome job. To be finally living my dream.

Nina xx

I have a request.

If you loved Blade as much as I love Blade, I would truly appreciate it if you would leave a review for Slay on the site where you bought it. Reviews help other readers decide whether to purchase a book, which in turn helps authors continue writing. It would mean a lot to me if you did leave a review. It doesn't have to be a long and detailed review – I think the minimum they require is about 20 words.

Thank you! xx

SLAY PLAYLIST

You may remember from Revive I mentioned how important music is to me when I am creating characters and stories. The songs below inspired Slay, but I have to admit to you that I listened to Taylor Swift's new album 1989 pretty much 98% of the time while writing this book. Her music and lyrics actually inspire a lot of my work. Storm was written to a lot of the songs on her Red album.

Apart from Taylor's music, the songs Dust to Dust by The Civil Wars & Superheroes by The Script really get me in the zone for Blade. Take a listen to the lyrics, you'll see ...

I'll Stand by You by The Pretenders
Burning Bridges by OneRepublic
A Thousand Years by Christina Perri
21 Guns by Green Day
Dust to Dust by The Civil Wars
When I'm Gone by 3 Doors Down
Ghost by Ella Henderson
Animals by Maroon 5
Love Runs Out by OneRepublic
Far From Home by Five Finger Death Punch
Pieces by Red
Light It Up by Rev Theory
Bad by David Guetta
Stronger (What Doesn't Kill You) by Kelly Clarkson
No One Ever Taught Us by Jason Reeves

City In Motion by Ron Pope
Angel by Florida Georgia Line
Closer by Nine Inch Nails
Superheroes by The Script
Tell Me How You Like It by Florida Georgia Line
Hurricane by The Fray
Making Memories of Us by Keith Urban
You're My Better Half by Keith Urban
My Heart is Open by Keith Urban

All my books have playlists here:
https://play.spotify.com/user/1299222556

FREQUENTLY ASKED QUESTIONS

I do a lot of promotional work online and chat with my readers at many online events. I always open up a thread for questions and find there are common questions, so I thought I'd answer some of them here.

Q. Why and how did you develop the Storm MC?

A. The original concept for Storm was a story based around Madison. She was the daughter of an MC President and had left town, however she wasn't originally involved with J. He was simply supposed to be a friend of hers sent by the MC to bring her home. It was never going to be a biker book as such and she was not going to return home with him. However, when J turned up, he took over the whole damn book. I'm sure you can imagine! He truly is a dominant man. So, I reworked the story and Storm was the result. Also, I always intended to write about alpha men and bikers just fit the bill and add that dirty to it that we all love..

Q. Will you write a book about Serena?

A. Hell yes!!! I love that chick. I aim to have her book out in 2015.

Q. What books do you plan to write next?

A. Next up I am working on a secret project that I aim to release very, very soon. However, I am not going to tell you what it is in case I don't manage to pull it off. After that is part two to Destined Havoc, Inevitable Havoc. Then I will write part two to All Your

Reasons (yes, finally more Jett!). After that is Illusive, which is Griff's book, and Command, Scott & Harlow's next book, which is also the last book in the Storm MC series. In amongst that, I have another secret project that I know you are all going to LOVE! Once Storm MC is finished (sob, we will miss these men!), I will write the first book in a new series – The Stone Brother Series. The first book will be Serena's book. Her guy is HOT and oh, so alpha – to the extreme!! I get freaking excited just thinking about writing that book! Her guy is Zane Stone and his brother is Blake Stone who you might recall is Madison's friend. Blake will also get his own book. I will also be writing more of Roxie and releasing it as I go. I am also considering writing a serial of some sort but hell, I am not sure when!

Q. Are you scared to read the reviews about your books?
A. LMAO, not anymore! My first book received so many negative reviews and I spent a lot of time reading them and working out where I needed to improve. One day, I will rewrite that book, but I am thankful to those reviews because they showed me what work I needed to put in to write better books. Slay is the first book I've written that I LOVED while writing. Mind you, it took me many attempts to get it right. I went through three different versions of characters for Layla to find the right Layla. I had deleted so many words and grown so sick of looking at the computer every day, and then one afternoon I sat down and just let my mind take over and the first scene where you meet Layla in the alley with the drunks flowed onto the page. I'd stopped plotting and planning her character and just let her evolve. After that, it was a mad rush to get the book finished to meet deadlines. So, in the end the majority of Slay was written in about two weeks. They were some long ass days! At least fifteen hours every single day. But, I got sidetracked on the question there... no, I am not scared to read reviews anymore. The way I look

at it now is that I compare books to music. I LOVE Macklemore but a friend of mine doesn't. Does that make him a bad artist? No, it simply shows we all have different tastes. Same with books. We all take something different from what we read. And I think a lot of that also comes from your experiences in life.

Q. Best line ever written?

A. Okay, so it may not be my best line ever written, but it has a lot of personal meaning to me so I love it hard.. "I smiled as I tasted freedom." Velvet says this in Revive. She is a strong woman but there's that one person in her life who still makes her shrink – her ex. And then there's the day she stops shrinking and can move out from under his shadow. She tastes freedom.

Q. Do you write on schedule?

A. The last twelve months has been a whirlwind of trying to catch my breath and catch up. I was working full time up until just before Revive was released so my schedule was pretty much work five days a week at my job and then write all night into the early hours. I also wrote pretty much all weekend, too. Now that I write full time, I am trying to establish a routine of Monday to Friday during the day. I'd love to have nights and weekends off again. However, I struggle to take time off. I'm kinda addicted to it all. But, Slay is my last book I have a deadline for and I won't be setting release dates anymore until closer to when I've finished writing the book. Hopefully, I will get myself into some sort of balance between work and life. The hard thing is trying to juggle writing with marketing. I love both, but I do need to cut back on some of it. When I am writing a book, I usually have a word count I try to hit everyday. I do know how many words I am aiming for for each book so I break it down. I tend to fall behind though so towards the end of the book, it's not uncommon for me to be writing 10k words a day.

Q. What advice would you give a new author?

A. Begin building your presence before you publish your first book. I started to build mine two months prior to releasing Storm. Be prepared for a lot of hours at first to get your work out there. Hell, the hours never really let up, but at first it can feel overwhelming. Watch successful authors in the genre you want to write in and see how they market their books. Start some of these practices yourself. Read The Naked Truth About Self-Publishing. And keep reading it after you release your book. That book tells you everything you need to know to get your name out there. Treat your writing like a business. Don't get involved in petty online drama. FARK. AVOID IT AT ALL COSTS. Don't even surf your Facebook newsfeed. Surround yourself with positive, switched on people in the industry and only read their online posts. I set notifications for the people I adore. Help each other! Share their work. Don't whinge about negative reviews. Nobody wants to read that. Everyone is entitled to his or her opinion on your book. If you aren't ready for that, DO NOT publish a book. You WILL need to grow a thick skin for this line of work. Keep learning and improving your craft. NEVER GIVE UP.

Q. Who is your favourite Storm man? Why?

A. Well, until Slay, it was Scott Cole. That man has everything I want in a man. He is completely alpha, but treats his woman as an equal. He is loyal, protective and bossy. But then when I wrote Blade, I fell for him HARD. He's an alpha with not an ounce of asshole in him. He will do ANYTHING for the woman in his life. Hell, he'll do *anything* for the people he loves. I didn't intentionally write it this way, but he and Scott have a lot in common. I love them both.

ABOUT THE AUTHOR

Nina Levine is an Aussie writer who writes stories about hot, alpha men and the strong, independent women they love.

When she's not creating with words, she loves to create with paint and paper. Often though, she can be found curled up with a good book and some chocolate.

Signup for her newsletter: http://eepurl.com/OvJzX
Join my readers club on Facebook:
https://www.facebook.com/groups/LevinesLadies/

She loves to chat with the readers of her book so please visit her or contact her here:

Website: http://ninalevinebooks.blogspot.com.au
Facebook: https://www.facebook.com/AuthorNinaLevine
Twitter: https://twitter.com/NinaLWriter
Pinterest: http://www.pinterest.com/ninalevine92/

ALL YOUR REASONS

This is the first book in my new rockstar series and will be available in early 2015.

Nina xx

CHAPTER 1

PRESLEY

As I take the call I've been waiting six months for, the people around me carry on with their lives as mine stands still. It's funny how that happens. How, in the blink of an eye, your life can change so completely and yet everyone else is unaware. If they were to look at you, they wouldn't know anything had changed.

I'm in the middle of running a photography shoot, and I've got people everywhere. In amongst the noise and chaos, my world is being tilted, and I'm struggling to focus on what's being said.

"Presley, are you listening to me?"

His question pulls me back into the conversation. "It's too late now, Lennon. I needed you to say this to me six months ago."

He sighs and it's as familiar as an old cardigan. It's the same sigh he's used on me numerous times throughout our marriage, the sigh that tells me how frustrated he is with whatever I am asking of him. "How can it be too late? We've been married for three years, that's not something you just give up on. I want you back, and I'll do anything to make that happen."

The pain his words inflict tears another hole in my heart. "The reason it's too late is because you should have been willing to do anything to make our marriage work while we were in it or when I told you there was a problem. But you didn't. You were too busy with your work to care about me and telling me six months later is not enough. You need to accept this is over and move on."

"That's not gonna happen, baby. You're mine and I'm coming home to show you how wrong I was."

"You're coming back to Australia?"

"That's what I just said. I'll be there next week. Once we finish up with the tour."

Now it's my turn to sigh. He just doesn't get it. "And that's why we'll never work," I say softly.

I know him so well I can almost hear his brain thinking and I can picture his brows pulled together in confusion as he asks, "Why?"

"Because if you truly loved me and wanted me back, you wouldn't be waiting for the bloody tour to end." I take a breath before adding, "Don't come back, Lennon. I don't want to see you." I bite my lip as I prepare to end the call.

Darla, my assistant, is watching me closely, and she raises her brows, questioning if I'm okay. She knows the last thing I need on this shoot is for my concentration to be challenged. And she can probably tell from my body language and facial expressions that's exactly what's happening. She's worked with me for a long time and been my friend for longer. She knows me well. I nod at her to indicate I'll be okay, because I will be. This isn't the first time my husband has screwed with my concentration. I'm well versed in dealing with it and getting through my work, in spite of it.

Lennon's patience gives way. I'm surprised he's lasted this long with that short fuse of his. "Presley, you don't know what you want half the time," he snaps. "We're meant to be, and you'll see that when I get there."

"Goodbye, Lennon," I say and hang up because otherwise we could be going back and forth all day. He just doesn't listen. I knew it while we were together, but since we broke up, it's become even clearer to me.

Darla approaches. "You okay, boss?"

"That was Lennon," I say.

Her eyes widen. "What did he want?"

"Apparently, after all this time, he's decided he wants me back. Says he's coming home in a week or so to show me how much."

"That bloody asshole!" She's never been a huge fan, not after she saw the way he always put our marriage second to his career.

"I feel like this truly is the end now, you know?" I don't know why I feel sad about this all of a sudden. I've spent the last six months trying to get over him, and I've started moving on, but after that conversation, it feels more final. I look at Darla with resignation. "I don't know, maybe deep down I still hoped he'd come and fight for me, but what he's doing doesn't feel like enough. Does that sound stupid?"

She madly shakes her head. "No, it doesn't, and you're right... this is all too little, too late."

I slowly nod. "Yeah, it is."

We stand in silence for a moment, both lost in thought about the demise of my marriage. Eventually, Darla claps her hands together. "Okay, back to work. We're going to get this shoot finished and then we're gonna go out and get drunk."

I shake my head and grin mischievously at her. "No, you might be going to get drunk... I'm going to get laid."

Laughing, she agrees, "Yes, you are. And I might just do that, too."

★★★

I finish applying lipstick to my lips, place it back in my purse, and then run my fingers through my long, blonde hair, messing it up as I go. The straight hair trend shits me to tears; give me messy, wild hair any day over that perfect, boring look. Stepping back from the mirror, I assess my outfit for tonight; skintight black leather pants, heels, and a slinky red sleeveless top. I've finished it off with an assortment of bracelets and my silver Tiffany heart tag necklace. *Yeah*, I grin, *tonight I'm going to score.*

"Presley, babe, you made it."

I divert my attention from the mirror to the voice behind me. Shit, I'd forgotten she'd be here tonight. Jade Garcia. Supermodel. Shallow bitch from hell. *God, give me strength.*

Before I can reply, her food deprived friend interrupts. "You're the photographer from today's shoot, aren't you?"

Full points to the vapid supermodel wannabe. I bite my tongue on so many witty remarks and instead, simply reply, "Yes." Well, okay, perhaps they weren't witty, so much as catty. I can be one of the cattiest bitches you'll ever meet. That could be why I don't have a lot of friends. That and the fact that I truly dislike most people I meet.

Jade starts gushing to her friend. "Presley is one of the best photographers I've ever worked with. They had to pay a small fortune to get her to work on this shoot."

I tune her out; I've heard it all before, and I'm over it. I'm also over working with models and clients with no imagination. This shoot bored me to fucking tears, and I won't be in a hurry to work with them again.

"I've got to meet another friend, Jade. I'll see you around," I say as I begin to make my way out of the ladies' room.

She raises her eyebrows. "A Valentine's date?"

"God, no!"

"You don't like Valentine's Day?"

"What's there to like? A commercialised day that puts pressure on people to buy shit that supposedly proves how much they love their partner. I've never celebrated it and don't ever plan to," I reply, noting her stunned expression.

"Wow. I've never met a woman who doesn't love Valentine's Day." Her previous awe of me has been replaced with disdain. If I'd known it would be this easy to change her opinion of me, I would have shared my thoughts earlier.

I shrug. "Well, now you have. Love's an everyday experience; it's something shown in the mundane things you do for your partner. It's not found in a fucking overpriced bunch of flowers picked up on the way home from work because you know if you don't get them that day, of all days, your life won't be worth living."

Jade's eyes are glazing over; I probably lost her at mundane.

"I'll catch you later," I say as I push open the door and exit the room, not waiting for her response. With a bit of luck, I'll never have to see her again.

The cool air of the club hits my face and I welcome it after the heated stuffiness of the crowded ladies' room. It's Friday night and pumping in here. Everyone is celebrating the end of the work week. I'm celebrating the beginning of my holidays. Three months of no work. Three months of doing whatever the hell I want. *Bliss.*

I make my way to the bar and order a bourbon and Coke. After slamming it down in two gulps, I motion to the bartender to pour me another.

"Hard day, sweetheart?"

Turning to see who is speaking to me, I am momentarily speechless while I take in piercing blue eyes and gorgeous features. Whoever this man is, he has the ability to turn me on just by being near me because I am turned way the fuck on right now. As electricity sparks through me, I imagine running my hands through his dark hair and laying kisses along that chiseled jaw. Need and desire swirl together and I decide that he will be mine tonight.

"Hard week, more like it," I answer him just as the bartender brings me another drink. Before I can get cash out of my purse to pay for the drink, the guy lifts his chin at the bartender, who nods and walks away without taking payment. I'm still trying to find cash in my purse and the guy puts his hand over mine, stilling it.

"Why was your week so bad?" he asks, his hand still on mine.

I move my hand away. "Thanks for the drink."

He flashes me a smile that shoots more electricity through me. "You're very welcome. Now tell me about your week."

I sigh. "I'd rather not talk about it. Let's just say that dealing with pretentious, self-centred people for twelve hours a day, five days in a row, is enough to make me consider moving in with the Amish and adopting their way of life."

He chuckles. "I hear you. It sounds like we've been dealing with similar people all week."

I cock my eyebrow. "Oh, no. I fucking win this one, dude. I've been working with models who couldn't work out their left from their right half the time."

He nods, another smile forms on his face that would melt my panties if they weren't already melted. "You win. I could think of nothing worse than working with models."

My gaze sweeps over him, taking in his jeans and black t-shirt that both hug his body. He's rocking muscles I am fighting not to drool over; muscles I need to hold my hands back from because all they want to do is touch. Those muscles are covered in tats, and I squint to try and read what one of them says. It looks like a quote written in cursive on his forearm, but I struggle to work out what it says.

He sees me looking and holds his arm out as he tells me what it says. "Fate loves the fearless."

I grab hold of his arm and position it so I can read it better. The moment I touch him, I feel it, and I know he feels it, too, because his eyes show it. There's an undeniable spark between us, and as soon as it hits me, my body lights up at the thought of sleeping with him.

As I let go of him, he leans his face close to mine and asks, "You feel that?"

Not letting go of his eyes, I nod. The slow burn of desire is eliciting a hunger in me I haven't felt for a long time. And I sense he wants me just as much as I want him. "I do," I finally answer him, slightly breathless.

The beat of the music surrounds us, and the crowd threatens to drown us, but I am lost to the moment and almost unaware of everything else as we search each other's eyes. I'm sure I detect warmth and kindness in his. Odd that I'm getting all that when I've just met him, but I would swear it on a bible.

He slowly moves his face away from mine and drinks some of his drink. As he places the glass back on the bar, he says, "I'm Jett."

"Presley."

A smile tugs at his lips. "Your parents are Elvis fans?"

"My mother is and my father is blinded by love. She could have called me Elvis and he wouldn't have blinked."

This inspires a laugh out of him. "Your parents are still happily married?"

"Yeah, go figure. How many marriages do you know of that are still going strong after thirty years?"

His eyes twinkle. "My parents are still happy after thirty-five years. I guess you and I are like some weird science experiment. It kinda sucks, really."

Frowning, I ask, "Why?"

He throws the rest of his drink back, his eyes still twinkling. "When you don't come from a fucked-up family, you can hardly blame your issues on your parents, can you? Nope, you and me, we have to own our fucking issues."

I burst out laughing. "You are so right. Shit, pass me my drink, I can't cope with this knowledge."

Shaking his head, he holds my drink away from me. "Bad idea, sweetheart. You have no one to blame your alcoholism on except yourself. I suggest you give up alcohol straight away and find a new vice that's not as socially unacceptable as alcohol addiction."

Oh, this is fun. I raise my eyebrows. "What do you suggest?"

He doesn't even hesitate. "Sex addiction. Take that shit up. Much easier to hide from public view. And a lot more fucking fun than dealing with hangovers."

"I wouldn't know the first thing about taking that up. You think you could help me with that?"

He pulls a face like it's the hardest question he's ever been asked. Nodding, he says, "Sure. You want to get started now?"

My core clenches at the thought, and I lean into him and say, "You've no idea how much I want to get started on that now, Jett."

He sucks in a breath, and his hand curls around my neck. "You sure? Because once I'm finished with you, you're going to have an addiction that will be hard to kick."

"I'm more than sure. But if my newfound addiction gets out of hand, you might have to step up and help me break it."

"Oh baby, I can't think of one good reason to break that kind of addiction. No, I'll just step up and feed it. Can't have you fighting cravings, can we?"

Now it's my turn to suck in a breath. "Jett, it's fun to stand here and flirt with you, but I've gotta say, I'd rather you take me back to my hotel and fuck me."

He grins. "I thought you'd never ask."

Grabbing my hand, he begins to lead me away from the bar but I pull back and stop him. When he gives me a questioning look, I say, "I need to let my friend know I'm leaving."

"Sure."

I dial Darla. She's in this club somewhere, but I haven't seen her for a good hour. A couple of moments later, after I've spoken to her, Jett and I leave the club. I'm barely containing myself; I haven't been this excited for sex in a long time.

★★★

Thank god the hotel I'm staying at is close because Jett can't keep his hands off me and I'm about to explode with desire. We stumble through the door to my room and he pushes me up against the wall before pressing his lips to mine in a searing kiss. He tastes so good. I could spend hours devouring his lips and mouth. When his tongue tangles with mine, I moan and thread my hands through his hair. He groans and grinds his erection against me.

He breaks our kiss and cradles my face with his hands. His eyes search mine, and he murmurs, "Fuck, you're beautiful. How the hell are you not already taken?"

I run my finger over his lips. "Maybe I'm too much of a handful for just one man."

"Perhaps whoever tried wasn't enough of a man to know how to handle you right."

I grin at him and pull his face back to mine. Brushing my lips over his, I say, "I get the feeling you're a smooth talker, Jett."

A laugh escapes his mouth, and his eyes crinkle as he smiles. "I've been accused of that before, sweetheart, but don't let it turn you off." He moves to whisper in my ear. "I'd really like to help get you started on your new addiction."

As he moves his face back away from mine, I say, "I don't give a fuck if you're a smooth talker. Sweet-talk me all you like, so long as you back it up with an orgasm or two."

He quirks an eyebrow. "Only two?"

"Well, feel free to give me more. I won't complain." I give him a wink and then reach for his belt and undo it. A moment later, I've got his jeans undone and am stroking his cock while watching his eyes close with pleasure.

"Fuck...feels good," he groans.

I bend and take him in my mouth. This man is well endowed, and I'm consumed with lust. Usually I like to draw sex out, make it last, but tonight I'm rushing to the finish line. I need him inside me. Now.

As my desire takes over, I stand, push his jeans down and rip his shirt off. His eyes snap open as he kicks his jeans to the side. "Someone's eager," he murmurs.

I'm not even slowing down. My top is off faster than he can blink, and my shoes and pants follow soon after. And then I'm standing before him in my underwear, almost panting with need. I trail my fingers down his chest, taking in the tattoos covering his body. There's hardly an inch of him not tattooed, and as much as I'd love to stand here discovering what they all are, I don't have time for that tonight. No, tonight is all about getting as many orgasms out of him as possible. "We're in for a long night," I promise.

"I'm down with that."

"I thought you might be."

He reaches out and slips his hand inside my bra, pushing the cup aside so my breast is exposed. His thumb rubs my nipple, and a moment later, his mouth is on me, sucking, licking and gently biting. As he pushes the other cup out of the way so he is holding both my breasts, he asks, "You know what they call women with tits like yours?"

"No, enlighten me."

Looking up at me, he says, "Dangerous."

"Really? That's the best you've got?"

Straightening so his face is close to mine, he slides one hand around my neck and grips me there while his other hand cups my cheek and his thumb rubs over my lips. He brings his lips to mine and lightly kisses me. When he speaks, his voice is growly and sends delicious sensations to my core. "Really. Tits like these have been known to make a man do stupid things. We lose all fucking reason when we see them, and to hold and taste them, well fuck, that just sends us over the edge, sweetheart." He pauses and his eyes hold mine for a moment. They're speaking to me, silently. They're flashing desire and telling me how much he wants me. "Pretty fucking dangerous," he adds before leaning in to kiss me again.

I'm consumed by his kiss and his need. I have the same need. As he kisses me, I push his boxers down and then move my hands to take my panties off, but he has other ideas, and his hands are on mine, stopping them. I break the kiss and give him a questioning look. "You don't want them off?"

"I do, but I will have that honour," he answers me and then hooks his fingers in my panties and begins to slowly pull them down.

I watch in pleasure as he begins to lay kisses down my body and then kneel in front of me. He removes my panties and then stills, taking me in. His eyes on my pussy do amazing things to me, and I tingle with anticipation. If his eyes can do that, I know I'm in for a hell of a treat when he gives me his mouth.

When he takes his first taste of me, I sway a little, and his strong hands grip my legs, steadying me. He holds me as he runs his tongue from one end of my pussy to the other, and it's a good thing he does because I'm experiencing a heady rush of hunger. I'm not sure my legs would hold me up without his help. And then he pushes his tongue inside and my mind explodes with light and my body pulses with ecstasy.

I grip his hair and moan. Wild lust courses through me. I can hardly hold myself together as he works his magic with his tongue, and I know it won't take long for him to bring me to orgasm. His hands glide up my legs to hold my ass, and as he grips me there, it's almost like he's trying to pull me closer to him. It's not possible, though; Jett has his face buried in my pussy as deep as he can. He's got talents a woman can only dream of and I'm disappointed this will only be a one-night stand. I'd like to sample these talents again.

When he stops what he's doing, I want to push his face back to me. I'm about to beg him to keep going when he asks, "Do you have any idea how fucking good you taste?"

"No, but I'll believe you so long as you keep tasting me."

His eyes remain on mine as he begins to massage my clit with his finger. "I wasn't sure if you might prefer my finger to my tongue."

Oh good god, he's going to drive me insane with lust. "That's a hard choice. Maybe you should decide."

His eyes sparkle with mischievous delight. "Mmmm.... let me see." His finger is inside me a second later, and I close my eyes as I let the sensations wash over me. "Feel good?" he asks.

I nod because seriously, I can't even form a thought at this point, let alone a word.

"Good," he murmurs, and then he replaces his finger with his tongue.

"Fuck...Jett...don't fucking stop," I moan, my eyes still closed, my hand gripping his hair.

And then he takes me on a ride I never want to get off. His tongue and his fingers work together to bring me to orgasm. When it hits, I realise I've been missing something in my life. Jett gives me an orgasm like I've never had, and I scream his name as I shatter into a million fucking pieces of bliss.

My legs give way again, and he swiftly moves to stand up and hold me. As his arms go around me, his lips crash down on mine, and he kisses me into blissful oblivion. I am completely consumed with this man; tonight, he is owning my mind and body in a way no man ever has. And we've only just gotten started.

When he ends the kiss, I open my eyes to look into his. He's watching me with a look I can't quite put my finger on but I ignore it and say, "You think my tits are dangerous? I think your mouth is."

He laughs and murmurs, "Wait till you have my cock, sweetheart. I promised you an addiction you'll struggle to break, and I always keep my promises."

"Can't wait," I whisper, the effects of my orgasm still messing with my ability to form thoughts.

"Neither can I," he says, letting me go. His eyes wander down to my bra, and he reaches behind me and flicks it undone in one easy movement. "I'm not sure one night with these tits will be enough," he says as he slides my bra off. He lets it drop to the floor and bends to kiss my breasts again. The passion he kisses them with tells me he really can't get enough and that turns me on even more than I already am.

I reach for his cock and grasp it firmly before I begin to move my hand up and down his hard length. His breathing picks up and he stops what he's doing and straightens. Smiling at him, I bend to take his cock in my mouth.

The minute I wrap my lips around him, his hand lands on my head and he groans. "Fuck, Presley..."

And then my phone rings.

I ignore it and keep sucking him. No way am I letting anyone interrupt us tonight.

"You wanna get that?" he asks, although I can tell he doesn't want me to.

I swirl my tongue over him, and he sucks in a breath. "No. Whoever it is can wait 'cause I've got more important things to do."

"Thank Christ," he mutters as his eyes flutter shut.

My phone stops ringing but then starts again.

Bloody hell.

We both continue to ignore it, but when it rings a fourth time, I swear and let him go. "Sorry, I'll tell them to fuck off and be right back."

He rakes his hand through his hair, frustrated, and smacks me on the ass. "Hurry up, my dick fucking needs your mouth."

I love his dirty talk and answer my phone begrudgingly. "What?" I snap without even looking to see who it is.

"I've hurt my fucking ankle." It's Darla. *Shit.* I can tell from her voice she's in a great deal of pain.

"Where are you, hon?"

"I'm in my hotel room, just got back, but I tripped in the bloody gutter and twisted it. Are you able to come to my room and check it out? I don't think it's broken, but I need a second opinion."

My gaze shifts to Jett's hard on. *Fuck.*

He catches my gaze and gives me a questioning look. I frown and give my attention back to Darla. "Sure, I'll be there in a minute."

She sighs. "Thanks, babe."

"Of course," I say and hang up. There's no way I can let my friend down in her hour of need. She's been there for me every step of the way through my marriage break-up, and although I have an aching need for Jett to fuck me, Darla always comes first.

"You're leaving?" he asks, but there's no anger there.

"Yeah, sorry. My friend's twisted her ankle, and I want to make sure she hasn't broken it." The regret is clear in my voice.

"Shit," he says and begins to get dressed. "I'll come with you."

"What?"

"I'll organise for someone to pick her up and take her to the hospital so you don't have to worry about it. You can just take care of her while I sort this out for you."

Mind blown.

"Thank you, I appreciate it," I murmur, surprised at his offer. I'm more surprised at the way he's handling this, though. If I'd stopped mid blow job with my ex to run off and check on a twisted ankle, he'd have been pissed and wouldn't have hesitated to let me know.

"No worries."

We get dressed and then head to Darla's room. As we wait for her to answer her door, I say, "Sorry about this."

He grins. "It's all good, but you owe me and I'll be collecting."

Hell yes. I return his grin. "I like the way you think."

Before he can say anything else, Darla answers the door and I take in her distressed state. Mascara is running down her cheeks, along with tears. Darla never cries so I know this is bad. I take one look at her ankle and suspect she's broken it. "Shit, Darla, that looks nasty." I usher her to a chair and then dial down to the front desk and request for ice to be brought up to her room.

I'm so engrossed in helping her, I forget to introduce Jett so he does it for me. "Hi, I'm Jett."

She smiles through her tears. "Goddamn, you scored well," she says to me with a wink.

Jett laughs, not even slightly thrown by her remark. I get the feeling he's heard this before. "It's good to - "

Darla cuts him off. Her eyes have widened and she looks like she's about to hyperventilate. "Oh my god, you're Jett fucking Vaughn!"

"Who?" I ask, taking in her excitement and his blank look.

She's excited, but the pain has taken over again, and she can't answer me, so I look at Jett who is watching me with another look I can't read. Usually I'm good at reading people, but this is the second time tonight I've not been able to read him.

He scrubs a hand over his face. "You didn't know, did you?"

My brows knit. "Know what? I have no idea what either of you are talking about."

"Fuck," he mutters.

"Are you going to tell me?" I ask, wishing one of them would fill me in.

Darla's pain subsides enough for her to answer me. "He's the lead singer of Crave." That means nothing to me, and when she realises that, she exclaims, "God, Presley, how can you not know who Crave is? They're one of the best known rock bands in the world. You of all people should know who they are."

Jett steps in. "Not everyone has heard of us, Darla. I do occasionally find someone who doesn't know me."

She rolls her eyes. "Well, now you're just being humble. Everyone knows who you are." She gives me a pointed stare. "Except Presley which is odd because - "

I cut her off. "I don't know every rock star in the world." I give her a dirty look and then look at Jett. "Sorry."

He shakes his head. "No, I loved that you didn't know."

I send him a wicked grin. "I'm not into rock stars so we can just pretend I don't know."

He chuckles. "You're on." And then his phone rings and he turns away to take the call.

Turning my attention back to Darla, I bend down and ask, "How are you feeling, hon?"

Her face is etched with pain. "I've never been in so much pain. Do you think it's broken?"

"I have no clue. Jett's organising a car to come pick you up and take you to the hospital."

She looks at him in awe and then gives me a dreamy grin. "He's got a good reputation, you know. Goes through women, apparently, but a nice guy regardless. It's so nice of him to do this for me."

"Oh god, you know that most of the shit you hear in the press is crap so I don't know why you listen to that rubbish."

She shrugs. "It's Jett Vaughn, babe. I've been following him for years. I can't believe I've met him, but bloody hell, why did it have to be when I look like shit?" She pauses before her eyes light up again and she adds, "Fuck, I can't believe *he's* your one-night stand."

I laugh and wink at her. "Yeah, he's the guy I had my lips

wrapped around when you rang."

"How the hell did you get so lucky?"

I'm just about to answer her when Jett comes back. "Sorry to interrupt, ladies, but I've got a car waiting downstairs for us." He looks at Darla. "I'll carry you down if you'd like."

I'm sure she's about to burst from either pain or excitement and I would bet good money on the latter.

She's tiny, and he easily carries her to the car. Me? I'm still in shock this man gave up a blow job to take my friend to the hospital.

Want to learn more about my other books and where to buy them?
Visit my website for all the details and buy links:
http://ninalevinebooks.blogspot.com.au

Made in the USA
Monee, IL
16 August 2020